THE
MONA LISA
SACRIFICE

Also by Peter Darbyshire

Has the World Ended Yet?: Stories
Please
The Warhol Gang

THE MONA LISA SACRIFICE

PETER DARBYSHIRE

The Book of Cross 1

First edition 2013
New edition 2024

Published by Poplar Press
an imprint of Wolsak and Wynn Publishers
280 James Street North
Hamilton, ON L8R2L3
www.wolsakandwynn.ca

Acquiring editors: Ashley Hisson, Jennifer Rawlinson, A.G.A. Wilmot
Cover design: Michel Vrana
Cover image: Angel: ZU_09 / iStock; Background: Portrait of Mona Lisa photographed by Gwengoat / iStock; Plus assets from Worn 80s Paperback Textures by Jeff Finley
Interior design: Jennifer Rawlinson
Author photograph: Pacific Newspaper Group
Typeset in Caslon Pro and Gibson
Printed by Rapido Books, Montreal, Canada

10 9 8 7 6 5 4 3 2 1

The publisher gratefully acknowledges the support of the Canada Council for the Arts and the Ontario Arts Council. We also acknowledge the financial support of the Government of Canada through the Canada Book Fund and the Government of Ontario through the Ontario Book Publishing Tax Credit and Ontario Creates.

Library and Archives Canada Cataloguing in Publication

Title: The Mona Lisa sacrifice / Peter Darbyshire.
Names: Darbyshire, Peter, 1967- author. | Roman, Peter, 1967- Mona Lisa sacrifice.
Description: New edition. | Series statement: The book of Cross ; 1 | Previously published: Toronto, Canada: ChiZine Publications, 2013. | Originally published under the pseudonym Peter Roman.
Identifiers: Canadiana 20240427521 | ISBN 9781998408054 (softcover)
Subjects: LCGFT: Paranormal fiction. | LCGFT: Thrillers (Fiction) | LCGFT: Novels.
Classification: LCC PS8557.A59346 M66 2024 | DDC C813/.6—dc23

Rood was I reared. I lifted a mighty king,

Lord of the heavens, dared not to bend.

With dark nails they drove me through: on me those sores are seen,

open malice-wounds. I dared not scathe anyone.

They mocked us both, we two together. All wet with blood I was,

poured out from that Man's side, after ghost he gave up.

– "The Dream of the Rood," trans. Jonathan A. Glenn

IN THE BEGINNING

In the beginning was an angel, a church and a knife.

I had hunted down the angel, Remiel, in Barcelona. He was working as a living statue, one of those street performers whose job it is to separate tourists from their money before someone else does. His office was a wooden pedestal on La Rambla, the pedestrian boulevard by the harbour that every visitor has to hit before they start exploring the real city. He was tucked away among the kiosks that sold everything from postcards and magazines to live birds. A silver robot stood on a box to the left of him, while a clockwork man dressed in gears, wheels and pistons was on his right. Remiel was made up like a demon with golden skin, bat wings and two tails, holding a leather tome bound with three locks. He looked like just another out-of-work circus performer vying for tips. Apparently even angels have to make a living these days.

If you've been to Barcelona, or any other city with a tourist district, you know the scene: people with cameras and sunburns wandering around while living statues, jugglers, magicians and pickpockets compete with each other to earn a few of the local coins.

And me.

You wouldn't notice me. I'd be just another passing face, another man from somewhere else with a hat, sunglasses and backpack. I'm a pretty convincing nobody, thanks to centuries of experience.

But Remiel turned his head and scanned the crowd as soon as I caught sight of him. Angels have a sense for each other. He was looking for me. Trying to find me like I'd found him.

1

The problem was he was looking for the wrong thing. I'm not one of them. I can never be one of them. I'll let you worry about whether that's a curse or a gift.

I ducked into a kiosk and pretended to look over a selection of fridge magnets depicting La Sagrada Familia, the city's famous Gaudí church, while keeping an eye on Remiel in the mirror on the sunglasses stand. He fluttered his wings and lashed his tails, which prompted people in the crowd to applaud and toss money onto the mat at his feet. But he wasn't acting for them. I knew his demon form wasn't a disguise – he wasn't wearing makeup and using props like all the other performers. He wasn't even using a sleight to hide his real form. This was actually one of Remiel's incarnations. And he was genuinely agitated at sensing my presence but not being able to find me. I would have been amused by the situation if I wasn't so damned desperate for grace.

He hopped off the box and gathered up his mat and money in one smooth motion. He looked around some more as he put them in a shoulder bag he draped off one of his wings. Then he made his way through the crowd and into a side alley. I followed him, careful to keep clear of the people filming his exit. You never know when some enterprising law enforcement officer will think it's a good idea to look at people's cameras after a crime and then track you down at the bar or airport lounge where you happen to be enjoying a few drinks. And then you have to come up with answers to all those questions that are so difficult to answer.

After all, it was a photo that had led me to Barcelona. Printed on a piece of paper and tucked inside an envelope with no return address, delivered to a hotel in Prague where I'd been staying to ride out a heroin withdrawal. I'd wanted to cultivate an addiction so I could forget about various things I no longer wanted to remember, but my body had rejected the drug. It had worked for only a few weeks, hardly enough time to forget who I was, before my body started cleaning it out of my system. Healing me like it always did. Just doing its preprogrammed job. You'll have to trust me when I say I can't recommend going through withdrawal while you're still high.

A cleaning lady slipped the envelope under my door, because I'd instructed the hotel staff to stay away from my room until I checked out. Strange things can happen when I'm seeing things. The man at the front desk told me later the envelope had just shown up on the counter with nothing on it but the alias I was using at the time. It was written in blood, but I didn't point that out to him. And if he noticed, he was professional enough to not say anything. I won't share that alias right now in case I want to use it again. Although, all things considered, I probably won't. When I opened the envelope I thought for a moment that maybe I was still hallucinating. There was Remiel, golden-skinned and red-eyed on La Rambla, smiling into the camera as he spread his wings for the tourist shot. The first angel I'd seen in years. Even through the photo, I could sense his grace – the heavenly essence that made him what he was. I yearned for it far more than I ever could heroin or any other drug. It was time for me to chase a new high.

On the flight to Barcelona I wondered what had happened to the owner of the camera. I figured it was another angel who sent me the photo because who else would know the truth about both Remiel and me? But there was no way Remiel would have knowingly posed for one of his own kind. Angels didn't particularly trust each other these days, and with good reason – they were always trying to kill one another. Which meant some real tourist had taken the photo and then given up the camera for it to reach me. Hopefully it was just a straightforward theft. I'm tired of people dying on account of me.

I don't trust the angels any more than they trust each other, which is why I assumed I was walking into some sort of trap as I followed Remiel away from La Rambla. But he had grace hidden inside of him, and that's the one addiction my body can't resist. Besides, when you're not capable of really dying, even if you want to, you tend to grow a little cavalier about threats.

Remiel wandered through the old stone buildings of the city's Gothic Quarter, leading me through streets so narrow the evening sky was just a memory overhead. We went past produce and clothing stores, a bookstore with a cat sleeping on a crate of books outside, a sex store with live mannequins modelling clothing in the window and a row of wine bars. Remiel kept looking back, trying to find me, but I stayed hidden in the crowd, stopping to look at a poster advertising a concert, slipping into a group of people stumbling out of a nightclub who asked each other if it was evening or morning, stepping briefly into a tourist shop to buy a hat of a different colour.

It went on like that for a while, as Remiel led me out of the Gothic Quarter and across the city to the Gaudí church. I wasn't expecting that destination. I'd thought he'd take me to an abandoned building somewhere, like the apartment tower where I'd found Abraxos in Chechnya, its lower floors knocked out by tank shells. Or like the walled-off chamber in the Paris sewer where I'd killed . . . what was that angel's name? The one that had torn out his own eyes and tried to recite T.S. Eliot to me even as I strangled him. I like Eliot as much as the next lost soul, but that wasn't going to stop me.

So rather than hide, Remiel headed for the most popular tourist spot in the city. There's no accounting for the logic of angels.

Remiel changed into a different incarnation along the way, stepping into the shadows of a doorway, then emerging a second later as a man of average build, with dark hair and glasses. He'd also traded the gold skin for street clothes, and the wings and tails for a Starbucks cup. He kept the shoulder bag with the money, though. He looked like anyone else in the crowd. But he wasn't. Neither of us were.

The sky was dark now, and the ticket booths at the entrance to the church had just closed. Remiel went around to the exit at the back. The rear of the church is what everyone recognizes from the postcards, with its towers that look as if they were dreamed up by insects, or maybe mad angels. Or maybe mad insect angels. But they weren't. I knew Gaudí, and you'll have to take my word for it that he was no angel. Besides, angels generally aren't all that creative when it comes to making things. They're more inclined to destruction.

Remiel lingered by the gate as the last of the tourists filed out of the church and into buses for the trips back to their hotels and air conditioning and rooftop wine bars. I went past him on the other side of the street and tried not to stumble too much as my body tugged me in his direction. I needed grace. I sat on the patio of a café across from the church and ordered a glass of red and a bowl of gazpacho. You can't go wrong with the wine or the gazpacho in Spain, even at the tourist traps. I watched Remiel look at the statues carved out of the walls of the church. Angels have always had a thing for statues. I don't know what it is; maybe they see them as kindred spirits: "Hey, you look human but you're not. And your creator's been dead for ages. You're just like me."

All right, to be fair, no one knows if God is really dead or not. But he's definitely been MIA for a very long time.

If Remiel still felt my presence, he didn't seem concerned now. He leaned against a wall and waited until the last of the buses had pulled away and the guards had locked the gate, then he pulled out a phone and talked on it for a while. I sipped my wine and savoured my gazpacho, enjoying the good things in life while I considered whether or not he was calling for help. I decided he was probably just faking the call to look like he wasn't waiting for the guards to go back inside. It's what I would have done.

When the guards set off on their rounds, Remiel put away the phone and tapped the gate with one hand. It opened enough for him to slip through. Locks aren't much good against his kind. And a whole bunch of other kinds. He headed toward the wall while I pretended to watch the traffic and considered ordering another glass. I'd really missed Spanish wine.

Remiel reached the wall and started to climb it, pulling himself up one of the statues tucked into the numerous alcoves on the church's exterior. It would have been quite the scene if not for the fact that he disappeared as soon as he touched the wall.

That is, he disappeared to most people. But if you've been following along it should be clear by now that I'm not most people. I expended a bit of the little grace I had left to sharpen my vision and found him again. He was still there, climbing, but now he looked like part of the wall. His skin and clothes matched the colour and texture of the stone. Even his bag was camouflaged. When he moved sideways across a statue to secure a better foothold, he became that statue for a second. He was just another forgotten symbol of the past.

I threw discipline to the wind, like usual, and ordered another glass. I needed something to fill the new emptiness left behind by the grace I had just used.

By the time I'd finished the second glass, Remiel had disappeared for real, into an opening in one of the spires. His nest, no doubt. I chuckled at my own wit, which prompted the waiter to bring me the bill.

I paid up, waited for a lull in the traffic, or at least as close to one as you could find in this city, and went after Remiel.

He hadn't closed the gate completely behind him, so I slipped through and crossed the open area on the other side as quickly as possible before the guards came back. I pulled the hat lower on my head to conceal my face from any cameras. They were probably hidden all over the church. Maybe even in the eyes of one of the statues. That's where I'd put them.

I ran to the church and leapt onto the wall, grabbing hold of the same statue Remiel had and pulling myself up along the same path. If it was good enough for him, it would do for me. It wasn't that different from rock climbing. I moved over saints and angels I'd long since forgotten, although a few of the faces looked familiar. I stayed clear of the nativity scene – that one always makes me a little uncomfortable.

I didn't try to hide myself like Remiel had. I wanted to save my grace for what was to come so I just hoped no one was watching me at the moment. If they were, well, the heat in Barcelona can play tricks with your mind. And if someone was filming me, hey, there are always crazy tourists in every city trying to climb things they shouldn't. Hopefully I'd be just another novelty video online. I was too hungry for Remiel's grace to worry about it.

It took maybe a minute and a half to reach the opening where Remiel had disappeared. I paused for a few seconds beneath it while I caught my breath, perched on a stone outcropping like I was another statue. I wasn't in the best shape, given my most recent attempts at self-annihilation, but I wasn't in the worst shape either. There was a time when I wouldn't have made it halfway up the spire before falling off. Of course, in those days I probably would have been drunk as well.

I tore myself away from such fond memories and the view of Barcelona in the evening. It was time to get on with things.

I reached into my backpack and took out the knife I mentioned earlier. It was a standard hunting blade I'd bought in a shop as soon as I'd arrived in the city. Some people think you need special weapons to kill angels but you don't. They bleed and die like the rest of us. The trick is getting the chance to use a weapon against an angel at all. They're strong and quick and just generally nasty. But so am I.

I went in through the opening in the spire, fast and rolling.

It was a small stone chamber, with no doors or other entrances, as if Gaudí had designed it specially for someone like Remiel. Maybe he had. I took it all in with one glance: The bookshelves piled high with books, the mattress and pillow on the floor, the empty bottles of wine in a corner. Remiel waiting for me in the middle of the room.

This time he was a glowing winged man in robes. He'd opted for the classic look, perhaps as an appeal to any sense of nostalgia I might have. But like I said, I wasn't one of his kind. And I've never been the sentimental type. Maybe he suspected that, because he also held a glowing sword with flames lighting up the edges. Very showy. He moved so fast even I couldn't see him – what did I tell you? – and then there I was, impaled to the floor, the sword's blade embedded in me and the stone underneath.

Fuck. Those flames *hurt*.

Luckily, everything was going according to plan so far. Well, my plan didn't *specifically* involve getting pinned to the floor like some sort of collector's exhibit. But I wasn't surprised by it either. I didn't presume to think I was going to get through that window unscathed.

"You're getting predictable in your old age," I said as cheerfully as I could manage with a magic sword burning my insides. It's important to remain positive in moments like this, if only to make your opponent pause and consider your sanity for a second and thus potentially give you an opening. Which is exactly what happened. Remiel studied me, frowning, and I used that second to grab his robes with my left hand, pulling him down enough that I could bury my knife to the hilt in his stomach with my right. He grunted and grace escaped his lips and his wound at the same time.

The grace – to most people it just looks like a shimmering in the air, a trick of the light. If they even notice it at all. But to me it's so much more. It's the stuff light and life are made of. It washed over me and gave me a boost, although one that was more psychological than anything else, given the small amount of grace he lost. I felt like a man dying of thirst in the desert who's just spotted a water hole. A feeling I actually know from experience, unfortunately.

"Thanks, I needed that," I told Remiel.

His eyes widened at my words and he finally recognized me. "My lord," he said. Involuntarily, I suspect. The angels don't honour me like they used to. Not since I'd started hunting them.

Then he wrenched the sword free of the floor for another swing. But I was ready for it. I grabbed onto his arm and let his motion pull me back to my feet. The sword remained in me because of that, but it wasn't the first time I'd used this move so I managed to stay standing and conscious. Although I'm comfortable enough with my masculinity to admit there may have been a little screaming involved in the process.

So there we were, his sword still in me, my knife still in him, our free arms locked in a wrestling pose. It was the stuff statues are made of.

"This is a lovely place you have here," I managed to spit out. "Very cozy."

Remiel's eyes flicked to the window. Considering the odds of an escape, no doubt. I used the distraction to headbutt him in the face. He didn't flinch. Okay, so much for that trick. I didn't even bother kicking him in the balls. Experience has led me to believe angels actually like that.

He tried to twist my right arm to an angle where it would break. Hell, if I were a normal human he probably could have torn it off but I was using the last of my grace to keep me strong enough to match him. He suddenly let go of both the sword and my arm and smashed his hands into my ears.

It's bad enough when regular people do that. When an angel does it . . . well, I was shot in the face once in an alley in New Orleans and the bullet hurt less. And was that blaring sound coming from cars outside or horns in my head? I staggered and my grip slipped on Remiel, which allowed him to rip the sword from my guts. I screamed again, because the only thing that hurts worse than a flaming sword going in is a flaming sword coming out. But I wasn't done yet. I still had the knife, which I yanked out of him to make it useful again.

Remiel just grunted and swung the sword back in preparation for what looked to be a decapitating strike. Or maybe a body-cleaving blow. They have a similar windup. He smiled a little, his lips burning like the sword now. He thought he had me. Angels tend to be cocky like that.

I dropped underneath the swing, which wasn't as easy as it sounds given the wound in my stomach. I made more unmanly noises and his blade shaved a few hairs off the top of my head. I managed to keep moving, spinning around into a foot sweep. Angels have never been much for martial arts that don't involve flaming weapons – they think it's beneath them. Remiel was no different. I took his feet out and he fell back into the bookshelf, sending it to the floor. He spread his wings to try to keep his balance, but I grabbed one of them as I rose and twisted it. I must have broken something, because the wing suddenly bent in a way I knew it wasn't meant to bend. Remiel wouldn't be flying out of here.

He hissed in pain and swung with the sword again but I kept going, throwing myself into a flying knee that took me inside his guard and into his midsection. The move opened my wound some more, so it probably hurt me more than him, but his breath whoofed out and I inhaled deeply. It was cloves and honey and all things nice, and it made me think of other times – for a few years there had been a market stall in Cairo where you could actually buy bottled angel breath. Anyway.

I continued my winning streak by driving my knife into his left eye, smashing the blade through his skull and into the wall behind him. Now Remiel was the one pinned. With typical divine stoicism, he didn't cry out, which just showed he was more of a man than me. Or less. Whichever. He just glared at me with his other eye and reached up with his left hand to try to pull the knife free. I caught his arm and held it with my right hand. So he dropped the sword in his other hand and tried again. Which is what I was expecting. I caught the sword with my left hand – all the years I've spent on battlefields have made me ambidextrous – and stepped back to give myself room. He pulled the knife out of the wall and his eye with the sort of sound you'd expect a knife coming out of an eye to make. And I gave him the same decapitating stroke he'd tried to give me. Only mine was successful. His head flew off and landed on the bed, and his body fell to its knees, where it remained, grace spilling out of it.

I leaned on the sword for a moment, catching my breath, holding my free hand over the wound in my stomach. No matter how many times you've been stabbed or impaled, it always hurts worse than the last time.

"Your heart didn't really seem in it," I said to Remiel's head, but he didn't answer. He moved his lips in silent prayer and stared at me with his good eye.

The tricky thing about angels is you can kill them but they don't really stay dead. I could have cut Remiel into different parts and spread them around the world, but some life would have remained in each of those parts thanks to his grace. And eventually those parts would have found their way back to each other through some means or another, and he would have found a way to be reassembled. And then he'd be a very angry angel. As long as he had the grace, he couldn't truly be killed.

But the grace was why I was here.

I dropped the sword and went over to the bed and picked up his head by the hair. He was weeping tears from his good eye now, blood from his ruined one.

"If it had to be someone," he said, "I'm honoured it's you."

"I'm not who you think I am," I told him, and I put my lips to his and kissed him and drew all of his grace out of him.

What can I say of the grace? It's not only the lifeblood of the angels and their kin, it's the most incredible high imaginable. Bliss, pure bliss. Imagine the best orgasm you've ever had. The best heroin high. The rush of adrenalin you get when you jump out of a plane. The smell of spring in the air. The calmness of meditation. It's the power of creation. It's all that's left of God in the world. It makes living bearable. For a time, anyway.

When I was done with the head I went to the body. I drained him until he was empty, and then I fell onto his bed in a stupor and lost myself in memories of other times.

SOME THINGS NEVER CHANGE

I dreamed of the last time I'd visited Barcelona. I'd been stabbed that time, too.

I'd been lying drunk in an alley in the Gothic Quarter. There weren't any tourists around that night. Probably something to do with all the screaming and gunshots in the surrounding streets. I remember toasting the one star I could see with the dregs of my wine bottle. That was back when you could still see stars from cities. A long time ago.

I don't remember how I got there or where I went after. I don't remember what year it was. I do know there was a war going on, but then there's always a war going on, isn't there? I wasn't involved, though. I was just trying to forget myself and what I was, as usual, and I was doing a reasonably good job of it.

Until the soldiers came down the alley. Three of them, with stained uniforms and jaunty caps, holding rifles with practised ease. One of them carried a flashlight, the old metal kind that was big enough to be a weapon itself. Although I guess it wasn't old at the time. They stopped and looked down at me, and I toasted them with the empty bottle as well.

"Comrades," I said. I suppose that was my mistake. I meant it as a brothers-in-arms endearment, but they took it in the political sense. Always the way.

The one with the flashlight squatted beside me and shone the light in my eyes. "We are not your comrades," he told me. "Your comrades are warming the streets with their blood."

The Spanish – they can get poetic when they're riled up about something.

He put the flashlight down on the ground and I sighed. I knew where this was going, and he didn't surprise me. He pulled out his knife and thrust it into my side in one motion, like he'd had plenty of practice.

Soldiers – why are they always stabbing me?

I swore and spat and went through all the motions you usually go through when you've been stabbed. Then I went to finish the bottle before I remembered it was empty. "I don't suppose you have any more wine?" I asked.

The soldier who'd knifed me blinked a few times, then pulled the blade out of me and stared at it. It was covered in my blood. If he wiped it off on my shirt, I was really going to have to do something to him.

"Water will do," I told him. "I can make my own wine."

He stabbed me again, this time in the stomach. Now he was getting annoying. He was ruining my clothes worse than I'd already ruined them. So I hit him over the head with the bottle and pushed his body off me when he fell. I pulled myself up the wall to my feet as the other two fumbled their rifles to their shoulders.

"Don't shoot me," I said. "I'll be forced to –" But I didn't have time to finish because they went ahead and shot me despite my warning. One in the chest, one in the stomach. Good centre of mass shots, which would have killed me eventually if I hadn't done anything about them.

Luckily, I was too drunk to feel the pain. I just looked down at the blood leaking out of me and shook my head. I didn't bother finishing my warning. I don't know what I would have said to them anyway. I wasn't really in the mood for this.

I caught my blood in the bottle. It would do as well as water when it came to making wine. I stumbled off down the alley, looking for a quieter, darker place to heal myself and keep on drinking. The soldiers watched me for a moment, then ran off in the opposite direction, leaving the fallen one behind.

No, definitely not comrades.

AN ANGEL SPEAKS IN RIDDLES

The memory faded away as I came out of the grace stupor in Remiel's chamber. The wound in my stomach had faded away, too, and I felt so rested it was like I'd slept for hours even though it had likely only been a few minutes. The grace had worked its magic on me like it always does. I reflexively looked around for Remiel but there was nothing left of him but dust. And the sword lying on the floor. But its flames had gone out and the metal was dull and black.

Now that I was full of grace once more, I felt bad about what I'd done to Remiel. Guilt always came with the grace. Oh well. I sat up and tried to shrug it off. Tomorrow would be another day.

"An epic struggle," said a statue in the window, "if there had been anyone to watch and sing it down through history after."

I tried not to jump too much. After all, if he'd wanted to do me harm, he could have done it while I was lying there dreaming of past lives. I studied him as I got to my feet.

He was a stone angel, looking as if he'd stepped right out of the wall of the church. Remiel and I may have climbed right over him. I wondered how long he'd been there, how much he'd seen. I was surprised I didn't feel the pull of grace from him, but I was refreshed after Remiel, so maybe that had something to do with it. Who the hell knew with angels?

"Which one are you?" I asked.

"Some know me as Cassiel," he said. He didn't seem concerned about the sword, or the fact I'd just killed one of his brethren.

I searched my memory for angel trivia. "The watcher," I said.

"At times," he said. "In times."

Ah, he was that kind of angel. The kind who talks in riddles.

I tried to figure out what he was doing here and realized there was really only one answer.

"I'm guessing you were the one who sent me the photo," I said.

"A photo was taken," Cassiel said. "A photo was delivered. An angel was slain. Events were set into motion."

I stretched and measured the distance to the sword. Cassiel continued to watch me but didn't move. I didn't pose much of a threat now. I was sated, the hunger in me gone for a time. I had no desire to harm him. Not yet. Although if he kept talking the way he did . . .

"What do you want?" I asked him. "Why all the setup to bring me here?"

"Those are two questions," he said. "Two very different stories."

"Let's start with the first," I sighed.

"I want *Mona Lisa*," he said without changing expression.

All right, that was a new one. But I just shrugged it off. Some angels collect souls, others apparently collect art.

"It's in the Louvre," I told him. "Shouldn't be too much of a problem for the likes of you."

"That is but a shadow," he said. "A haunting."

I shook my head. "Let's just cut through the parts where I try to puzzle out what the hell you're talking about," I said. "Tell me what you really want."

"I want the real Mona Lisa," he said.

I studied him and he studied me right back from his perch in the window.

The real Mona Lisa.

Maybe he was suggesting the painting in the Louvre was a fraud, like a certain Picasso in one of the American galleries, but I had a feeling he was talking about something entirely different. Angels aren't usually the type to have an interest in art. They prefer bombs and military aircraft and tanks and that sort of thing. I don't know – maybe explosions are art to angels.

"What's the real Mona Lisa? Is it some kind of weapon?" I asked, following that line of logic.

"You will help or you won't help," Cassiel said. "What you know about Mona Lisa will not affect the outcome."

I tried not to sigh again. It was times like this that I preferred the company of demons. They could get you into a lot of trouble, but at least they were straight talkers.

"All right, let's take a step backward for a moment," I said. "Why me?"

"You can do it or you cannot do it," Cassiel said. "Either way, a final outcome."

I worked my way through that. "So I'm the only one capable of finding the Mona Lisa?"

"Those are your words," he said. "Not mine."

I thought about killing him just to make him shut up. But I do love a good mystery.

"Maybe others can find the Mona Lisa," I said. "But I'm the only one who can actually pull off whatever it is you want pulled off."

"As I said," Cassiel agreed.

Now we were getting somewhere. And it didn't even involve burning bushes or turning people to salt or any of the usual angelic attempts at communication. "Why give me Remiel then? If you knew where I was, why not come to me directly?"

"You are sated," he said. "We are negotiating now."

"So you lured me with Remiel," I said. "He was the bait to get me here so we could have this conversation. And the thing that kept you safe."

"That is an acceptable version of events," Cassiel said.

"All right," I said. "So we're negotiating. We'll talk price in a moment. First, what do you want me to do?"

"As I said," Cassiel said.

"Find the Mona Lisa." I nodded. "Do you know who has it?"

"The information you seek is irrelevant to your decision," he said.

Of course. Why would that matter?

"How about location then?" I asked. "Any idea where it is?"

"The only thing certain is uncertainty," Cassiel said.

"The only certainty I'm feeling right now is that this sounds like a job best avoided," I said. "I don't care what you're offering –"

"I will deliver you Judas," Cassiel said, then stepped back out of the window and fell from sight.

He didn't need to wait for an answer, for he knew once he mentioned Judas that I would be in.

I hated Judas more than I hated the angels for everything he had done to me.

I hated Judas more than I hated the angels for what he had done to Penelope.

I hated Judas more than I hated myself.

THE SERPENT IN THE GARDEN

I know what you're thinking.

You're thinking I can't really be him. Christ. And you're right.

I'm not him – or Him, if that's your preference. I'm what he left behind, the body that he used for his earthly incarnation and then abandoned when he died. The afterbirth, if you will.

I'm who woke up in the burial cave after Christ shuffled off this mortal coil. I'm who left that cave and went out into the world to wreak more mayhem than miracles. Not Christ, but a lost soul trapped in Christ's resurrected body.

Whose lost soul? I don't know. I woke up in Christ's body in the cave with no memories. No memories of my own, at least. I still had some of Christ's memories. They came to me as I lay there on the cave floor in the first moments of my life.

I remembered Christ sitting with Judas at a wooden table in a small room somewhere. A few lamps burning olive oil and some cups of wine. No one else though – no apostles, no serving staff, no painters taking down the scene to preserve it for the ages. Just Judas and Christ. Only I remembered it as Judas and me, because that's just the way things work in this body of mine.

I hadn't known what Judas was when I was Christ. I had thought he was just another mortal in search of meaning to his empty life. He'd shown up at a speech I'd given outside a temple, about the evils of moneylenders. A lot of good that accomplished. When I was done and the crowd had wandered back to their market stalls, Judas came to me and offered his hands for whatever work I needed. And so I put him to work. And he was loyal and faithful to the cause, and he quickly became my hands in the world. He arranged the public events and brought in the crowds, first in the dozens and then the hundreds. He paid the soldiers to look the other way. And we spread the gospel and converted the followers of the dead and dying gods to my growing army of the faithful. And it was good.

Until there we were, sharing wine I'd made, resting after a long day Judas had arranged of impressing my followers by having me walk on water and raise the dead. I was out of grace thanks to the day's activities, but when I was the real Christ I just had to wait for it to regenerate. If you're one of those who is supposed to have it, like I used to be, it comes back on its own. You don't have to get involved in all the messy business of slaying angels and such.

But Judas had left me no time to replenish my grace.

"You're going to fall," he told me in the room that night, gazing into his wine like he was reading entrails. "Just like all the others who believed themselves eternal."

I thought I knew what he was talking about. My job as Christ was to save humanity. I wasn't supposed to die for their sins – that's just empty revisionism. I was supposed to convert them all and spread the Garden out over the earth. Yes, there used to be a Garden of Eden and it was on the earth. Still is. As the song goes, there's a parking lot in its place now.

"Patience, my friend," I said. "This is just the beginning of the voyage. We'll reach our hallowed destination in time."

Yeah, that was the way I used to talk. Unbearable.

"No, I mean I'm not going to let you do it," Judas said and chuckled. He looked at me and showed me his true self for the first time. His eyes went black, like a serpent's, only even darker. His skin took on the hue of a corpse. Even his shape changed, twisting into something gaunt and skeletal that was not quite human. And his voice became a thousand different voices, all whispering in unison. "I will turn your dreams to ash and dust, just like the dreams of all the saviours who have come before you."

I pushed myself away from the table, from him. "What manner of abomination are you?" I cried. But I knew the answer from his words even as I asked the question. He was something older than me, something older than the Father and the angels. Perhaps even older than the demons. But I wasn't exactly sure what. A minor god of a people long dead, perhaps. One of the countless tricksters who roamed the earth, wreaking mischief and havoc. Or perhaps something even more ancient and alien. Something the world had forgotten.

"I am the serpent in your garden," Judas said. Then came the sound of an armoured hand pounding on the door, and I knew I was betrayed. And I didn't have so much as a breath of grace to defend myself.

"But I could have saved even you," I told him.

Judas toasted me with the wine. "The thing you need to learn," he said, "is that not everyone wants your salvation." He got up as a human once again and opened the door. And the rest, so they say, is history.

If ruining things for all of humanity wasn't bad enough, Judas also came to me in the form of the Roman legionnaire who stuck the spear in my side while I was on the cross, dying that first time. He tried to get the other legionnaires to join him in poking me, but they were too busy betting who would die first: me, the thief on my left or the political agitator on my right. The agitator was preaching an early form of communism, if you must know, but, obviously, the world wasn't ready for it yet.

There were more crosses planted around the hill. Skeletons hung from them, picked clean by the birds. Skulls littered the ground underfoot. The very earth seemed to be made of bones. A sign of what we were to become. From dust I was born and now, it seemed, to dust I would return.

The angels were there, of course. Perched on the crosses in the hundreds, watching me die. They had cast sleights so no one would notice them, but I saw them. They were there for me, after all.

They could have stopped the entire event. They could have rescued me from the cross. They could have slaughtered the Romans and put Judas in my place. But they did none of these things. They just looked on and did nothing. I have no idea why they didn't save me. Perhaps because I was human, in a way. Perhaps because it was the Father's will. Perhaps because they were already fallen.

When the other legionnaires got bored of waiting for us to expire and went off in search of some wine and camp whores, Judas climbed up the cross to look at me face to face. And there were those black eyes again.

"I see you have an honour guard," he said in that chorus of voices, glancing around at all the angels. "Or are they here for one of the others?"

"You have damned the world," I said, "when I would have redeemed it."

He spat on the bones beneath us. "You and your kind damned my world many ages ago," he said. "Now I'm damning yours. I will spread chaos where you would have spread your precious garden."

"You cannot bring back that which is gone," I said. "This is meaningless."

He leaned in close enough I could smell his breath. Meat and blood and all things nice. "You are preaching to the converted on that front," he said.

"Soon I will be nothing," I said. "And humanity along with me. But your kind, whatever they may have been, will still be nothing as well."

"We are all nothing in the end," Judas said. "Just like in the beginning. It's what we do in between that matters. And today I have done something that matters a great deal."

"I curse you for all the ages," I told him. "You will never know peace again. Everything you love will be taken from you."

Judas kissed me on the lips. "And you, little monkey," he breathed. Then he gouged out my eyes and threw himself off the cross, and I went painfully and tediously into that good night.

And that should have been it, except that I woke up in that cave sometime later, about as far from paradise as you can get, not knowing who I was, not knowing where I was, with nothing in my mind but those memories. I should have been dead, but instead I was born.

I used to be Christ, but now I wasn't. I knew I wasn't him in the same way you know a dream wasn't real when you wake. I woke in that cave trapped in a body that wasn't mine, a lost soul with no memories of my own. I didn't know how I'd gotten there, or where or even what I had been before, but I knew I wasn't Christ.

I was born and I yearned for something to fill the void inside me. The void that Christ had left. I was born and I hated. I hated Judas instinctively. Perhaps because of the memories of what he had done to Christ. Perhaps because I suspected he played some role in me being trapped in Christ's body. That hate has never faded, even now, but then he's given me plenty of reasons over the centuries to keep on hating.

I had hoped Judas dead after our last encounter, after Penelope, but if what Cassiel told me was true, then it seemed Judas was still alive. And Cassiel didn't strike me as the type to make things up.

Cassiel probably knew I'd do anything to get my hands on Judas, to corner him in a little chamber like I'd cornered Remiel. Remiel wasn't personal. Remiel was just grace.

But Judas – Judas was personal.

A VISIT WITH THE *MONA LISA* AND OTHER CURIOSITIES

Every quest has to start somewhere, but luckily this one had an obvious starting point: the *Mona Lisa* in Paris. The one that Cassiel seemed to think wasn't the real Mona Lisa.

So I took Remiel's money from his shoulder bag and I slept on a bench in the Barcelona train station. Only one pickpocket tried to take the money from my pants during the night, and I caught a couple of his fingers and broke them without opening my eyes. After that, no one else bothered me.

I took the first train to Paris in the morning. As we pulled out of the station we passed an old steam locomotive with a single passenger car sitting on one of the side tracks, empty of travellers or crew. Both locomotive and car were painted white, with crimson wheels. They were waiting for someone to board. I knew this because I'd been warned about the train by a Spanish sculptor I'd once raised from the dead to ask about some of his missing works. I thought maybe if he knew where they were I could find them and sell them to afford more wine and lovers. I'd tell you his name but I've forgotten it. Just like history has forgotten him.

The sculptor didn't know what had happened to the missing works, and he no longer cared. But he did tell me about the white train, maybe because a railway ran past the cemetery where I raised him, and maybe because I'd brought wine with me to the cemetery. He said the white train went to Paris, but a different Paris. The Paris of people's dreams and fantasies, the perfect Paris. The Paris that didn't exist and you would never find unless

the back of my right leg and into the sand, pinning me. I cried out in pain and the crowd cried out in delight.

"The gods be damned," I said, turning my pain into a scream of rage. "Why are you doing this?" He was going to slay me again and I still didn't know what was going on.

Judas moved behind me, and now I couldn't see him.

"For the same reasons I killed you," he said. "Or at least I thought I killed you."

I reached back and tried to pull out the sword, but he smashed the other blade down onto my arm, breaking the bone. I made various unmanly noises at the pain and fell forward, into the sand. The crowd began to chant his name: Commodus. They'd always been a fickle lot.

"You're going to destroy them." I spat into the sand. "Just like you destroyed everything Christ could have given humanity." He may have been the emperor, but he was still the same Judas underneath.

"They have tried to create a golden age," he said, "but they cannot help their nature. They dress in the robes and fineries of upright citizens, but they are still beasts ready to turn upon each other." He slammed his knee into my back and held me down against the earth. "Listen to them shriek at each other. They *want* the chaos of the arena. Did you hear them cheer when I came down here amid the blood and beasts? This is where they want to be. It is their nature." He ground me deeper into the sand. "This empire will burn like all the others. I may be the flame, but they are the kindling."

"You're mad," I gasped.

"Civilization is madness," Judas said. "A delusion that you all share, thinking it will hold off the night. I remind humanity of what you are – monkeys killing each other in the dirt. *I'm* what you should be praying to because I'm the natural order."

"That's what this is all about?" I said. "You're feeling left out because people have moved on to other gods?"

He put the blade of his sword against my throat. "You'd best pray to one of those other gods now," he said. "For I won't save you."

"Answer me one thing before I die," I said, gasping for my last breaths of air.

"Perhaps, if the question is interesting enough," he said, pausing.

"Who am I?" I asked.

Judas chuckled. "You? You're just another dead monkey." And he drew the blade across my throat and held my face into the sand until the blood drained out of me.

I died with the roar of the crowd in my ears.

And I awoke to the sound of my own screaming, alone under the earth.

I thrashed wildly, reaching out for Judas in the darkness, trying to find a weapon, trying to crawl away, all at once. But I was held by the grave. Dirt flowed into my mouth, choking off my screams, and I blindly clawed my way out, until I burst forth into the light.

I pulled myself halfway from the grave and spat the dirt out of my mouth before I threw up on the ground. I took deep, heaving breaths. More sobs than breaths, really. I looked around, expecting to find myself in Hades. Instead, I found myself in a shallow grave beside an olive orchard. A crow laughed at me from a tree, and I heard a donkey bray somewhere in the distance. Not exactly what I'd expected of the afterlife.

That's when I realized I couldn't die. Not for good, anyway. Judas may have killed and buried me again, but my body wouldn't let me stay dead. My body's supernatural healing powers extended all the way to resurrection.

Since then I've learned the length of time I'm dead depends on how much grace I've got in my system. Sometimes it takes hours, sometimes years. But so far I've always come back to life, whether or not I've wanted to.

I brushed the earth from me and screamed some more. At what had happened to me. At what I had become. Then I threw a clod of dirt at the crow to shut it up and walked away from the grave to figure out where I was.

I was a day's walk from Rome, but it seemed an entire age had passed by the time I returned to the city. I walked through the gates in search of Commodus or whoever Judas was now, but he was gone, and the city was torn apart. Armed militias clashed with each other, while soldiers got drunk in the public squares. People fucked in the alleys. Villas burned here and there. And everywhere was graffiti announcing the death of the emperor. Some said he'd been killed by a slave he'd taken to his bed, while more creative pieces described in pictures how a group of his animal lovers had torn him apart and consumed him. The official notices posted in the squares said he'd been strangled in his bath by his wrestling partner, Narcissus. I didn't know which of the stories were true.

Nobody recognized me. Nobody seemed to be in charge. I knew Judas had created this chaos somehow. The empire was falling into ruin, and nothing could save it now. And I also knew Judas wasn't really dead, not any more than I was.

He was gone, but I understood now how to find him.

I left Rome and went out into the world, just another forgotten dead man. I went in search of more war and chaos; in search of Judas.

I went in search of myself.

A DEAL WITH A GORGON

And now here I was, centuries later, sitting on a dusty window ledge in a museum, with a few more memories and experiences but still no real idea of where I'd come from or even how I'd come to be. Or, more importantly, why I'd wound up in the body of Christ. It was the sort of thing that could get you down if you let it.

The window beside me turned dark and cool and a woman announced over the PA that the museum was closing. I waited until the sounds of people in the hall faded away before I opened my eyes and looked around. It was just Victory and me.

Victory isn't her real name, of course. And she isn't just a statue. She's a gorgon who was turned to stone through some misfortune she won't discuss. All she's ever told me is it wasn't a mirror. Apparently that whole business about reflected gazes is a myth. You just can't trust the people who make up the myths. Who knows – maybe her condition was caused by the gorgon equivalent of osteoporosis. At any rate, you'd be surprised how many statues and gargoyles are more than just statues and gargoyles.

I watched her and waited for the security guard to make his pass through the area. He blew Victory a kiss when he did so, and I had to smile and shake my head. If he only knew.

When the guard was gone, I hopped off the window ledge and went over to Victory. I summoned a bit of grace and blew it into the space where her head should have been. A face formed there, flickering, insubstantial, like a ghost. It writhed in and out of existence, so I could only catch glimpses of it. High cheekbones. Eyes and lips like a snake's. Which matched the writhing hair you'd expect of a gorgon. I could have used extra grace to make her more substantial, but I'd learned over the years to conserve it. Angels were in short supply these days, and you never knew when you'd stumble across another one.

I didn't bother averting my eyes. Victory's gaze had never done me any harm, other than make me feel slightly uncomfortable. Besides, she'd told me once the gorgons all had different powers and hers wasn't her gaze. Of course, she wouldn't tell me what it was. Everyone has their secrets.

"It has been a long time, hydra," she said. Hydra was her pet name for me because she found my inability to die amusing. At least someone appreciated it.

"It hasn't been that long," I said. It had only been a couple of decades since I'd gone to her for help with the Perseus affair. Perseus – now there was a monster.

"Every second of time feels like an eternity to us," she said.

Victory always used the plural when talking about herself and the other gorgons. She said they lived in each other. Like the Holy Trinity, she'd explained to me once, but I told her I didn't know what that meant.

"Every time I visit you I learn something new," I said.

"The things we could teach you in the flesh," she said. "Have you come to give us life and limb again at long last?"

"I'm afraid not," I told her. "I don't think the world is ready for that."

"It has never been ready." She sighed, and I somehow felt her breath on my skin. The hair on my arms and neck stood up, and I had to restrain myself from stepping back. "But we are ready for it. The things we have dreamed of doing all these centuries –"

I motioned for her to keep it down because her voice was starting to rise, and she frowned at me. "When we were free of these earthly chains, we sang until the very sky was rent open," she muttered. "No one dared to order us into silence then."

"Now they'd just put you in a crate with soundproof walls," I told her. "Look, this isn't a social call. I need your help."

"Ah," she said, and the snakes on her head hissed at me. "Men and their never-ending quests. We have seen so many of your kind over the ages.

Always with swords in your hands instead of gifts."

"Rumour is you ate the one man who actually wanted to be your suitor," I said.

"We were young and impetuous then," she said with a smile. "And he was so very meaty. We are far more refined these days."

"Give me what I need and I'll bring you a cup of tea next time," I said.

"Replace cup with flagon and tea with blood and we may be able to work something out," she said.

I wasn't sure if she was joking or not but what the hell. That's why people donate blood, right?

"Tell me what you know about the Mona Lisa," I said.

"Go down the hall until you hit the washrooms," she said. "Turn left and then –"

"Not that one," I said. "The real Mona Lisa."

Victory fell silent then as she considered me, which was a first. She's usually a very talkative gorgon. I suppose being locked in stone for most of your existence makes you chatty in your few moments of reprieve. Even her snakes were quiet as they all watched me. I tried not to look at them and cast my gaze about the hall instead, checking for other security guards on their rounds. It was only a matter of time.

"What is the nature of your quest?" Victory finally asked.

"A certain angel has taken an interest in the Mona Lisa," I said. "If I can deliver it, he will give me something I really want."

"The name of this angel," she said.

"Cassiel," I told her. "The watcher."

Now she was silent for even longer, and her snakes coiled around each other.

"You know him," I said. It was an observation, not a question.

"We know him," Victory said.

I shouldn't have been surprised, and yet I was.

"We will help you," Victory said before I could recover enough to ask the obvious follow-up question.

"Wait a minute," I said. "*How* do you know Cassiel?" I wasn't going to leave that one alone.

"You must earn your answers in the time-honoured manner," she said. "With a quest of our own devising."

I sighed. There's always a catch.

"Can I do the questing part later?" I asked. "After you give me the information and I get this other quest out of the way? I mean, it's not like you're going anywhere."

"Find our head," she said.

I paused. I wasn't expecting that.

"You mean your missing head?" I asked. "The one all the archaeologists and scholars haven't been able to find?"

"Find our head and we will reward you with the information you so desire," she said.

"I can't say I have any idea where to look for your head," I admitted.

"This is why it is a quest and not a mere errand," she said.

"What do you even want with it?" I asked.

Her hair hissed at me again. "We don't ask you why you're so attached to your head," she said.

"What I mean is it won't do you any good," I said. "You'll still be stone." I paused again. "Won't you?"

"We miss it," she said simply, and I couldn't take issue with that.

I thought things over, but I didn't see as I had much of a choice.

"All right," I said, "but you can't keep it here. I don't want the curators finding it and putting this place under constant surveillance."

"Oh, you don't need to bring it back to us," she said. "Just destroy it once you've found it."

"You want me to find your head and then destroy it?" I asked. "I'm having trouble following your logic."

"We are trapped in separate pieces," she said. "Our spirit torn asunder with our body. Perhaps if you destroy our head, you will free us and we can be one again."

She didn't need to say anything about her missing arms for me to imagine what might happen if I actually did manage to find her head. Every good quest comes in trilogy form, after all.

"And if it doesn't free your spirit?" I asked. "What if destroying your head destroys what's left of you?" I wasn't just talking out loud here – I would actually miss Victory if she were gone. We had our differences, her being a gorgon and me being, well, whatever I was, but we went back a long way. There were a lot of memories.

"Then we will live on in our sisters," she said. "Like Medusa."

I took a step back involuntarily. "Medusa's in there with you?" I asked.

"She is one of us," Victory said. "She is all of us."

"I see," I said, although I really didn't.

"Our time here is fading," Victory said. "Free us, hydra. Free us and you will be rewarded."

And then she was gone and it was just me and the stone statue again. The sounds of someone whistling down the hall meant it was time to be going anyway. I blew Victory a kiss and got the hell out of there.

I left via an emergency exit that set alarms ringing – nothing wrong with giving the guards a little excitement to distract them from their cameras – and lost myself in the Tuileries Garden and the light rain outside. I ignored a handful of young men smoking a joint underneath some trees who mistook me for a lost tourist and yelled insults at me about – well, my contemporary French is a little shaky. I think they commented on the cut of my pants, but I wasn't really certain. I'd long since given up getting in fights over such things. There were always young men ready with a quick insult somewhere. They were legion. And I'd learned very early in my life that it was best not to attract too much attention to myself by doing things like getting in brawls with strangers on city streets. Sometimes it attracted the attention of the authorities. And sometimes it attracted the attention of things far more dangerous.

IN THE POPE'S DUNGEON

I'd gone to Victory for help because we have a history together. We'd met in a dungeon under the Vatican well before it was ever called the Vatican. That was back in my early days, when I was still learning how to use the powers Christ had left me.

I'd been in the dungeon because of a brawl with some drunks in a tavern. I can't even remember where it happened, other than it was someplace in the south of what's now known as Italy. I'd travelled to the area because there was a good deal of rioting and burning of villages and such in the region at the time. I'd figured there was a chance Judas was behind it all and still lingering around. Whatever time I didn't spend scouring the countryside for him I wasted away in wine and lovers more fallen than me.

Imagine Christ's grace taken away from you, but you can still feel it, or at least its absence. What can I compare it to? Imagine your wife or husband or kids killed but their ghosts haunting you every day. Imagine living your life in the rain and dark with only the memories of sunshine. Imagine having the epiphany in church that God exists, that Christ really was here – only they're never coming back again. All right, that one's not so hard to imagine.

Sometimes, the only thing you can do is drink. So that's what I did.

I'd had a few too many of this particular tavern's homemade ale, and they had gone to my head. And every other part of me. For some reason I'd started comparing battle scars with a few of the other drunks. We tried to outdo each other with longer, nastier wounds. I was expecting to win, given all the times I'd been knifed and hacked and stabbed and such over the years. My scars fade with time, thanks to my miraculous body, but I was always adding new ones, so I had a pretty good collection to show off. But then the tavern keeper himself, a big, bald brute of a man, lifted his tunic to show a vicious red line running from his throat to his groin.

"I lay on death's doorstep for an entire winter," he said, "but the bastard wouldn't let me in." He laughed. "If you think this is bad, you should see the other poor soul."

My new drinking partners all toasted him and agreed that he'd won. But I wasn't ready to give up yet.

"Piss on your scar," I told the tavern keeper. "I've had far worse wounds than that. I just heal better than you sickly lot."

The tavern keeper snorted and poured himself a victory drink. "If you'd ever had a worse wound than mine, you'd be dead."

"I've been dead plenty of times," I said. I tried to drain my cup in a dramatic fashion, but it was empty. Story of my life. I smashed it down on the table instead. I forgot my usual caution about revealing too many personal details because of all the drinks I'd had. "But they haven't made a weapon yet that can kill Christ for good." I thought about that for a second, then added, "Or me, anyway."

For some reason they took offence at my words, and one of the other drunks hammered me with his stool a couple of times. I threw my goblet at him but hit someone else, and then suddenly the whole tavern was involved. It was everyone against everyone, because that's just the kind of place it was.

And then he came out of the crowd at me. I've never known his name. He was old, hunched in a robe and cloak, with grey stringy hair that covered half his face, over the eye socket that had been melted shut. To this day I wonder who did that to him, or if he did it to himself.

As soon as I saw him I felt that familiar hollowness inside. For a few seconds, I thought it was fear. But then I found myself stumbling toward him instead of away.

He stopped and looked at me as the mayhem continued around us. "You are Christ?" he asked.

"Christ is dead," I said. "So the world's going to have to make do with me." I threw a punch at him that he caught with one hand and held there in the air. He showed no signs of exertion. A charge ran down my arm at his touch. I wanted to pull him into an embrace, but I settled for spitting at his feet. "And what mockery of nature are you?" I asked.

"I'm an abomination," he said. "Just like you."

And then one of his hands lashed out from underneath the cape with a knife, and I had the best scar in the room.

I resurrected chained to the wall of a cramped dungeon cell. I was hungry as hell, and had no idea where I was, or why I was there. I wondered if the one-eyed bastard had been a friend of Judas's, sent to warn me off his trail, but then the guards came in with the pope, and I knew I was in an entirely different sort of trouble.

You see what I mean about attracting the wrong kind of attention?

I didn't know he was the pope at first, of course. He had to introduce himself to me and explain we were in a secret dungeon. I'd tell you his name, but to do so runs the risk of raising him from the grave. Let dead popes lie, I say.

Even then, I thought perhaps that he was Judas in disguise again. I went so far as to suggest as much, which earned a few well-placed blows from one of the guards. But then the pope asked me how I'd managed that resurrection trick, and I realized he didn't know anything about me. Which I guess explained the chains. When you're in the pope business, it's probably better to play it safe when dealing with things like me. For all the good that it did him in the end.

"I'm Christ," I told the pope. "Or at least I used to be. Now I don't know who I am." I didn't see any point in withholding information. Maybe if I was honest with them they'd free me. Or at least give me a drink. Or maybe he'd find some way to put me out of my misery for good.

"I don't think so," the pope said. He held a cloth to his nose while he studied me. I'd soiled myself in death again. "I don't think Christ would return in such a lowly vessel."

I shrugged as best as I could in chains. "It's kind of hard to explain, but in some ways I never really left."

That obviously wasn't good enough for him, because he waved at his torturers to start setting up their equipment. "Tell me what you really are," he said.

"And here I was hoping you could tell me," I said.

He nodded at his men and they went to work on me. They crossed themselves before they started. Tough spot for them to be in, I suppose.

What to say of that time? They did their thing and I did my part by screaming a lot and adding more stains to the floor. At the end of our little session, nobody was really satisfied.

"I will give you time to rethink your answers," the pope said, and I skipped my usual witty response on account of what they'd done to my tongue.

It was while I hung there in my chains after they left that I first noticed Victory. My door had a hole with bars in it, and I could see into the cell across the hall. Victory was chained to the wall in that cell, although she was a statue even back then.

"Help me get out of here and I'll take you with me," I called out to her when I could speak again, but she didn't say anything in response. I figured she was more than just a statue if she was locked up in the pope's dungeon, but I had no idea at the time exactly what she was. Life's full of little surprises.

The torches in the hall had nearly all burned out when the pope returned with his torturers. They lit new torches, but I couldn't decide if that was a good thing or a bad thing.

"Could you at least give me something to eat before we start again?" I asked. I was desperate for something, anything, to fill the emptiness inside me. It had been a long time since I'd killed the angel in the arena, and everything I'd taken from him was gone.

"Whatever you are, I doubt it's earthly sustenance you need," the pope said and settled himself onto a stool one of his guards had carried. It's never a good sign when the guy in charge makes himself comfortable.

"Let us begin with a fresh page," he said. "Who are you?"

"I already told you I don't know," I reminded him. But this just wasn't one of those times honesty paid off. His men did their thing once more, and I did mine, and then the pope called a break.

"If you were the real Christ, you would have borne this suffering with dignity," he said to me.

"If I were the real Christ, I would have had you crucified by now," I said. "And I would have added a hot poker up your ass for good measure."

And then he got up off the stool and took the tools from his men and went to work on me himself. And I was forced to concede that if the pope thing didn't work out for him, he had an excellent future as a torturer.

At the end of it all he brought in the one-eyed man who'd stabbed me in the tavern. "Find out what this thing is," the pope told him, "and I will put an end to your suffering."

I never did find out what the one-eyed man's suffering was, because he came at me then and I used a little trick a fellow gladiator had shown me in the pits and caught him in my chains. He was old or weak, or maybe both, otherwise I never could have held him. Or maybe he just wanted to be caught.

I twisted the chains so hard a little gasp escaped his lips. And in that breath was a bit of grace, just like what I'd taken from that angel in the Colosseum. When I breathed it in, my body screamed for more. I may have even screamed aloud. Every part of me yearned for what was in him. And the grace made me stronger, so I twisted the chains even more, until the skin on his neck tore open as he struggled, and the grace poured out.

The pope and the torturers just stared as I strangled the life out of the angel. I guess it wasn't the sort of thing you saw every day, even in a pope's dungeon.

And then a bit of grace splashed out of the cell and onto the statue across the hall. And a spectral face formed there above the stone body – Victory, although we didn't know each other by name at that point. She began to shriek in Greek, and the pope and his men turned white when they looked into her cell. And then they fled and didn't return.

I finished killing the angel and taking his grace. Then I sundered the chains and stood there for a moment, just savouring the feeling of the light in me. I didn't feel hungry anymore. I didn't feel empty anymore. I'd forgotten what it felt like to be whole.

I went out into the hall to the other cell and kicked down the door. That spectral head shrieked some more, but I didn't know enough Greek to make sense of it.

"I don't know what you're saying," I said, "but I'm a man of my word." That was a bit of a stretch, but I figured no one deserved to be in this dungeon, no matter what they'd done. No one except for Judas.

I dragged Victory out of the cell and up the stairs, into a small fortress filled with soldiers. But they all ran away too when Victory screeched at them. I realized she must have been someone special indeed in her day.

So we went back out into the world. Her head eventually faded away and she was a statue again, but I knew how to summon her now. I was learning how to use the grace. I took her to a special antiquities dealer and blew a bit of grace into her to call her back. And she came, shrieking once more, but she calmed down when she saw she was in a shop instead of a dungeon cell. The dealer just nodded like he'd seen this before and dropped some coins into my hand.

"I'll check up on you again," I told Victory, and waved at her in case she didn't understand. I tossed a couple of the coins back to the dealer. "See if you can teach her a language that people actually still use," I told him, and then I gave her enough grace to keep her around for a while.

After all, you just never know who your friends might turn out to be.

And then, because I knew who my enemy was, I went back outside and after Judas once more.

THIS IS THE WAY
YOU SUMMON ALICE

I walked until I hit the Champs-Élysées, and then I made my way down it as the dawn lit up the city. I found a café that had opened early and went in for another espresso and a pain au chocolat this time. I figured I'd earned it. I was hungry for more, for a proper meal, because it had been a while since I'd had one of those. But I was used to being hungry.

I could see the top of the Eiffel Tower from my table. Most people think it's just an old communications tower. It is, but most people have no idea what it was used to communicate with. It's probably better if they don't know, but who am I to say?

I drank my espresso and ate my pain au chocolat and thought about Victory's request.

I understand what it is to be separated from your spirit. I don't mean Christ – he's more like a fading dream to me these days.

I mean Penelope.

I wasn't entirely honest earlier when I said the only things that make life bearable for me are grace and death. There's also Penelope. Or rather, there was Penelope.

Penelope who raised me from the dead in her own way, and who's dead now herself.

I finished my breakfast and made my way to the Montparnasse Cemetery. I wandered it for a while and listened to the sounds of the city fade. I thought of the last time I'd been here, with her. It was after the Nazis had been driven out of the city and everyone thought maybe it had been the war to finally end all wars.

Today was sunny, with clear skies, but that day had been grey and wet, more of a Copenhagen day than a Paris postcard. We were looking for angels, but the only angels we found were on gravestones. I revisited them all now. They didn't have any more to say to me this time than they did back then.

I stopped in front of Baudelaire's grave and nodded my hello to him. Penelope and I had kissed there that day, in this same spot. Our breath had been visible in the air, and a breeze had lifted her hair around our heads. It was a moment I wanted to last forever.

But I've learned very few things in the world last forever.

And now it was time to see Alice. I couldn't put it off anymore. I left the cemetery and waved down a taxi. I asked the driver to take me to the nearest library. He eyed me a little – I guess his fares didn't usually want libraries – but I threw some money on his lap and then we were friends again.

When he dropped me off at the library, I patted the stone lions flanking the stairs to its entrance. You never know. If they were really something other than sculptures and came to life some day I'd like them to have fond memories of me.

Then I went up the stairs and through the doors in search of Alice.

Here's the thing about Alice – you can only find her in libraries. Well, and sometimes bookstores. But that depends on the bookstore. She's a little moody about them. She likes most libraries, though, so that's where I tend to look for her first.

This is the way you summon Alice: You find the right book in the library and start to read it. That'll bring her to you from wherever it is she hides in libraries. Simple, right? So what's the right book? That's the hard part and it depends on the library. Sometimes the book even changes in the same library. In the New York Public Library's Epiphany Branch it had been a biography of Lewis Carroll for years, and then one day I tried it and it didn't work. It took me three weeks to find the new book, a copy of Alberto Manguel's *A History of Reading*. Also, the book has to be mis-shelved. Did I mention Alice was moody?

And yes, I said summon. Alice is a lot like a demon in some ways, except she's not a demon. And she doesn't have any grace in her, which is why I've never tried to kill her and we're still friends. But she's definitely not human. In fact, I'm not even sure she exists. It's a strange little world we live in sometimes.

I'd never been in this library before, so I had nothing to go on. At least it was a small neighbourhood branch. It would probably only take a few hours to skim the stacks, looking for the books out of place.

I started in the fiction section. Whenever I found a book that wasn't where it was supposed to be, I took it from the shelf and read a few pages, then looked around. When Alice didn't appear, I put the book back and moved on. I'd been doing this for about forty-five minutes when a woman wearing a librarian's name tag came over and asked me if I needed any help. I was reading a passage from Donald Barthelme's *Snow White* at the time, but she had a look on her face that said we both knew I wasn't there for the great literature.

"I'm looking for an old friend," I told her. "Only I'm not sure where to find her."

She folded her arms across her chest and gazed at me. It was a look I recognized well from all the time I'd spent in libraries. She was trying to decide whether she should go back to her mystery novel or call the police. They usually went back to their mystery novels, because reading a book is always better than filling out paperwork. But some had read too many of those mystery novels and saw danger everywhere.

While she was still making up her mind, a chorus of young voices wailing together came from the children's literature section.

"Never mind," I said, putting *Snow White* back on the shelf. "I think I know where she is."

I followed the sounds of children crying until I found Alice sitting on a stool in an open area of the library. She was wearing a dress with stains on it that could have been blood, as well as a top hat. Today her hair was blond, although there were streaks of mud in it. She looked like she was barely out of her teens, which was the same way she'd looked when I'd met her many, many years before. She was reading from an ancient leather tome to the weeping children seated around her. At least I think it was leather.

It could have been human skin. And the stool was a giant mushroom that looked like a real giant mushroom.

"And that's how the world will end," Alice said as I walked up. She closed the book and slipped it into one of the shelves beside her and the children cried even harder and ran for their parents. None of the librarians seated at a nearby desk even looked up. I think Alice casts some sort of charm on them so they recognize her as one of their own. They're a mysterious bunch, librarians.

When Alice saw me, she clapped her hands together and ran over to give me a hug. I tried to think of the last time I'd seen her. Athens, maybe? When she had sported the shaved head and the military uniform?

"Cross!" she said. "Have you come to tell me you've finally found what you were looking for? I hope so. I want to see what it is."

"Hold on," I said. "I want to know how the world ends." I looked for the book she'd been reading to the children, but I didn't see it on the shelf. It had vanished.

Alice giggled. "You should know how it ends," she said. "You were the one who wrote the book."

I shook my head. "I've had the good sense to never write anything more than a few lines of romantic drivel," I said. "I've certainly never tried anything as ambitious as a book." And I would never try. The novelists I've known over the centuries have all been drunks and vagabonds. Or insane. It's best to stay clear of that business.

"You didn't write it in this story, silly," she said, ruffling my hair. "You wrote it in one of the other ones."

"Oh," I said. "Of course."

She looked around and then leaned close to whisper in my ear. "But I like you better in this one. You're too mean in the other one. I think running all those armies and torturing all those people is getting to you."

"I can only imagine," I said.

I'd once found Alice by reading an article in a magazine about multiple universes. When I'd finished the article, Alice was sitting in the chair beside me, wearing a bridal gown and knitting a hat for someone who had a head at least three times the size of mine.

"They have it all wrong," she'd said that time. "There aren't any other universes. There are only other books."

Make of that what you will.

Now she stepped back and twirled her hair with a finger. "So what brings you here?" She looked around. "Where are we anyway?"

"Paris," I told her, and then I added the year. Just in case.

"Ohhh, I like Paris," she said and smiled. "You should see the things people do in the stacks sometimes."

"I need to find out something," I told her and pulled her into one of those stacks.

"Me too," she said, nodding. I waited, but she didn't say anything else. That was Alice. So I carried on.

"I don't suppose you know where Judas is?" I asked.

"Of course I do," she said, pulling some of her hair out of her head with that same finger. "He's where he always is."

"And where's that?" I asked. I tried not to get my hopes up.

She tapped me on the forehead. "In here, of course." Then she noticed the hair wrapped around her finger. She stared at it like she didn't know where it'd come from.

Whenever I asked Alice about Judas, she always gave me an answer like that. Maybe she was trying to be philosophical. And you thought the books were hard to read.

Right, next.

"You know the gorgon in the Louvre?" I asked her.

She nodded again. "I've read everything about her," she said. "Even her diaries. She just needs to find the right lover."

"That could be tricky," I said. "And it's not my problem. But I do need to find her head."

"Oh, that's easy," Alice said. "It's where it's always been. Well, not always of course. Because once upon a time it was on her neck and shoulders."

I waited. Patience is a virtue and all that, especially with Alice.

"And after that, of course, it was at the bottom of the sea until the kraken found it and wore it as a charm for one of its tentacles. But then Ahab cut that tentacle off when he fought the kraken. So I guess it wasn't that good of a charm."

"I thought all the krakens were dead," I said.

"Not the ghost krakens," she said, rolling her eyes at me.

"Of course," I said. "Pardon me."

"And then what happened to it?" she said, scrunching her eyes tight. "Hmm, let me see."

I watched a mother try to pull her son into the children's section, but he screamed and ran away at the sight of Alice.

"Oh yes," Alice said. "Then a sea diver found it and took it back to his tribe. They all thought it was the skull of one of their gods, but she's not really a god, you know, she's –"

"Condensed version?" I suggested.

Alice pouted at me. "I don't know why I should help you after what you did to the Library of Alexandria. I rather liked that library."

"If we're talking about the real Library of Alexandria, I already told you that was an accident," I said. "Besides which, look at all the ones I've helped you find in the meantime. Remember Marlowe's secret library?"

"Oh, I do remember that!" Alice said. "I keep it in between a journal entry of a dream that Anaïs Nin had about Venice and a book idea that Fitzgerald wrote down on a scrap of paper while he was drunk but forgot about when he was sober. The British Museum."

"You keep those memories in the British Museum?" I asked.

"No, I keep those memories in here," she said. She took off the top hat and stared inside it. "At least I did. Now where did they get to?"

"The British Museum?" I prompted her.

"No, I just told you they're not there," she said. "But that's where the gorgon's head is. Only it's not really a head anymore. It's just a skull now, if you can even call it that." She put the top hat back on, then paused as a thought struck her. "Don't you think it's odd that museums don't have muses?"

"Where in the museum is it?" I asked.

Alice smiled at me. "Why, where it's supposed to be, of course."

"All right," I said. I wasn't going to get anything else out of her. I kissed her on her cheeks, in the French way. "Until next time. Hopefully it won't be as long a wait."

"You can't have things worth waiting for without the wait," she said.

She turned and walked off into the stacks, disappearing behind a display of Tintin comics, and I went back out into the street. I had a train to England to catch.

PENELOPE

In case you haven't noticed, I find it hard to talk about Penelope even though she's been dead for decades. There's not even anything left of her. No body, no grave anywhere, marked or unmarked. Even her photos are all gone. All that remains of her are my memories.

Penelope and I in the forgotten graveyard in the forest where we met, the morning mist burning away between us as we looked at each other across the simple crosses shoved into the ground.

Penelope and I at the bow of a ship in the Pacific, watching the sun set until we were alone in the darkness. Our own little world.

Penelope and I sitting on a blanket under a row of cherry blossom trees beside the Kamo River in Japan during the annual hanami, toasting the other people around us with sake. The lights of the lanterns better than any stars.

Someday all my memories will fade and I'll have nothing left to remember her by. I hope that's the day I die and stay dead.

But I won't rest until I find Judas and kill him. Kill him like he killed Penelope.

HOW NOT TO STEAL
A GORGON'S SKULL

I took the train to London. It was quick, but not nearly as scenic as the ship crossings of earlier centuries had been. Once we were in the tunnel under the ocean, there was nothing to look at but my own reflection in the window, and I'd had enough of that view some time ago. I settled for reading the back page of the paper that the man across from me was browsing. It had the latest update on a politician caught bedding someone he shouldn't have been bedding, and ads for the home furnishings of your dreams. The usual fare. At least the train was warmer and drier than taking a ship.

I thought about what Alice had told me. I wasn't exactly enthusiastic about trying to find Victory's head in the British Museum, let alone destroying property of the state. As far as I knew, the Royal Family still had a bounty on my head for the Avebury incident. Hopefully, I'd be able to get in and out of the country before they even knew I was there.

I closed my eyes and tried to nap. It's a habit from my days in various armies around the world. No matter what cause you're dying for, one thing always remains the same for soldiers: get your sleep while you can because you don't know when you'll get a chance next.

I dozed for maybe half an hour or so and then something woke me. One of those feelings of danger that I've learned to trust. I tightened my grip on my backpack – experience has taught me to always keep a hand on my luggage, even when sleeping – and opened my eyes without moving, looking around for the source of the danger. For the attack.

But there was nothing other than the man across from me. He'd put the paper aside and was looking at a Sotheby's catalogue of paintings. *Old Masters*, the cover said over a rendering of a man wreaking havoc in a field with a scythe. I didn't recognize the painting or the artist, but that was usually the way. The truly good paintings usually get tossed on a fire or locked in a room somewhere. Same with the good artists.

The man glanced up at me and nodded when he saw I was awake. "We're almost there," he said in English, but with an accent I couldn't place.

I sat up and looked around. I couldn't see anything out of the ordinary, just other people reading and sleeping and sharing snacks. I wondered if maybe I'd just had a bad dream.

I looked back at the man across from me. "Are you a collector?" I asked, gesturing at the catalogue.

"Dealer," he said. "Coming back from the fair in Maastricht."

"How was it?" I asked.

He shook his head. "I wouldn't call this year a success. The attendance was very poor, the offerings substandard. All the good works are being kept under lock and key these days."

I studied him for a moment. Then I said, "I take it you couldn't get a booth to sell your wares."

He studied me right back. "What makes you think that?" he asked.

I shrugged. "I've known a few dealers in my time. I know the standard line is always the show was a success, even when it wasn't. It's all about the buzz. So I'm guessing you're not a large enough dealer to earn a spot in the show, but you're large enough that you cared to attend. Maybe your competition got in and now you're in danger of losing clients. If you didn't have any stake in it, you wouldn't have bothered attending and you certainly wouldn't bother bashing an industry event to a stranger you just met on a train."

Sometimes you have to find your own way to pass the time.

He smiled, just enough to show his teeth. "Are you an artist or another dealer?" he asked.

"I've never had enough business sense to be a dealer," I said. "And I haven't been an artist in a very long time."

"Are you responsible for anything I would know?" he asked.

"I doubt it," I told him, "unless your specialty is Roman sewer paintings."

He looked puzzled at that, and I moved on before he could ask any more questions. Another thing I've learned is that it's always better to be the interrogator than the interrogated.

"I'm still a bit of an art buff though," I said. "I try to keep up with the latest news. I read in a magazine recently that half the famous artworks hanging in the big galleries are fakes. You think that figure's right?" That was a bit of a lie. I hadn't read it in a magazine. Jackson Pollock had told me that, back before he'd made it big and still drank in bars. But the general idea is correct.

His mouth worked for a bit, and I couldn't tell if he was trying to hold back another smile or a grimace. "Most galleries have access to specialized equipment and labs for testing pigments and fibres and such," he said. "And experts that cannot easily be fooled. So I think you can be confident that the major works are genuine. But it's impossible to test everything in a gallery's collection. It's simply too time consuming. That's where dealers such as myself are invaluable. We have first-hand knowledge of many works, and close relationships with –"

"So you think it's possible then," I said.

"Anything is possible," he said, "but that doesn't make it probable."

The train started to slow, so I figured it was time to get down to it. "Let me ask you a question then. If the *Mona Lisa* hanging in the Louvre were a fake, where do you think the original would be?"

He sighed and shook his head. "I can assure you it's not a fake."

"It's been stolen before," I pointed out. "The real one could have been replaced with a forgery."

"You cannot even conceive of the range of tests they must have done on that painting to ensure its authenticity," he said. "The team of experts they would have assembled. It's more valuable than entire countries."

"Humour me then," I said.

"Whatever on earth for?" he asked, frowning and drumming his fingers on his catalogue.

"Let's say someone came to you to sell it," I said. "What would you do with it?"

There. That made him pause.

"Turn it in for the reward?" he said, in a less than convincing tone.

I rolled my eyes.

"Well, if we're speaking hypothetically," he said. "I guess I'd try to find a private collector for it."

"How would you do that?" I asked.

"I'd put the word out to my higher-end clients that I have a special work available," he said. "For private auction. I wouldn't have to name it. People talk. They figure things out."

"This actually happens?" I asked.

He shrugged, and we emerged from the tunnel, into the light. A landscape of industrial parks around us. The usual rain. Billboards obliterated by graffiti. Ah, England. As pastoral as ever.

"America," the art dealer said.

"What about it?" I asked.

"I'd take the *Mona Lisa* to America," he said.

I looked at him and he looked out the window.

"The collectors there buy history like they buy everything else," he said. "But then they make it disappear. They take the things we love and hide them away until the world forgets them."

An odd statement, I thought, but he did work in the arts.

He didn't look away from the window until the train came to a stop. We said our goodbyes and went our separate ways. I made time for breakfast at a pub – eggs and potatoes and toast and tea. I sat at the window and watched the rain blur the world outside. I thought about Cassiel and why he wanted the painting so badly, but I still didn't have any answers. I thought about Judas and wondered where he was at this very moment. I thought about friends I'd had in London who were all long gone now. It was only then that I realized the feeling I'd felt on the train had faded. Whatever threat there'd been, if any, was gone now. So be it. I had other things to worry about.

When I was done brooding, I went out into the rain and made my way to the British Museum. I stood in line behind an endless column of children in school uniforms screaming and taking pictures of each other with their phones. I just gazed around and did my best to look like another tourist. Which I was, in my own way.

When I finally made it inside, I wandered around like everyone else. I wasn't sure where the skull was, so I was going to have to find it. I spent the morning browsing the Egyptian wing. I studied stone sculptures and a pitted flint knife that looked like it had seen plenty of use in its time. I read a sign on a glass case housing a sarcophagus with faded paint. The sign said the occupant of the sarcophagus had been destined to become a god upon his death. I hoped he'd had better luck than me.

Morning turned to afternoon, which I whiled away checking the relics and statuary dedicated to Indian and Asian deities in their respective rooms. The British Museum has a lovely collection of jade, by the way, if you ever get the chance to visit.

I found the skull in a glass case in a corner of one of the galleries, surrounded by young boys in blazers who were daring each other to knock over the case. I knew it was the correct one right away – it shone with a light no one else seemed to notice. A light like grace but not grace at the same time. One of those things that only I could see. Yep, had to be the one. How many magical skulls could there be in the British Museum?

No, don't answer that.

I studied it for a while, wondering if all gorgon bones were made of crystal. Then I read the placard on the wall, which told me the museum acquired the skull from a French antiquities dealer who claimed to have discovered it in Mexico. It said toolmarks in the crystal later revealed it was made this century and thus a fraud. Clever, that. Hide one of your most prized possessions in the open by saying it's not prized at all. I assumed it was one of the museum's most prized possessions anyway – I'd never been in their storerooms. Maybe the museum had better things in its collection than gorgon skulls.

The boys moved on and I did as well. I didn't want to stand out from the crowd and be noticed. I wandered a few more rooms until I grew bored. A note to curators: the textiles and clothing of the fifteenth century aren't any more interesting now than they were back then.

I went for dinner in a pub down the street. It was in a basement and had the usual elements: dark corners, bad ale, drunk bankers. I had a feeling I'd been in this very place before, but I couldn't recall for sure. So many pubs over the centuries.

I ate as much of an uninventive pizza and drank as much of the afore-mentioned bad ale as I could before it repulsed me enough I had to push it away. When I reached into my pocket for some money, I discovered I didn't have any left so I reached into the pocket of the banker sitting beside me and took his money instead. I didn't even use any grace. You pick up a few tricks spending time in the places I have. I left a big tip and then strolled the streets for a bit.

I visited a bookstore with no name in an alley with no name. The owner sat in a wheelchair behind the counter and nodded at me when I came in, even though it had been several years since I'd last been there. We'd never talked but we were like old friends. Maybe because we'd never talked.

I spent an hour or so going through a water-stained copy of Chandler's *The Lady in the Lake*, rereading all my favourite parts. I didn't buy it, be-cause I was always on the move and I'd given up collecting books long ago. On the way out, though, I left more of the banker's money on the counter while the bookstore owner was on the phone. Just doing my part to keep the arts alive.

I went back to the museum and, to make a long and repetitive story shorter and less repetitive, I wandered around some more and then pulled the same trick I had in the Louvre, hopping up on a ledge and using a bit of the grace I'd taken from Remiel to make people think I was a statue. Hell, I could make a decent living as a living statue on La Rambla myself.

I passed the time by going over my mental list of the various things I was going to do to Judas when I finally caught him for good. It was a very long list. Eventually the lights faded and the museum emptied of everyone except the guards doing their rounds, which looked pretty similar to the rounds the guards in the Louvre had made. When everything was sufficiently dark and quiet, I hopped off the ledge and made my way back to the skull.

As usual, I didn't have a plan. When you're stealing magical skulls from the British Museum, you kind of have to make things up as you go.

I studied the display case for a bit and considered my options. I didn't really see any, as I'm not an antiquities thief. I've never had the patience to learn the subtle skills. So I just shrugged and used a bit of grace to harden my hand, then punched it through the glass and grabbed the skull. They probably had a double in the storeroom anyway. No visitor would be the wiser once the staff had cleaned up.

Alarms sounded as I pulled the skull from its case and tried to crush it in my hand. No luck – it was as hard as diamond. I wasn't really surprised. Gorgons never make things easy for you. I tried breaking it against the wall, but all that did was leave a head-sized indentation in the wall. I was going to have to figure out a way to destroy the skull but I didn't have time now so I just shoved it into my backpack and used a bit more grace to heal my bleeding hand. I went through the nearest exit, which took me into the Great Court with the cafés and souvenir shop, all closed now, of course. I didn't see anyone, so I headed for the front doors. Once outside, it wouldn't take me long to disappear.

But as I made for the exit a metal door slid down over it. I could hear others thumping into place in other areas of the museum.

Yeah, a backup plan might have been a good idea.

I headed into the Egyptian wing in search of another exit. That's when I ran into the museum's night watch. The lid of the sarcophagus I'd looked at earlier had been pushed open, and the mummy inside – the one that was supposed to have become a god – was clambering out, decayed bandages and all. Okay, so it hadn't been any luckier than me.

It swivelled its head to look at me as I came to a stop, and I felt my skin actually wither a little. I didn't want to imagine what that gaze could do to normal people, and I didn't want to stick around to find out what it could do to me given time. I turned and ran back the other way, cursing, as the mummy smashed its way through the glass display case to come after me. Just once I'd like to break into a museum and have to deal with human guards only. I ran back through the Great Court and into the Enlightenment gallery on the other side, which is two levels of books and sculptures and other relics behind more glass cases lining the walls. The only windows were on the open upper level that overlooked the ground floor, but they had metal doors covering them now too. At least there weren't any more mummies. Or any other guards for that matter. I guess the museum security staff figured old Ramses was enough to deal with intruders. I hoped they were wrong on that count.

Speaking of which, here came the mummy, lurching into the room after me. I looked around for something to defend myself with, but there weren't any swords or firearms or flamethrowers handy. The books would have to do. Sorry, Alice. I broke the glass covering a bookshelf on one wall and grabbed a dusty tome from it, then pulled a lighter from my backpack and made my own version of a Molotov cocktail. I know what you're thinking, but if the books were that valuable they wouldn't have them sitting around where someone like me could do what I was doing, would they?

I tossed the burning book at the mummy and waited for it to catch fire and run screaming away from me, destroyer of the supernatural. The book bounced off its chest and the mummy shambled through the flames without so much as sparking. All right, so much for books saving the day.

Bookshelves, however . . . I pulled some more books out to give myself a foothold and then climbed up, pulling myself from one shelf to another, until I was out of reach of the mummy. It stared up at me, making my skin feel all dried and chapped again, but showed no signs of having taken up rock climbing in the centuries since it'd died. I swung myself over the railing to the second floor and waved at the mummy, then used a bit of Remiel's grace to unlock one of the window shutters. A bit more broken glass and I found myself in the night outside, heading away from the museum with a stolen treasure in my pack.

Some things never change.

No, I'm not going to tell you the story about the night I stole the Constitution of the United States from the National Archives. Maybe some other time, if you buy me a drink.

Besides, I put it back. I only needed it for a quick summoning ritual. And the less everyone knows about that the better.

I went down the street to the Holborn Tube station and lost myself in the crowd of revellers and red-eyed bankers heading home. When a train pulled into the station I held back and looked around, as if I were waiting to meet someone disembarking. As soon as the train pulled away and everyone on the platform headed for the exits, I hopped down onto the tracks and ran into the tunnel in the direction the train had come from.

I knew I didn't have much time before another train arrived, but I didn't need it. I only had to run for a minute or so before I reached the next station. Although it wasn't a station any living being has used for a long time. It was a ghost station, dark and abandoned, the entrances to the streets above sealed shut. It wasn't a ghost station in the supernatural sense – there were no real ghosts, no trains other than the ones that passed through to the other stations. It was just a station that had been shut down by the authorities. But I remembered it from other lives I had lived in this city.

There are *real* ghost stations under London, of course, but they are deeper down, hidden among the government bunkers and secret tunnels and the Other London. There's more than one underground beneath the city.

I pulled myself up on the empty platform and pressed myself into the far corner of the station, against a wall, as the next train went past, a blur of light and faces peering blindly out at me. Petals on a wet, black bough. Then it was gone and I was left in the darkness again.

I pulled the skull out of my backpack and saw that it was still glowing, but now the glow pulsed in a regular pattern, like a heartbeat.

I tried to destroy the skull once more, hammering it into the wall. Not with all my strength, because that would have shattered the wall, but with enough force to shatter a human skull, let alone a crystal one. It simply bounced off and grinned that skull grin at me when I looked down at it. They made these gorgons tougher than they appear.

I had to get creative, which I didn't really want to do, because it would mean using even more grace. But a deal with a gorgon is a deal with a gorgon. That is, it's best not broken.

I raised the skull to my lips and blew a little grace into it, just enough to give me something to work with. Or so I thought. The glow pulsed quicker for a few seconds, and then the skull melted away in my hands before I could do anything. But it wasn't truly gone. In its place hung Victory's face, like when I'd summoned her at the Louvre, only much more real and terrible now.

How do I describe what she truly looked like? There was fire and smoke and snakes made of fire and smoke and a gaze that was broken glass and a mouth that looked like it opened into Hell when she smiled at me. She was one of the most beautiful things I'd ever seen, even though the mere sight of her nearly killed me and would probably stop most people's hearts.

I could see now why she'd been separated into pieces. And I wondered who had been capable of such a feat.

"Impressive, hydra," she said. "To be honest, we didn't think you would succeed where so many others have failed. You are indeed a hero."

"No, I'm not," I said. I didn't know what she meant by "others," but now was not the time to press for details. "I've lived up to my end of the bargain. Time for you to tell me what you know about the Mona Lisa."

She laughed, and the sound was like knives digging into my ears.

"You may not want to learn the truth," she said.

"I'm pretty sure I don't," I told her. "And yet here we are."

"We like you, hydra," she said, and her snakes lashed out at me, sinking their spectral fangs into my eyes. I couldn't help but flinch. "We suspect we could find ways to make it worth your while to return our other limbs to us."

"I'm enjoying the single life these days." I coughed at all the smoke in the air. Another train went by, and more faces stared out at us. I wondered what they saw. "Mona Lisa?" I said.

"She is our sister," Victory said.

I had to let that one sink in for a moment.

"Mona Lisa was a gorgon?" I said.

"She is the most powerful among us," Victory said. "So much so that her spirit lingers even in those inferior portraits the mortals insist upon painting."

Yeah, I noticed the plural too.

Victory sighed. "But even our power is as fleeting as human lives. Once we ruled over men, and now we are nothing but prizes in men's collections. That is the way of it, though. Everything passes from one realm to another." Her snakes went for my face again, but this time they caressed it. "Even you, our special one. Even you."

So, I'd been played by Cassiel. I thought he had me chasing after a secret painting when in fact he had me chasing after a secret gorgon. I wondered what other secrets I didn't know about.

"Can you just find her in there with the rest of you and ask her where she is?" I asked. "That would make my quest a little easier."

Her snakes all drooped on her head and Victory closed her eyes. "She is not among us."

"But if Medusa is in there with you –" I said.

"She is far from us," Victory said. "Farther than Medusa and the other dead ones. She has been taken."

"Taken?" I said. "Taken where?"

The snakes spread themselves out and looked in different directions. They hissed at things I couldn't see.

"We do not know where she is," Victory said. "She was torn from us during the Windsor Castle fire."

I had a vague memory of watching footage of the fire on the news years ago. I thought it had been a construction accident, but I should have known better.

"She has been lost to us ever since," Victory added, and the snakes continued their search.

"Who took her?" I asked.

She opened her eyes again and looked at me. "If we knew that, we would have gone on the hunt ourselves," she said.

I felt a chill at the thought of that. An angry group of gorgons was not to be taken lightly. Just ask anyone who's ever encountered the Bacchae.

All right. One step at a time.

"What was she doing at Windsor Castle?" I asked.

"We are not certain," Victory said. "She was blind, deaf and mute at the time, her powers bound, so we could not tell. She had been held captive in another realm for a long time, so we had no contact with her. Those few followers we still have told us she was a guest of the queen when she returned to the land of the seasons, but she was taken again before we could find out what happened to her. And now she is gone once more, and even the queen's representatives don't know where she is."

"Are you sure they're telling you the truth?" I asked. I decided to leave alone the revelation that the gorgons still had followers.

"Yes," Victory said, in a tone that suggested . . . well, I don't know what it suggested, other than something not particularly pleasant had probably happened to the queen's representatives.

"A guest of the queen." As I knew well, the Royal Family's guest accommodations could be anything from a castle to a dungeon cell deep underground with no entrance or exit. And I suspect the latter was more likely if Mona Lisa was blind, deaf and mute at the time. The Royal Family. Damn.

"I really wish you would have told me all this before," I said.

"But then we wouldn't have had this lovely time together," she said. "Come. Kiss us before we go."

So I did. When a gorgon tells you to kiss her, it's generally a good idea to comply.

Her lips burned mine, and her snakes bit at my face, and when I looked into her eyes from this distance, my heart actually stopped for a second.

"If only you had been the one to slay us," she breathed.

"One last thing," I said. "Why does Cassiel want to find her?"

"We cannot say for certain," Victory said, "but we assume it's because they were once lovers." And then she was gone, blown away by the wind of another train going past.

I stood in the dark, empty station for another moment, thinking things over.

Mona Lisa was a gorgon.

A guest of the queen.

Cassiel's lover.

It was only then that I realized I'd been so preoccupied with learning about the Royal Family connection that I hadn't even asked who'd held Mona Lisa captive before that. I hoped it was a minor detail.

I shook my head and tried to come up with a plan as trains came and went. I had to talk to a member of the Royal Family to figure out what was going on here. But I knew none of them would speak to me. Not any of the living ones, anyway. Which left me with only one option.

It was time to raise the dead.

LOOKING FOR AN ANGEL IN THE MIDDLE OF NOWHERE

When I said earlier that Penelope raised me from the dead I meant it figuratively, not literally. But I was dead and buried in that graveyard in British Columbia when she showed up just in time for me to resurrect.

It was the 1940s. I don't remember the exact month or year. I've never been that good with time, given that it's meaningless for me. I had tracked down the angel Gabriel to a lair in the Rockies, just a little north of the Canada-US border. It was a cave high in the mountains, and a tricky spot to reach. The cave entrance was hidden from the ground, so most people wouldn't even know it was there. But I'm not most people, et cetera. Also, I saw him fly in there one sunset.

I found him in the cave but he was waiting for me, probably on account of the avalanche I caused on the climb up. It made a lot of noise, and I suppose I didn't help things by using some grace to melt my way out of it. So when I stepped into the entrance of the cave he was ready for battle. I only had time to register the homey touches he'd made – renderings of dead angels in blood on the walls, an ice sculpture of the true face of Christ, a cross made of bones taller than me – and then he came hurtling out of the depths and smashed into me, carrying us both out into the night sky. He knocked the climbing axe from my hands, which ruined my plan a little, as I'd been intending to lodge the axe in his skull, and then we fought, grappling with each other and exchanging blows as we fell.

Normally this was the point of the story where I'd get the upper hand, but Gabriel was stronger than me, especially when I'd wasted half my grace on things like melting my way out of an avalanche and he had an ice sword so perfectly clear and polished it may as well have been invisible. I certainly hadn't noticed it before he rammed it through my heart. I've no doubt I'll beat him someday, but that day was not the one.

I woke with dirt in my mouth and cold all around me. I opened my eyes but there was only more dirt. I'd been buried without the courtesy of a coffin.

It wasn't the first time, of course. I'd lost track of the number of times I'd been tossed into some pit in the ground after dying. But it's not really the sort of thing you ever get used to. Try it sometime if you don't believe me.

I was still in one piece. Thankfully, I don't have to contend with being scavenged by animals and insects like most corpses. For some reason they leave me alone. I don't know why. I'm dead when they're ignoring me, remember?

Waking up after dying is like waking up from a deep sleep: you come to slowly, and it takes a while for your mind to start working, to recognize where you are. But when you wake from sleep you tend to be in the same bed or corner of the bar you passed out in. You pick up where you left off. When you wake up from being dead, however, you're usually in someplace different. Like a grave. It's a bit disorienting. You also tend to remember the last thing you were thinking of before you died. In that case, it was getting skewered by Gabriel in the night sky, so I woke up screaming and swinging my arms to fend him off.

It turned out I'd been buried in a shallow grave, because my belated attempts at self-defence caused me to erupt from the ground. I spat dirt from my mouth and wiped it from my eyes. When I could see again I looked around. I was sitting in a graveyard in a forest somewhere. Simple wooden crosses surrounded me, leaning from age or maybe the weight of the moss covering them. Some had already fallen to the ground. Mist wreathed everything, and steam rose from my skin.

I pulled myself the rest of the way out of the ground and brushed the dirt from my clothes. I was still dressed in my climbing gear, but it was too warm for that now. It felt like a summer morning. So I'd probably been dead for six months or so. Time enough for Gabriel to disappear again.

I did a quick inventory. The knife I'd never gotten around to using during our battle was gone, as was my wallet. I'd been robbed, probably by whoever it was that dragged me to this graveyard from wherever it was they'd found my body. They'd even taken my boots. I couldn't fault them for that though. Good boots were hard to find in those days.

Well, I'd woken up in worse situations.

I took another look around, and that's when I saw the woman at the edge of the graveyard. She was standing behind a camera pointed in my direction. Most people would have run screaming at the sight of someone erupting from a grave like I just had. But she simply lifted her head from underneath the focusing cloth and looked at me.

"Well, you are almost the strangest thing I've ever seen," she said.

I was caught off guard by her presence, so I didn't know what to say to that. She filled the silence by crossing the graveyard to hand me her canteen. I drank from it without taking the time to thank her. We studied each other as I guzzled the water. She wore sensible clothes – and definitely unladylike for the time. Trousers, a long-sleeved shirt, a vest for her camera gear, a safari-type hat. Good, worn boots. Her skin was tanned and un-marked by makeup. If she was wearing perfume, I couldn't smell it through her sweat. There was something familiar about her, even though I didn't think we'd met before.

"Do I know you?" I asked her when the water was gone.

She smiled. "I hope that's an honest question and not just you being flirtatious," she said.

"It's as honest as I get," I said. I tipped an imaginary hat. "Cross."

She curtsied with an imaginary dress. "Penelope," she said. Yes, the same Penelope I've been going on about.

I studied her a few seconds longer, but if I did actually know her, it wasn't coming back to me.

"What are you doing out here?" I asked, handing her the empty canteen.

"I was going to ask you the same thing." She looked at the grave once more.

I shook my head. "I don't really remember," I said, which was truthful enough. "I was climbing and fell. I guess someone must have found me and thought I was dead. But obviously I'm not." Yeah, I was really going to have to work on better cover stories for moments like this.

"You're wearing winter clothes," she pointed out.

"It gets cold in the mountains," I countered.

"Not that cold," she said. "Not this time of the year."

I decided it was probably time to change the direction of the conversation. "Where are we anyway?" The morning sun was burning away the mist now, but I still couldn't see much more than the trees around us.

"In the woods, in a graveyard," she said.

"Thanks, but I'd already figured out that part," I said.

"We're in British Columbia, Canada," she said. She reached out and brushed some dirt from my hair. "About a day's hike from the mountains."

All right, so Gabriel hadn't thrown me that far then. Not that it mattered. He was too long gone to track him now. I'd have to start over.

I looked back at her and found her eyeing the hole in my jacket where Gabriel had run me through. At least she didn't say anything about that, which saved me from having to come up with another bad lie.

"You look hungry," she said. "Come on, I'll take you back to the cabin for something to eat."

"You still haven't answered my question," I said.

"What's a nice gal like me doing out here?" she asked.

"What's a nice gal like you doing out here, taking photos of graveyards?"

She smiled at me again. "I'm looking for an angel."

ALWAYS EXPECT
THE UNEXPECTED WHEN
RAISING THE DEAD

I went back out into the tunnel between trains and climbed onto the platform at the Holborn station. A man and woman in evening wear were the only ones to notice me. They stared and then in true British fashion pointedly looked away, carrying on a conversation about the production of *Doctor Faustus* they'd just seen. I've always liked Marlowe, so I was tempted to stop and explain to them the play was partly biographical and based on moments of Marlowe's life. But then I would have had to explain he wasn't a spy in addition to being a scholar, as the common myths went, but was instead a demon hunter in addition to being a scholar. Not the sort of conversation you wanted to have with people when you were trying to maintain a low profile in the country. Especially if you'd just been seen climbing out of a Tube tunnel. I kept my knowledge to myself and got on the next train. The well-dressed couple waited for me to board before choosing a different car.

I switched lines at random for an hour, in case there was any pursuit I hadn't noticed, and tried to remember my London geography. I got off at the Archway station and made my way to the Highgate Cemetery a few blocks away. I walked along the fence until I found a lamppost with a burned-out light. I stepped into the shadows, climbed the fence and dropped into the shrubbery on the other side. Although shrubbery may be too polite a word. The bushes swallowed me up, scratching and gouging me with thorns and sharp branches as I came down, and loomed over my head like deformed trees when I'd landed. The cemetery was one of those rare places in England where the caretakers allowed plants to grow wild rather than cultivating and grooming them. It was wonderfully atmospheric and all, but it did make skulking about a little more difficult.

I moved through the undergrowth in a random direction. I didn't have a destination in mind, although I'd been here many times before. I'd visited Karl Marx's grave a few times to read him the latest news from the papers, until it got too crowded with students and their bottles of cheap wine – and the news grew too unpleasant for Marx's taste. I'd brought a few bottles of wine myself to the grave of Adam Worth, a criminal artist I'd once worked with. Yes, artist – there's no other way of describing him. I don't know if the rumours that Conan Doyle modelled his Professor Moriarty on him are true or not, but it wouldn't surprise me. Worth wasn't much of a criminal sort these days – death has a way of mellowing out most people – but he still had plenty of stories to tell from his younger days. And he had fewer visitors than Marx, partially because he'd been buried in a pauper's grave, under a pseudonym. Such is the legacy we leave.

This time, though, I wasn't looking for any of my old friends. Instead, I was searching for someone entirely different, someone I didn't even know. But I'd know her when I found her.

Something crashed through the undergrowth ahead of me as I moved, and I paused to see what direction it took. In addition to the usual ghosts and ghouls and assorted creatures you find around graveyards, Highgate has a few unusual residents. The Highgate Vampire is a myth, but some of the other supernatural sightings in the area have more truth than ale to them. Whatever it was moved away from me, and I proceeded on, only tripping and falling over gravestones a couple of times. I wondered if anyone even remembered these dead out here, lost in the overgrowth. Ah well, to some a battlefield or a watery grave, to others a forgotten coffin in a patch of London soil. What did it matter?

Besides, the forgotten dead were what I was after. And I found what I was seeking a few minutes later: a mausoleum covered in vines and moss and cradled in the roots and branches of the trees around it. A woman's name I didn't recognize, and which I won't repeat here to respect her privacy, chiselled above the rotted wooden doors. I opened the doors with a touch of my hand and a breath of grace and, hoping no one heard the squeal of the rusted hinges, went inside.

It was a simple stone tomb, with benches along the walls and shelves with dead, petrified flowers in stone vases. There was a stone coffin in the centre of the room, which I pushed the lid off of to reveal the desiccated corpse of a woman. Let's call her Eurydice. Her funeral dress was little more than rags now, and the locket she held in her clasped hands was dull and in need of a polish. I took it from her and opened it, even though I already knew what it contained: a lock of hair. It was always a lock of hair in these older places. I put it back in her hands.

Most people think raising the dead is actually that – bringing a dead body back to life. But it's a little more complex than that – I'm living proof. When you raise the dead, you not only bring a body back to life, you also have to put a soul into the body. Sometimes the soul wants to come, other times it doesn't. It all depends where it is now. So it can be a relatively straightforward procedure – for the likes of me, anyway – or it can be a little more arduous.

But here's a trick of the trade: You don't have to put a soul into the body that originally held it. You can put a soul in any body.

Which is why I was here, lifting this stranger's corpse into my arms and out of its resting place. I needed a vessel for the soul I wanted.

I bent my head and kissed the corpse on the lips, breathing more grace than I wanted to let go into her. Then I slumped to the floor with her and tried not to think about the emptiness welling inside me again at the loss of the grace. I tried not to think about what I had just done, because it was all a bit personal. I distracted myself by composing a few lines of poetry in my head while I waited. It seemed a moment fitting for poetry. I didn't bother writing them down, though. The best poetry is always the poetry that never gets written down.

Eurydice gasped and I looked down at her again. Her flesh was lively once more, pale but with the flush of blood in her cheeks now. Her cheeks that weren't sunken anymore. Her body shook as she remembered how to breathe again. I pulled her into a sitting position and untangled her hair as best I could, then brushed the dust off her clothing. She wasn't exactly presentable, but sometimes you just have to make do.

I opened her eyes and looked into her to make sure there was nothing there, that her original soul hadn't been called back to her during the resurrection, or hadn't been hiding in her all these centuries. It happens sometimes. But there was nothing in her. She was as empty as a mannequin. So I called the soul I wanted and waited.

You have to be careful about the order of these things. If you bind a soul into a body without resurrecting the body first, you wind up with a zombie. Which, to be honest, frightens them more than you. The things you learn from trial and error over the years.

No matter what you do, though, the dead are always shocked to return. It's not a natural state of affairs for most people. Especially when they're brought back into someone else's body. But there was no helping it in this case – the body of the soul I was calling was far from here, and under heavy guard. The Royal Family looked after their own, even in death.

But it was a member of the Royal Family I needed. If Mona Lisa had disappeared while a guest of the queen, whatever that meant, then maybe a Royal would know what had happened.

The woman in my arms blinked a couple of times and then her eyes focused. She took a deep breath and sat up. She gazed around the tomb, then at me. I tried to smile as warmly as I could.

"Hello, Princess," I said.

It was Diana, of course. Princess of Wales. Or maybe former Princess of Wales. I'm not sure if that family keeps their honorifics after death. I called her because she was the only one of the Royals who would ever deign to converse with me, unless you counted threats of evisceration as conversation.

She finally looked down at herself. And then she screamed.

I slapped my hand over her mouth. It was the middle of the night in a cemetery, but I'd left the door to the tomb open. And it *was* the middle of the night in a cemetery. If passersby on the street outside the walls didn't hear her, something else might.

She glared at me over my fingers and struggled to break free of my arms. She even bit me hard enough to draw blood. It wasn't the first time someone had done that to me, though.

"I know it's not your body," I told her. "But I can't exactly get to your body and I need to talk to you. I have some questions."

She narrowed her eyes at me and then nodded. I removed my hand from her mouth and helped her to her feet.

"I have a few questions of my own," she said. She looked down at her clothing and adjusted it, blowing some more dust out of the seams. "Starting with why you chose to resurrect me in such a form."

"I'm sorry, Princess," I said. "I've fallen on hard times, or I would have made certain you awoke in proper attire."

She gave me that look of hers. "When have you not been a victim of hard times?" she asked. Then she noticed the locket she was still holding and opened it.

"It came with the body," I said.

"I gathered," she said, tossing the locket into a corner of the tomb. She glanced around again and sighed. "You could have at least raised me someplace a little nicer. The last time I was raised was in a spa. There were fresh berries, tea and baths. A little more appropriate, I would think."

I refrained from asking who had raised her last. You have to remember your manners around royalty, especially royalty you've just raised from the dead. And don't ask them what it's like being dead. In fact, don't ask anyone who's been raised about what death is like. Just trust me on this.

She went to the door of the tomb and stared out into the night. She sniffed the air a few times. "We are in England."

I didn't ask how she could tell. A royal secret, no doubt.

"Highgate Cemetery," I said.

"I trust this body is of proper standing then," she said. "That's something, at least." She looked back over her shoulder at me. "Unless it's some former flame of yours."

"I don't think so," I said, then added, with a straight face, "but I can't remember them all."

She smiled a little. "As roguish as ever, I see," she said.

I shrugged. "I am what the world makes me," I said.

"I should like to see this world again, I think," she said.

I came up beside her and offered her my arm. "I would be happy to be your escort," I said.

"Of course you would," she said.

We left the tomb and, because she was a princess, we strolled down one of the walkways rather than struggle through the underbrush. The night sky was bright enough from the city we could make out the grave markers lining our way, and she stopped every now and then to check the names.

"I had no idea he was dead," she murmured, inspecting one of them. "I'll have to look him up."

I didn't bother with the names myself. I was too busy keeping an eye on the bushes around us, and the angels perched on gravestones here and there. They looked like they were just statues, but I wasn't taking any chances right now. Nothing came out of the night to bother us, though. I guess no one wanted to mess with the son of God and a resurrected princess of the Royal Family.

I opened the gate at the end of the walkway and we left the cemetery and went down the street. We passed some drunks sitting in a bus shelter and a few couples walking arm in arm, but no one paid us any attention, other than a few glances at Diana's dress. It was London, after all. They'd probably seen stranger.

I didn't say anything for a while, giving her time to get used to being alive again. I knew from personal experience how disorienting that could be sometimes.

"I would like to see the river," Diana said after a time, so I hailed a passing taxi and had him drive us down to the Thames. Diana stared out the windows as we drove.

"What year is it anyway?" she asked.

I told her and she nodded, and the taxi driver only glanced at us once in the mirror before looking back at the road. I gave him a good tip for not asking any questions when we got out but not so good that he'd remember our faces.

We walked along the Thames and I told her all the news I could think of since she'd died, skipping the minor wars and sticking to the European sphere. I wasn't going to keep her alive long enough to cover it all. I offered to tell her what I knew of the Royal Family but she just smiled and shook her head.

"I get regular updates," she said, and I bowed my head and said nothing else on the subject.

We stopped on the Millennium pedestrian bridge, which she murmured approving words about, and watched the sky turn from charcoal to a lighter shade of grey.

"So why exactly have you called on me, Cross?" she asked, watching a tug pull some barges down the river. "Or have you offended so many people you're forced to turn to the dead for companionship now?"

"I don't think I'd fare any better with them," I said, and she laughed.

"No, I don't imagine you would," she said.

I looked up at the sky, watching planes rise from Heathrow to disappear into the clouds overhead. "It's a personal matter," I said, "but I am unable to manage it on my own."

"I believe they have medication for that sort of thing now," she said.

"If I am guilty of roguishness, it may have something to do with the company I keep," I said.

"Yes, yes, get on with it." She smiled a little.

"I need to know what the queen was doing with Mona Lisa," I said.

I give her credit – she didn't even blink.

"I don't know what you mean," she said. "The *Mona Lisa* is in the Louvre."

"The real Mona Lisa," I said. "The one that disappeared in the fire at Windsor Castle. The gorgon."

"So you *have* been talking to the family," she said. "However did you manage a rapprochement?"

"I haven't been in touch with them," I said, "as you can see by the fact I still have all my limbs."

She turned and leaned on the rail to look at me directly now. "Who else could have told you?"

"A statue," I said. Sometimes honesty is the best policy. Mainly because it confuses people.

"I see," she said. "And what do I have to gain if I tell you?"

"I brought you back to life," I pointed out.

"But not for long," she countered.

"I don't have the grace necessary to sustain you," I said. "At least not in the life to which you are accustomed." I gestured at her rags.

At least she had the goodwill to laugh again. "So what did you have planned?" she asked.

"I was going to find a nice bench overlooking the water where you could watch the sun come up once again," I said. "I thought it would be nice for you to retire on the dawn."

She glanced back at the sky, which showed no signs of letting the sun shine through the clouds. "That would have been a nice view," she said. "In theory."

I shrugged. "Even I can't control the weather."

"What will you give me when you have more grace and time?" she asked.

"Dinner and dancing and all that," I said. "Whatever you desire."

"You have no idea what I desire," she said. Which was true enough. Perhaps I could have guessed when she was mortal, but death had a way of changing people.

"Very well," she went on. "A date in the future then. But you had better raise me in finer clothes next time."

I bowed my head.

"So what is it you want to know?" she asked.

"The angel Cassiel is willing to trade me the whereabouts of Judas for Mona Lisa," I said. "I trust you know of my interest in Judas."

She raised an eyebrow. "As in the biblical Judas? I would have thought him long dead."

"He's not what he seems," I said.

She nodded. "Who is?" she said. "And what is Cassiel's interest?"

I shrugged. "Who knows with angels?" I didn't see any point in telling her what I knew. She was going to give me the information I wanted or she wasn't. The little detail about Cassiel and Mona Lisa being lovers once wouldn't change that. Besides, it was good to have secrets sometimes.

"Indeed," Diana said, in a tone that suggested she knew I was holding something back. I imagine it was just like life at court.

"So I would know of Mona Lisa's relation to the queen," I said. "And I will work out the rest later."

"She was tribute," Diana said. "Meant for the queen's collection."

"Tribute? Tribute from whom?" I asked. And collection? What sort of collection would include a gorgon?

"The faerie queen," she said. "Part of the pact to keep peace between their realms. They exchange tribute every century."

I damned Cassiel under my breath. I damned all the angels under my breath. Why wouldn't they just come out and tell people this sort of thing?

"But something happened this century," I said.

Diana nodded. "There was an attack," she said. "It wasn't the gorgon. She was delivered to the castle in an iron crate and with her eyes and tongue torn out, her ears branded shut, her mouth sewn closed. She was powerless. It was something else."

"What would be powerful enough to attack the Royals?" I asked.

Diana shrugged. "I wasn't invited to that particular event, so the details are unclear to me. But the castle was damaged. Guards were slain. And after, the gorgon was gone."

"The fire at the castle wasn't any ordinary fire then," I said.

"The family released a story about construction work causing it," she said. "And they told the families of the dead guards there'd been accidents, although they said the deaths had happened all over the city so as to divert attention. The ones who asked questions they paid off. The ones who asked too many questions, well . . ."

I nodded. There'd been a time when the Royal Family wouldn't have bothered with the payoffs at all, when they'd just have gone for the unspoken option.

"So what did happen?" I asked. "You must have an idea."

She studied me for a moment. "No one's really certain," she finally said. "Some believe the faerie stole her back. But I don't put any faith in that."

"Why not?" I asked. "It seems like a perfectly faerie thing to do."

She smiled a little. "I had a faerie acquaintance. He assured me they were pleased to be rid of Mona Lisa."

I shouldn't have been surprised the princess had a faerie lover, but I was. And the fact the Royal Family probably knew about it – they had spies and eyes everywhere – brought me some amount of pleasure.

"I had drinks with the Queen Mother once after the fire," Diana went on. "She told me she thought it was another collector. But she wouldn't discuss names." She shook her head. "I don't know who or what would have the courage or the resources to raid the queen's collection."

"And none of your subjects in your current kingdom have any insight into the matter?" I asked.

"I am currently a princess in a land of kings and queens," she said. "But thank you. Unfortunately, no. It is as much a mystery in the afterlife as it is here."

We were quiet for a moment then, as I thought things over and the princess breathed deep of the morning air. I didn't bother asking where the faerie had found Mona Lisa. They were always finding and binding things. It is their way – it makes their court more lively. Actually, it makes their court. But it was unlike them to give up a prize like that.

I sighed. I could see only one course of action. "I'm going to have to talk to the queen," I said.

"She'll have you crucified again," Diana said. "And that's just for starters."

"I meant the faerie queen," I said. "I'm running out of clues, and I have a feeling she has the last one."

"Perhaps," she said. "Or perhaps you could let go of your obsession with Judas."

"I tried that once," I said. "It didn't work out." Which was true enough in its own way.

She opened her mouth to say something else but then looked over my shoulder. "Friend of yours?" she asked.

I turned to see a man wearing a coat and hat walking toward us. I had time to register the bandages flapping around feet and face, eyes burning at me – the mummy from the British Museum. Then it lunged at me, grabbing on to my jacket with both hands and carrying us both over the side of the bridge with its momentum. I managed to knock its hands free of me as we fell, and we hit the river separately.

I'd once wasted an afternoon taking a tour boat up and down the Thames. The guide told us the water of the Thames was actually quite clean, that it just looked dirty from the sediment stirred up by the tides. He said you could dip a glass in it and once the sediment settled at the bottom, the water would be clear enough to drink. I didn't believe him.

Don't swallow the water, I told myself as I sank under the surface. Don't swallow the water.

The mummy reached for me again as we went down, some of its bandages floating free around it now, but I kicked off in a random direction and it faded away. I dove deeper and zigged this way, zagged that way, hoping to lose it in the murk, until my lungs couldn't take it anymore and I rose back up into the light.

Directly into the path of a tugboat. I threw myself to one side in the water, it swerved the other way, and everything worked out. A man on the deck threw a life preserver into the water and hauled me in, pulling me up over the side of the boat. I spat up the water I'd swallowed and then looked back at the bridge, a few hundred feet behind us now. I saw the princess running away, disappearing into the city. I wasn't sure how much grace she had left, but it would probably keep her alive long enough she could cause some trouble. Oh well, what was done was done. But I was glad I hadn't raised her in her own body. An anonymous body turning up somewhere was one thing, but the body of a dead princess showing up outside the official tomb was something else entirely.

I thanked the man who'd fished me out of the Thames, and he just shook his head and muttered something about tourists. The captain of the tug steered us toward the nearest dock.

I squeezed the water out of my shirt and watched the wake of the tug. There was no sign of the mummy, and no one else seemed to be looking for it. No one had seen us fall other than the princess. I wondered where the mummy was, and pictured it walking along the bottom of the Thames after me.

So, maybe there was something after all to the legends about pharaohs' curses.

The tugboat pulled up alongside a wooden dock long enough for me to disembark, and then the men went down the river without so much as a backward glance, ignoring my wave of thanks. No doubt some code of the sea thing.

I climbed the steps up to street level, before there were any more surprises, and lost myself in the crowd of people heading to their early morning jobs. It being London and all, no one paid any attention to my soaking clothes. I dried them with a bit of grace and then stopped at a pub for a breakfast of eggs and toast and black, black tea. The British do tea like the Spanish do wine. Which says a lot about their respective histories. I flipped through a paper while I ate. I tried to come up with a plan to deal with the mummy, because I had a feeling it was going to keep chasing me. The undead are kind of single-minded that way.

But I forgot all about that when I turned the page of the newspaper and came across a photo of the art dealer I'd talked to on the train. There was also a photo of a bloody knife. It was the knife I'd used on Remiel. The one I'd left behind in the Gaudí church.

I stared at the photos for a moment, then read the story that went with them. It said the art dealer had been coming back from the fair at Maastricht when he'd been stabbed to death in the washroom of the train. His eyes had been gouged out. A cross had been carved into his face using the knife. Police figured it had happened before the train had even left the station. A conductor said someone had hung an out-of-order sign on the washroom door shortly after boarding began. I thought again of the feeling of danger that had woken me on the train.

So the art dealer I had been talking to hadn't in fact been the art dealer. Who *had* I been talking to on the train then? And why?

The only witness to Remiel's death had been Cassiel. He was the only one who could have found the knife. But I couldn't think of any reason why he'd kill and mutilate the art dealer and pretend to be him to engage me in small talk.

I replayed the Barcelona trip in my mind, but I didn't see any moment where I thought someone else had been watching. And even if they had, why this?

And why the eyes and the cross?

There was only one answer.

I downed the rest of my tea and stared out the window, at the passing crowd.

Judas.

GHOSTS IN THE WOODS

Penelope took me back to her cabin, which was more of a shack in a clearing in the woods than any sort of proper structure. It took us an hour to hike there, and I didn't notice any paths among the trees, which meant people didn't come this way often. I offered to carry Penelope's camera gear for her, but she just laughed.

"If I needed a man to carry my camera, I'd be back in the city, sipping tea and waiting for you to hold the door open for me," she said. "Do you see any doors out here?"

I couldn't help but smile, despite feeling the way I usually feel after a resurrection. Hungover, hungry and angry. Yeah, she definitely had spirit.

"No doors," I agreed.

"Except for the one you came through," she said, eyeing my clothes again.

I still couldn't shake the feeling there was something familiar about her, but I didn't sense any danger, so I didn't know what to make of it. I put it in the back of my mind for the moment, because there was another subject I was more curious about.

"So have you actually seen any angels out here?" I asked.

It was a bit of a trick question. Most people who said they saw angels or gorgons or any of my other acquaintances were generally a bit mad. Or a lot mad. The smart creatures and gods had learned to make themselves invisible and blend into the crowd once humans had taken their place in the world and history. The ones that weren't smart were extinct. But every now and then I'd come across a person who had an eye for them. Usually, they worked in museums or libraries or for certain government organizations. But not all of them. And if Penelope *had* seen an angel, well maybe she knew which way Gabriel had gone.

"I haven't seen him yet," Penelope said. "But I'll find him someday."

Ah well. I'd have to search out Gabriel on my own again then. So it goes.

"And what will you do when you find him? Take a photo?" I nodded at the camera.

"The camera isn't for the angel," she said. "It's for the others."

"What others?" I asked.

"Whatever others I can find," she said. "Ghosts. Wood spirits. Faerie folk. I was about to take a photograph of what I think was a sasquatch when you erupted out of your grave and scared it off."

I considered her words and she looked back at me and smiled again.

"You think me mad, don't you?"

"Possibly," I said. "Why else would you want a photograph of a faerie?" I didn't add that faerie being what they were and all, there was nothing interesting about photos of them. They just looked like more people on the street. Or, I guess in this case, in the woods. Also, I was pretty sure sasquatches didn't exist.

She laughed. "There are many people in the world who are interested in such photographs."

I thought about that for a second, and then it all came together for me. "Spiritualists," I said, and she nodded.

This was the age when many people thought they could communicate with ghosts in the afterlife, or even see other things walking among us, if only they had the right equipment: Ouija boards and crystal balls and the like. Their hearts were in the right places, but unfortunately most of them were victims of fraudsters, willing to believe in doctored photographs of the faerie dancing in wood glens and such. As if the faerie hung around in the forests these days.

"Now you think me a fraud," she said, still smiling.

I shrugged. "I'm not one to judge what others believe. If they're interested in your photographs, so be it."

But I had a hunch there was more to the situation than that. If she wanted to create fake photographs, she could have done it much easier in woods closer to her home, wherever that was. So why was she all the way out here? Was she actually searching for a real angel?

We waded through a stream and mist sparkled around us. A rainbow arched overhead. I caught sight of the skull of a goblin hidden among the rocks in the water but I didn't say anything. She stepped over it without seeming to notice. Well, so much for her having the eye for such things.

"So why did you come all the way out here?" I asked her. "The wilds of British Columbia aren't exactly where I'd expect to find angels."

A clever bit of misdirection, that. Hopefully it would distract her from asking what *I* was doing out here.

She reached the other side of the stream and waited for me to cross. She looked at the rainbow, which would have made a nice shot, but didn't bother setting up her camera.

"I don't know," she said. "I just had a feeling. It's as if I were drawn here." She looked back at me. "What brought you out here?"

"We already covered that," I said. "The climbing accident, remember?"

Her expression said we both knew that was a lie, but then she turned back to the woods and we carried on anyway.

We eventually arrived at her shack, which looked like it was in danger of collapsing into itself. Moss grew on every surface, and the roof sagged in the middle. It looked as old as me.

"Did you build this?" I asked as she forced the door open. The frame was warped, so she had to put her shoulder to it.

She shook her head as she led me inside. "I'm a photographer, not a mad trapper," she said. "I found it here when I hiked in. The place was abandoned, so I made myself at home."

The inside was dark on account of there being no windows, but enough light came in through the open door I could look around while Penelope set down her camera gear. It was a simple affair: a table and stool made of rough pieces of wood, a bed in a corner, a stove in the other corner with some chopped wood nearby. Bottles of chemicals half-hidden by a curtain that was probably her darkroom area. Not your typical woman's dwelling.

And then there were the photos hanging from clotheslines on the walls. They were of meadows or forests like the graveyard where Penelope had found me. And they all had the things that would have made the spiritualists happy: will-o'-the-wisps that could have been real wisps or maybe just swamp gas. A footprint in mud that could have been the mark of some strange creature even I didn't know or simply a deformed bear. An insubstantial form moving between some crosses in another graveyard that could have been a ghost or could have been a trick of the light.

"How many graveyards are out here anyway?" I asked, looking at that photo.

"This area was home to a prospecting boom for a while," Penelope said. She took a can of beans from a box on the floor and opened it with a can opener from the box. She stuck a spoon in the can and handed it to me without bothering to warm the beans. "A lot of people died out here with their dreams." She shrugged. "But they left a lot of handy shelters."

She sat on the lone stool and watched me eat the beans, which didn't take long at all. They didn't do anything to stop the hunger inside me, but I nodded my thanks like they did.

"So what's your real name?" she asked.

"How do you know Cross isn't my real name?" I said.

"You carry yourself like you're hiding something," she said. "And you looked away when you told me your name. I've known enough men to recognize that as a sign they're pretending to be someone else, for whatever reason."

Maybe she did have an eye after all.

"It's a long story," I said, and she nodded and let it be. She picked up her camera gear and carried it to the darkroom area. I spent some more time looking around the shack. It was only then that I saw the photo tucked into one corner. A close-up of the rocks of a stream bed. The goblin skull in the centre of the photograph.

THIS IS HOW
THE FAERIE TRAP YOU

I didn't know how Judas was involved in my search for Mona Lisa, but I knew he was. I had no doubt he'd killed the real art dealer and then sat across from me in that train, masquerading as the dead man while he told me to go to America. I just didn't know why. I ran things through my mind again and again at breakfast, but the only answer I could come up with was that he had somehow learned about Cassiel's promise to deliver him to me if I found Mona Lisa. But then why show himself at all? Why not go deeper into hiding, so that even Cassiel couldn't find him?

It was impossible to think like Judas, which meant I'd never have the real answer. And, in turn, that meant there was only one thing I could do.

Carry on with my original plan like I didn't know Judas was involved.

I went to Heathrow and lifted the wallet of an American businessman from his pocket while he complained to someone on his phone about the bad weather. Like there was any other kind in England. I used his credit cards to buy a plane ticket to Dublin and a new backpack. I try to change my gear as often as I can while travelling. With all the DNA testing and drug dogs and chemical sniffers and such these days, you never know what's going to get you into trouble. I once got thrown into a jail cell in Turkey because of some traces of hash in my bag – and I'd stolen the bag from the pilot of a Lufthansa flight. No more of that. Do your part for the economy and buy new, everyone.

On the plane, I settled into my seat and ordered a couple of drinks. I pretended not to see the businessman whose wallet I'd stolen a few seats ahead of me. I didn't feel any vague sense of danger like I had on the train, so I just passed off his presence on the plane to one of those coincidences. And it was.

I figured the businessman had already cancelled his credit card, so when we landed in Dublin I stole a new one from an airport cop. I also took the cop's driver's licence because I'd be needing a car. I left the businessman's credit card in the cop's wallet. I was going to see the faerie, so I was trying to think like them.

I rented a car at the airport with my new ID and picked a random direction out of the city. I didn't know where I was going. Looking for the faerie is like trying to summon Alice. They're right here among us but you still have to search for them. And you never know what you're searching for.

I found them in the deep, dark hours of the night a short distance outside of Dublin. I could give you the exact location, but it doesn't matter. They wouldn't be there if you went looking for them. They won't be there if I go looking for them again. The faerie get bored easily. Let's just say this time they were camped out in an abandoned pub set back in a field shortly after Conolly's Folly. If you don't know that particular landmark, it's a strange archway made of stone slabs and obelisks on the grounds of Castletown House. Another faerie hangout for a while, because of the things it used to attract. These days, though, its only visitors are tourists.

I could tell the pub was abandoned by the boarded-up windows and "For Lease" signs nailed onto the walls. But even in the car I could hear the music and laughter from inside. And the parking lot was crowded, with only one empty space. That sort of invitation is a sure sign of a faerie pub. And if you're still not convinced, well then, you'll just have to trust my experience in this matter. I parked and stretched a bit while looking around for other signs of life nearby. But there weren't any, not even another car on the road. When I was done putting things off, I took a deep breath and went inside.

It was wall to wall with people. I had to tap a man on the shoulder just to be able to step inside enough to close the door behind me. They were a friendly bunch, though – everyone who looked my way toasted me with their drink, and when I finally made my way to the counter the bartender poured me an ale without me even asking.

Yes, definitely a faerie pub.

I leaned against the bar and sipped my drink, which tasted of flowers and spices and charcoal and a few other things I couldn't identify. The good thing about faerie ales is that no one glass tastes the same as another. They don't have the patience for mass brewing. Or recipes.

I looked around for a few moments before talking to anyone. I wanted to get a feel for the mood of things before I went to work here. You had to be careful with the faerie. They can buy you another round or stick a blade between your shoulder blades with the exact same smile on their faces.

A band on a riser in a corner played snippets of songs that sounded familiar – a lyric I recognized here, a drumbeat or a guitar chorus there. They switched from electric guitars to acoustic and then to banjos and violins. The stage was littered with instruments. The drummer turned to pots and pans sometimes, then back to his drum kit. It was a chaotic, never-ending jam session, and it should have been a mess, but I found myself tapping my feet to the hidden rhythm that began to emerge from it. I toasted them. They nodded at me and kept playing, sweat on their faces and soaking their shirts. Everything seemed pleasant enough so far, but I knew that didn't mean anything with the faerie.

The bartender pushed me another ale, and I discovered I'd finished the first one he'd given me already. Some of the people around me crowded closer. They asked me questions all at once.

"What year is it?"

"Are the Troubles still on?"

"Can you take a message to my wife?"

They smiled and laughed as they talked to me, but I could see the desperation in their eyes. I tried not to look too deep. They were the fey, people who'd been tricked and taken by the faerie, doomed to spend the rest of eternity entertaining them. More of them kept coming, crowding around me until I turned my back on them. Fools, every one. They were upset about their fate. Didn't they realize there were worse fates?

The band stopped playing their instruments all at once, and the singer stepped to the front of the stage and sang the first few lines of "Silent Night," only he sang the German version –

"Stille Nacht, heilige Nacht!

"Alles schläft; einsam wacht"

– and just like that I remembered huddling in a trench with my fellow soldiers at Ypres in the First World War. It was Christmas and we'd used candles to decorate the few trees that still stood. Those of us with whisky passed our flasks around, and we sang Christmas carols. I was with the Germans that time – you can't always pick the right side, or the winning side. Whichever. It didn't matter. Everyone from both sides was dead now. Everyone but me.

After a couple carols, the English in the trenches across the way joined in. We went back and forth with the lines, singing to each other.

"Sleep in heavenly peace.

"Schlaf in himmlischer Ruh."

It was one of those moments that happen sometimes in war, when soldiers realize we're all on the wrong side. We're all tired of fighting.

"Silent night, holy night.

"Hirten erst kundgemacht."

The next day we got up out of our trenches without our rifles and marched across the field, and we met the British halfway. They'd also left their weapons behind. We exchanged what gifts we could with them – jam, cigars, chocolates. It was almost enough to give me faith in humanity, until the generals ordered the artillery to start firing again.

"By the angels' hallelujah,

"Tönt es laut von fern und nah."

The men and women around me now started singing along with the song, and I wanted to join in. I wanted to relive that time. I wanted to recapture that feeling of belonging to a group that loved me and would die for me as I would die for them. I wiped the tears from my eyes. And I realized we were all singing the song now.

"Christ the Saviour is here.

"Christ, der Retter ist da."

This is how the faerie trap you.

I slammed my hand down on the bar instead. The singing didn't stop, but it did grow quieter. The bartender pushed me another drink but I pushed it back.

"Tell your queen her lover is here," I said, then corrected myself. "Former lover."

That did the trick.

Now the singing stopped and the room grew quiet. I turned and looked for her, but I didn't have to look too hard. People moved aside until there was an open aisle from me to a table in a far corner of the room. A red-headed lass with freckles and a mischievous grin sat there, surrounded by a group of men. The kind of woman every man desires but knows he can never keep. All of them wore muddy hiking clothes, like they'd been wandering the fields all day. Maybe they had been.

She was the most beautiful woman in the room. She was always the most beautiful woman in the room. Some had known her in the past as Titania, others as Gloriana. But those were all human names. To the faerie, she was simply and always the queen.

Me? I knew her as Morgana le Fay. And that was the root of my current problem.

The men at the table didn't have the same looks of despair as the others in the pub. Their mirth as they regarded me seemed genuine. I figured them for faerie rather than fey. I didn't recognize them, but I'd probably encountered them in the past.

She smiled at me, and I smiled back. Perhaps time had righted all wrongs between us.

"Cross," she said.

I toasted her with the glass. "My queen."

"Put him in irons," she said.

THE TRUE KNIGHTS OF CAMELOT

You may have guessed by now that Morgana and I have a bit of a history. In fact, it's a rather long history – it dates back to when I was one of the knights of Camelot.

As is usually the case, the legends have everything wrong. Camelot wasn't exactly what it's portrayed to be now. It wasn't some shining castle on a hill in a pastoral countryside somewhere. It was far from that. Very far.

I first heard about Camelot when I found myself drinking with Gawain in a roadside tavern somewhere in the English countryside. He was a haggard shadow of a man, gaunt and scarred, with tangled hair and a beard that hung to his belt. He wore a sword on his back, and the handle was well worn from use. My kind of fellow drinker.

At some point in the night, I asked him where he hailed from and he said Camelot. When I said I'd never heard of it, tears rolled down his cheeks.

"It's the most beautiful place in the world," he said. "The centre of civilization. Towers that reach the very heavens themselves. A thousand knights who each have more honour and martial skills than a thousand men combined. The most beautiful, pure women you'll ever meet. Magickers that build wondrous new devices that make life easier for all, not just the rich. Led by the greatest king of all: Arthur. It is the city of dreams."

It sounded like the place for me, mainly because of the thousand knights he mentioned. I was on the run from . . . well, that doesn't matter now. Let's just say I needed to surround myself with people who knew how to wield a weapon.

Gawain left me in the tavern at some point after I passed out on the table. I slept until the sun came in through a window and roasted my face a bit. The bartender looked like he hadn't left. Maybe he hadn't, but he was serving breakfast now. I asked him which way to Camelot, and he just shook his head.

"You don't want to go there," he said. "Nothing good comes of Camelot."

"You take care of the porridge," I told him, "and I'll take care of myself."

So he gave me directions and I gave him a handful of coins for the previous night, and I went down the road to Camelot.

Instead of finding Gawain's city of dreams, I found a small camp of tents by a river. More haggard, hairy men lay dozing by fires or tending to horses that looked as worn as them. A few of them glanced up when I rode into their midst, but none bothered to be friendly. Except for Gawain, who came stumbling out of some bushes and scratching at his privates. He stopped when he saw me, and I could see his mind struggle to figure out where he remembered me from.

"I think you may have exaggerated the charms of Camelot a little," I said to him, getting off my horse. It snorted a sigh of relief to be done with me and wandered over to the river for a drink. Gawain had the good grace to at least look a little embarrassed.

"He exaggerated nothing," said a voice from behind me. I turned to see an old man emerge from one of the tents. A ghost of a man, thin and pale, with a white beard that went to his knees. He leaned on a sword like a cane. The sword was as black as the blackest night. I noticed the others all looked at him with expressions that were equal parts respect and weariness.

"Whatever Gawain told you of Camelot was but a hint of its true glory," he said. "Because it cannot be summed up in mere words." And Gawain quickly nodded, no doubt happy to be let off the hook.

I eyed that sword for a bit and then looked around the camp. "What's this place then?" I asked.

"The foundation of Camelot," the old man said. "And we are its building blocks."

I didn't think this particular bunch of blocks would be able to hold up too much, but I kept the thought to myself. As I mentioned earlier, I was still on the run and needed to lose myself among men with weapons. And weapons were the one thing this group had plenty of. Perhaps the only thing.

"I take it you're the king of Camelot," I said. "Arthur." His sword looked like a king's sword, after all.

"In Camelot, every man is a king," he whispered. I wasn't sure if he was still talking to me or thinking out loud.

I shrugged it off. "I'd like to add my hand to your labours then. It sounds like a pleasant enough place to live once it's built."

His arm shook on the sword, and for a moment I thought he was in danger of falling and was trying to support himself with the blade.

"We do not need any more lost souls," he told me. "We have quite enough of those."

Some of the others lying around their campfires laughed, but not many of them.

"Trust me when I say I'm not like any other knight you've met," I said.

"I don't care," he said. "I don't want your death on my conscience." And he gazed around at the others like they were already dead. Like he knew things we couldn't.

But I knew how the drill worked in those days.

"Give me a test," I said. "To prove myself to you."

And the blade lifted off the ground for a moment, and I realized he wasn't leaning on it but was instead holding it down. I didn't really know what to think of that, so I didn't think anything at all.

"Let him free her from Meleagant and his minions if he wants a quest so badly, Arthur," said a man trying to hammer the dents out of his armour, and the others laughed.

Arthur did nothing for a moment, then nodded. "Do as Percival says and you may join us," he said. "Because if you survive that you're as cursed as the rest of us anyway." Then he went back into his tent and closed the flap behind him.

I looked at Percival. "Which way to Meleagant?" I asked.

"You can't miss him," he said, pointing down the road. "Just follow the skeletons to the haunted castle."

"And who does he hold prisoner?" I asked.

Percival grinned. "We wouldn't want to ruin the surprise for you." And the others waved their farewells to me. None waved harder than Gawain.

So I rode down the road, past the skeletons hanging in nooses from the trees, and to the castle made of black stone deep in the woods. Although it was more of a tower with a wall around it than a proper castle. I blasted the door open with way more grace than I needed to, just to be flashy. Which was a waste, because the guards were all under some sort of enchantment and unimpressed. They shambled at me and I hacked off a couple of their arms to scare them away, but they didn't seem to care. So I had no choice but to kill them all, and that turned out to be a lot of work, given that they paid no attention to their mortal wounds. Let's just say I could have built another wall around the tower with their body parts.

When I was done that and had caught my breath again, I went into the tower and encountered another group of guards. I sighed and got on with it. I could see why Arthur's gang of knights had laughed at me. This was an annoying quest.

So I took care of that lot and then went up the stairs, hoping there weren't any more guards. There weren't. Instead, there was just Meleagant in his sleeping chamber. An old man dozing on a bed with a young woman at his side. I ran my sword through him and the bed and lodged it in the stone floor underneath. He didn't make a sound as he died. He didn't even try to defend himself, not that he had anything to defend himself with in his bed. I don't think he was ever aware that I was in the room.

Now, the legends all say it was Guinevere, Arthur's love, that Meleagant had with him there in his castle, but it wasn't. Guinevere never existed. She was made up, just a character meant to balance out all the blood and gore of those tales. Guineveres never exist. Instead, it was Morgana in Meleagant's bed, although I didn't know who she was at the time. She was a blond woman back then, with blue eyes and all that. She woke up and smiled at me when I slew Meleagant, and said, "I didn't know I'd been waiting for you until now."

She didn't care that I'd just massacred Meleagant and all his men. She didn't care that I was covered in blood and gore and stank like a hellhound. She pulled me into bed with her, and then I did the things you do with a faerie queen in a bed with a man you've just killed.

I think she wanted to put me under a spell like she had Meleagant and his followers but, well, I'm who I am and she didn't know how to work her charms on me yet. So when we were done I put my armour back on and tied her hands with some ribbons I took from her hair and ignored her screams and threats as I slung her over my horse and took her back to Arthur's camp.

If you know your Arthurian legends, this story may seem familiar to you. Yes, I was going by the name of Lancelot back then. But the legends have taken a few liberties with the truth here as well. I wasn't pure of spirit and a champion of virtue. I was just my usual unkillable self, which meant I won most of my fights and the people who make up stories about such things had to come up with a good reason why I was so hard to kill. It's funny how close they were, and yet so far away.

Anyway, I took Morgana back to Arthur's camp and was met by a group of very surprised knights. They gathered around and stared in amazement when I dumped her from the horse to the ground outside Arthur's tent. Gawain actually crossed himself, because that's the way he was. Percival spat on the ground near Morgana but not, I noted, on her.

She swore and shrieked at us, and promised what she'd done to Meleagant was just the beginning of what she'd do to us.

And then Arthur came of his tent with that sword, and Morgana grew very still.

"My love," she said. "It has been too long."

"It has been an eternity," Arthur said, but I had the feeling he was talking about something else.

"Will you not put down that thing and hold me in your arms?" Morgana asked, and the knights all looked at each other.

"You know I cannot do that," Arthur said and raised the black blade. He seemed to be fighting against it, but it was a losing battle. It dragged him forward, and then it swung down upon her.

And met my blade. I had to expend grace to push it back because, well, that's the sort of blade it was. A strange thing, but I guess I'd seen stranger.

Anyway, I parried the blow and then dropped off the horse and stood between Arthur and Morgana.

"Killing her isn't part of the deal," I said.

Yeah, I was a real gentleman back then.

"Arthur, my love," Morgana said with a mischievous smile I'd come to know better over the ages. "I can give you something more powerful even than Excalibur." I took that to be the name of Arthur's weapon. It was the sort of blade that deserved a name.

Arthur managed to wrestle the sword back to the ground. "I am doubtful such a thing exists," he said, but it wasn't in any sort of bragging fashion.

"Free me and let me be on my way, and I'll give you the Holy Grail," she said. "The goblet used to catch the dying blood of Christ himself."

Nobody said anything for a moment. I wondered if she knew my secret. But she didn't know who I was back then. Not yet.

"It is but a myth," Percival said, and a few of the others murmured their agreement.

"It is lost to history," Gawain said.

I didn't really have any opinion on the matter. I'd heard about the Grail before, but I'd been blinded by Judas when I was dying on the cross, so I had no idea if anyone had caught my blood in a goblet or not. They could have showered in it for all I knew. But I was curious about whether or not it existed.

Arthur studied Morgana. "You know where it is?" he asked.

"It is not myth and it is not lost," she said. "I know where the Grail lies."

"Tell me," Arthur said.

"First swear you'll let me be," Morgana said.

Arthur nodded. He ran a thumb down Excalibur's length, and his blood disappeared into the blade. Now it seemed to settle down. I'll stick to regular swords, thank you very much.

Morgana sat up and slipped her hands free of her bindings. I wondered why she hadn't done that earlier. The faerie are a tricky bunch to figure out.

"The dragon has it," she said.

"A dragon?" Percival said and laughed. "Well, that's just perfect."

"Not *a* dragon," Morgana said. "*The* dragon."

The knights all looked at each other in confusion and scratched various body parts. I have to admit I was surprised. I'd never before seen a dragon and I believed them creatures of the imagination only.

"Where is this dragon?" Arthur asked.

Morgana smiled at him. "That is not part of deal," she said.

"Slay her and be done with her madness," Percival said. He moved to draw his own sword, but stopped when Morgana looked at him.

"You should be careful how you address a queen," she said. "There are worse fates than Meleagant's."

And Percival dropped his sword back into its sheath.

"Begone from my land," Arthur said. "Our arrangement only extends to the next time we meet, and not a second longer."

"Oh, I don't think we'll meet again," Morgana said, turning to leave. But she paused to look at me again. "Except for you. I will make you mine one day."

"I am ever at your service," I said.

"Yes," she said, smiling. "You will be."

And then she went into the woods and disappeared.

We were all silent for a moment. Then I cleared my throat to speak. "This Grail – what does it do?"

"It is a powerful weapon," Galahad said.

"It will cleanse the land of evil," Gawain said.

"It will bring us riches," Percival said.

We all looked at Arthur.

"It will return my soul to me," he said and stared down at Excalibur.

We all looked at each other but didn't say anything else, because there was nothing to say to that.

"Break the camp," Arthur said. "We go to find the dragon."

So we went out into the land searching for it.

And we found Merlin instead.

A PRISONER OF
THE FAERIE QUEEN

So things were going pretty much as I expected they would.

I was sitting at Morgana's table, bound in iron shackles, as the party went on around me. I could have freed myself easily enough – hell, I could have just left before the crowd pulled out the chains and piled on me – but I hadn't learned what I'd come for yet.

Morgana shook her head at me as she drank wine. "I can't decide if you're brave or foolish, Cross," she said.

"Are you *still* holding a grudge?" I asked. "That was centuries ago."

She arched an eyebrow at me. "To which incident are you referring?" she asked.

All right, that was a fair comment. Morgana and I had met again after our initial encounter. A number of times. But each meeting ended more or less the same way, so what was the point in bringing them all up?

"I think it's time we let bygones be bygones," I said. "Let's start over."

The faerie at the table laughed, which prompted the crowd in the room to laugh even louder. Even Morgana smiled a little.

"That would perhaps make sense if time in my realm was the same as time in yours," she said. "But it is not."

"Really?" I said. "I didn't know that." Honestly. I didn't know that.

"I remember our first meeting like it was yesterday," she said. "Because to me it was."

I winced at that. Maybe I should have come up with a Plan C.

Morgana finished off her wine and held out the empty glass. A man stepped out of the crowd with a bottle and refilled her glass. When he stepped back into the people surrounding us, I lost sight of him. Neat trick, that.

"We should crucify him again," one of the men at the table said. He was chewing on a haunch of meat, but it wasn't any meat I recognized. He cocked his head in an impossible way that reminded me of Puck, but I couldn't be certain it was him. "On the original cross," he added. "I know where it is."

"I'm not sure that would be penalty enough for what he's done," Morgana said. "Especially now that he has trespassed into my realm."

I bowed my head to her. "I would have gladly avoided your court the rest of my life, and then some," I said. "But I am on a quest and in need of your assistance."

The men all sat up a little at that and stared at me with wide eyes. The faerie loved quests. A quest gave them all sorts of opportunity to create mischief because a quest meant there was chaos somewhere in the land. And the faerie loved chaos. They were drawn to it like, well, like I was drawn to angels. That's why they loved the age of the knights so much. I guess there wasn't much for them to do these days.

Morgana, however, was less than impressed.

"Oh, of course you're on a quest," she said. "Show me a mortal man who isn't on a quest and I'll show you a man who's in the grave. And even that's not enough to stop you sometimes."

I shrugged. "I can't help my nature," I said. "Any more than you can help yours."

"This quest, does it involve horses?" the one with the haunch of meat asked, licking his lips clean. Yes, definitely Puck.

Morgana slapped him on the side of the head and he dropped the meat underneath the table. He frowned and ducked down to pick it up again. Who knew what mischief he was up to while down there?

"Let me guess," Morgana said. "It involves Judas."

"What in history doesn't involve Judas?" I said.

"Why don't you give him up?" she said. "Your life would be so much . . . simpler without him."

"Never again," I said. I'd learned my lesson that way, and it had cost me more than I ever could have imagined. Even if I was willing to give up Judas, he would never give me up. Not until he was dead.

"Never is ours, Cross," she said. "Not yours." She sipped her wine, and it left a crimson shine on her lips. I wanted to kiss it off. I shook my head to snap out of it.

"At any rate, it doesn't matter," she said. "There's no questing for you as long as you're a captive of the court. Now, what should we do with you?"

The faerie all spoke at once, eager to offer their suggestions of ways to torment me:

"Turn him into a stag we can hunt with knives."

"Make him dance until he wears his feet to the bone."

"Switch him with the babe of an ogre."

Morgana sighed. "I grow weary of those diversions," she said.

Puck popped back up with a grin on his face. "Let him go."

The others all looked at him.

"What do you mean?" Morgana asked.

"Let him go and render him none of the aid he seeks," Puck said. "And then watch him fail."

The others mulled that over.

"It's not bad," one of them said.

"But how will we watch?" one of the others asked. "Through a sprite?"

"But what if he doesn't fail?" another wondered. "Where's the fun in that?"

"You can do what you like with me," I said. "As long as you tell me one thing."

"You are hardly in a position to make demands," Morgana pointed out.

"Aren't I?" I asked and turned all of their wine into water. I threw in a gesture with my shackled hands to make it more dramatic.

"Paaagghhh!" Puck said, spitting out the mouthful of drink he'd just taken.

Morgana rolled her eyes and motioned the man with the wine out of the crowd once more. "Use your magic in my court again and you'll pine for the comforts of your mortal hell," she said.

"I want to know about Mona Lisa," I said. "The real one, not the painting."

Morgana shook her head and I was momentarily entranced by the curls in her hair, the way they caught the light.

"She's long gone from us," Morgana said. "We sacrificed her to the human queen as tribute." She smiled. "I was expecting to receive something truly prized in return, but I have to admit I didn't think it would be you."

I mulled over that word. *Sacrifice*. Exactly what kind of relationship did the queens have? Well, no matter. There were other issues at hand.

"I take it you didn't steal her back then?" I asked.

The music suddenly became discordant as the band members faltered and everyone glanced our way. I guess they were more sensitive to Morgana's moods than I was. The other faerie pushed themselves away from the table a little. Puck was grinning that odd little grin of his. No doubt ready to spring upon me at her command.

But she chose to spare me, either out of nostalgia for old times or a desire to inflict a worse fate upon me.

"Remember where you are," she told me. "We *choose* to live in peace through the tributes. We are not forced into it by your kind. We would not take back a gift freely given."

"I meant no insult," I said. "But I had to ask."

"Aye, I suppose you did," she said, and all was right with the music once more. Morgana twirled a lock of her hair with a finger. Damn, that was distracting.

"What's your interest in the gorgon?" she asked. "Are you seeking to violate her, too?"

So I told the story, skipping all the usual self-incriminating parts. Not that this group would have been one to judge. They had real skeletons in their closets. Animated, talking skeletons. But sometimes it's good to keep a few things to yourself.

"An angel," Morgana said when I was done. "That is intriguing."

"They're usually more infuriating than intriguing," I said. "But I'm not here to talk about them. I'm here to find out about Mona Lisa. Tell me about her and I promise I'll let you do what you will with me."

I meant that promise. I suppose I owed her, in some form or another.

But she just looked at me for a moment and then got to her feet. "Dance with me," she said, and the shackles fell from my wrists and ankles.

The band switched to some rollicking number I didn't recognize and couples emerged from the crowd to do their thing in the centre of the room. We joined them, as the others at the table began to clap their hands and shout to the music. I wasn't sure what she was playing at, but I went along with it. When in the court of the faerie queen . . .

We danced a dance I'd never known before. It was a mixture of old formalized moves – little bits and pieces from the French, the British, even the Persians, from when such things were in style. But we combined it with the abandon of the Irish, the joy of the drunk. I didn't know any of it but it came to me naturally in this place. And she smiled her fiery smile at me.

"Mona Lisa was given in tribute to us," she told me as we whirled about. "Just as we gave her in tribute to someone else."

"Who gave her to you?"

She spun close to me and wrapped her arms around my neck. "Who do you think?" she breathed. And then she moved away again.

I hadn't thought about where Mona Lisa had been before the faerie got their hands on her. So I did that now, as we danced. And the obvious cut in and waltzed with me for a moment.

"Da Vinci?" I said.

Morgana clapped her hands at me, and everyone around us clapped too.

"He sacrificed her to us and so we gave him the dreams he wanted," she said. "We sacrificed her to the human queen and now here you are."

The musicians onstage were howling into their microphones now, unintelligible words. The pace of the dance picked up. I was sweating. I tried to work things out, but I was having trouble thinking.

"What was da Vinci doing with her?" I asked.

She raised an eyebrow at me, and I noted everyone else on the dance floor doing the same to their partners.

"That's no concern of ours," she said. "You know da Vinci."

Fair enough. He was a special case. A mortal, but not like the rest of them. He was the only one to have found a way to immortality, for instance. For all the good it did him.

"All right then," I said. "So who took her from the human queen?"

Morgana disappeared into the mass of writhing bodies and then popped out a second later halfway across the dance floor. She had a fresh glass of wine in her hand now.

"Ah, that's the answer you really seek, isn't it?" she said. Her voice came from the mouths of all the dancers around me. "But the question is what you're willing to pay for it."

"Whatever you want," I said.

She disappeared again and then put her hands over my eyes from behind me. "Well, I do fancy your soul," she said. And she nibbled on my ear and then bit, hard enough to draw blood and make me curse. The music and clapping and dancing all increased as she licked the blood away, until the room whirled around me and I thought I was going to pass out.

But she held me up with hands on my head as strong as iron bars. "You took her," she told me. "You and your kind took her. Just like you've taken everything else. And now I've taken you."

She released me and it was as if she really had taken everything inside me. I didn't even have the strength to stand. I fell to the floor, slamming my head against the back of a chair as I went down. I lay there and watched blood from my cut trickle through a crack in the floorboards. I felt that old hollowness return, only this time it was worse than anything it had ever been. Worse than if I were drained of grace. Worse even than when I'd first awoken as myself. I howled at the emptiness inside me, tried to curl up around it to make it go away.

Then one of the dancers helped me to my knees. A woman with black rings on all of her fingers. She wiped the blood from my face with a napkin. And then a man pressed another ale into my hands. He wore a black ring on his ring finger. I finished the ale in one long swallow but it didn't help. Neither did the next one, or the one after that.

But I got drunk. So drunk I just joined the dance and laughed the night away with the rest of them, all of them wearing black rings that marked them as something, but I didn't know what. I climbed on stage and picked up one of the guitars leaning against the wall. It had been years since I'd held a guitar, but the music came back to me like I'd been playing in this place my entire life. I jammed with the band just like the time I jammed with Hendrix in that nightclub in New Orleans. And then I stumbled off the stage and fell into Morgana's arms. Her skin burned like ice. We were face to face, so close I could feel her breath on my lips.

"I told you I would make you mine someday," she said. "And so I have."

I tried to push myself away from her but I was too weak, and she laughed at me. I knew there was something I needed to do, something I needed to ask her, but I couldn't remember what it was.

"Not even Arthur could save you now," she said. Then she threw me into the crowd and I didn't remember anything anymore.

IN SEARCH OF THE HOLY GRAIL

Arthur.

I rode the land with Arthur and his knights, in search of the dragon. In search of the Holy Grail. We fought everybody and everything we encountered. With Arthur leading us, we could not be defeated. Or rather, with Excalibur leading us. For the blade seemed to give Arthur a strength like the grace in battle. When we drove the Saxons into the sea, he threw men from him one-handed and cut through the armour of others like they were wearing cloth. When we slew the werewolves in their dens, he cut the beasts in two with a single sweep of that blade. When the rest of us dropped to our knees in exhaustion in the battle against the hill giants, he fought on like a man possessed. I suspected he *was* a man possessed – by that blade. But when we weren't in battle he just lay in his tent, emerging only to eat a little and occasionally drink some of the wine or ale we'd taken from the dead. Excalibur always in his hand.

At night, around the campfires, I asked the others about Arthur. They all whispered different stories about his past. He was an ancient and immortal Celtic hero. He was a dead king who had somehow escaped the afterlife. He was a faerie changeling who'd been raised among humans. He was a simple farmer until he'd been cursed by a god for taking his name in vain. And so on. No one knew which story, if any, was true, because Arthur didn't answer questions about himself.

They'd all come to him in different ways. They were all lost souls like me.

Lionel had been part of an order of religious knights that had gone to the Holy Land to recover lost artifacts. He was the only one who had returned. He'd just cast his weapons and armour into the sea when Arthur had ridden up to him on the beach and told him there was a greater cause than even God himself he could swear his faith to – Camelot.

Percival was the bastard son of a knight who was raised by his mother alone in the woods. When he was old enough to lift a sword, he sought out his father and killed him. His father's men imprisoned him in a dungeon and tortured him for years, until Arthur broke down the door to his cell one day, Excalibur bloody in his hand. Arthur told Percival he'd been drawn to his screams, and then told him of a city where there were no dungeons, no torturers – Camelot.

Galahad had been entombed in an underground chamber for centuries, the victim of a druid who'd become smitten with the woman Galahad loved, until Arthur had freed him. Arthur said there were no dark magics in Camelot.

And so on. They were all men who had nothing else now. Nothing but Arthur. And his dream of Camelot.

When it came time to reveal my past to the others around the campfire, I just stared into the flames and said nothing. How to tell them the name I'd given them was a sham, the latest in a long history of lies? I wore identities like clothes in those days, trying on new lives and then casting them aside when they got too worn or dirty for my taste. I no longer searched for the man I'd been before I'd woken up in the body of Christ. I had lived too many lives since then. I knew who I had become, if not who I had been. A man not even Arthur could redeem. I remained silent because it was better than telling them the truth about me. And they let me be, because the dream of Camelot waited for them in their beds.

As it waited for me.

The dream was real. We shared it as we slept around those dying campfires. And Camelot was as wondrous a place as Gawain had described to me in that roadside tavern.

Tall spires that disappeared into the clouds. Men on flying horses soaring between them. Fountains of crystal-clear water in the streets lined with perfectly shaped stones. Merchants with stalls full of wonders from around the world – wonders even I had not seen before. The women were all beautiful, the men all handsome, the steeds all noble. It was the perfect city. The first night I dreamed it, I woke weeping. I couldn't wait to fall asleep again, to revisit it.

But, in the morning, it always faded away, and we woke cursing our fate on the cold ground beside our dead fires.

When I asked Gawain what the dream meant over breakfast one day, he shook his head. "Once it meant the future to us," he said. "It was the dream Arthur shared with us of the kingdom he meant to build. But no more. It can never be anything but a dream now."

"What changed?" I asked.

"Excalibur," he said, spitting on the ground and glaring at Arthur's tent.

"What of it?" I asked.

"The blade has stolen his soul," Gawain said. "It cares nothing for Camelot. It only cares for blood. And so it leads us from battle to battle and won't let us rest. There's not enough blood in the world to satisfy it. We destroy the world instead of building a new one. Camelot can never be anything but a dream while Arthur wields Excalibur."

His words made me think of Judas again. Not only the civilizations he had ruined over the ages, but also my own quest to find him. For while I was no longer obsessed with finding out who I once may have been, I was still driven by the need to find out *why* I'd woken up in Christ's body. I needed to understand what Judas had done, to understand the purpose of my very existence. I needed to find a reason to the madness.

"So get rid of the sword," I suggested. "I'll take it off your hands." Perhaps it would help me in the hunt for Judas. And if not, I knew a few kings with actual kingdoms who'd pay a pretty price for a weapon like that.

Gawain shook his head and looked down at the ground. "It is not so easy," he said. "The sword is his until he dies. That is the promise Merlin made to Arthur when he gave him the blade. But it is also the curse he laid upon Arthur. We just didn't know it at the time. He cannot be rid of the sword."

"Who is Merlin?" I asked.

"A magicker," Percival said, pausing as he walked by to relieve himself in the woods. "He came to us when we were burying Cador after the battle with those damned dwarves. He told Arthur he had a weapon so powerful that none of the knights need ever die again. A fang of the dragon, forged into a sword by one of the old gods, back in one of the ages before the new gods stole the world away from them. Better we had all died than take Excalibur from him, as we did. It is no gift."

"Well, then we should find this Merlin character and force him to take the sword back," I said. I had to admit the dream of Camelot appealed to me. I wouldn't have minded seeing it become real. "And it sounds like he might know where this dragon is that we're seeking."

Gawain and Percival looked at each other but said nothing. "What is it?" I asked.

"I will see Merlin again," Arthur said, limping out of his tent. "He promised me as much. He said he would take Excalibur back from me the day I die." And now it was Percival's turn to spit on the ground.

"This sounds like a real deal with the devil you've made," I said.

Arthur shook his head. "Even the devil would keep his distance from Excalibur," he said. A fish splashed in the stream, and the sword turned in his hand toward it.

I shrugged. "Well, there's an easy solution to all of this," I said. And now they all looked at me. I swear even Excalibur pointed my way.

"Let's kill Arthur," I said. And then, in case they misunderstood me, I explained my plan.

So we broke camp and rode for several days, to Stonehenge. Back then, it wasn't a safe, sterile tourist zone like it's become now. It was a dangerous, wild area with strange creatures found nowhere else in the world. It was one of those places where there really was magic in the world, before those things that used magic were killed off or learned to hide themselves.

It was also a graveyard. It was where kings and knights were buried. And before them warriors and chieftains. If there were any brave enough to take their bodies there and bury them, anyway. That was a quest unto itself in those days. But nothing was foolish enough to attack us as we rode there. I guess it was apparent that we were a band of desperate men who had nothing to lose. Or maybe all the things that were hidden in the mist out there could sense Excalibur.

We reached Stonehenge in the early evening, and by the time we'd set up camp amid those rocks, night had fallen. We set up a large fire in the centre of the circle and huddled around it for warmth. The cold of the night pressed in on us despite the fire, and the mist crept right up to the edge of the stones.

We built a funeral pyre and laid Arthur on it, Excalibur clasped to his chest. The sword kept shifting this way and that, like it was struggling to reach one or another of us. Perhaps all of us.

We piled wood under the pyre but didn't light it. Instead, we honoured Arthur. We took turns telling the others what a great man he had been.

Gawain told the tale of how Arthur had rescued him from the Green Knight, a man cursed to forever re-enact his own murder in a forgotten castle deep in a forgotten land. Gawain had wandered into the castle while hunting and become trapped, and forced to take part in the drama. He played the part of the murderer, cutting off the Green Knight's head night after night with an axe, and being slain by the beheaded knight in return, only to wake from the dead the following day in a bed in the castle to repeat the same thing. Until Arthur had walked into the middle of one of the murder feasts and lopped off the head of the knight with Excalibur, slaying him once and for all.

Tristan told the tale of how Arthur had rescued him from the ghost of Isolde, his past lover, who followed him around the land and rode him at night like a banshee. Arthur had sat by Tristan's side as he slept, and when Isolde came drifting out of the woods, he'd touched that blade to her. In the morning there was nothing but a pile of bones on the ground, and she bothered Tristan no more.

Galahad told the tale of how Arthur had helped him hunt down the druid that had entombed him, who had hidden himself among the forest animals by taking their shapes. The druid had tried to flee as a deer but Galahad's arrow had brought it down. When the druid transformed into a bear as Galahad approached, Arthur had touched his blade to the beast and drawn all the magic out of it, until it was just a man again.

And around the circle we went, until everyone had told a tale but me. I was silent once again, for Arthur had not yet saved me. I looked around the stones and out into the night pressing in on us, but no one stepped out of the darkness. Merlin, if he was out there, was not fooled.

Arthur had the same idea. He sighed and climbed down from his pyre. "It's no use," he said. "The magicker no doubt can sense that I'm still alive." And the others swore and broke out their flagons of mead.

"You likely tell the truth," I said. "But we have one hope left." And I drew my sword and ran him through.

Excalibur reacted almost instantly, hurling his arm up to parry the blow. But I was expecting the sword to do something, so I'd thrown some grace into my strike to speed it along. By the time Excalibur hit my sword to knock it aside, I'd already buried the business end in Arthur.

He didn't cry out, but Excalibur did. It screamed, which I found interesting. I've heard swords make plenty of noises before, but never that. And then Arthur's men screamed and drew their own swords.

Arthur stared at me, and then slumped to his knees. He planted Excalibur point first in the ground and slumped against the blade. And that's where he died.

"Say your last rites, betrayer," Gawain said, his blade against my throat, "for we will not say them for you."

"Let's just all calm down and wait a minute," I said.

"Wait for what?" Percival said, approaching me with a look of murder in his eyes that I'd seen too many times in my lives.

"I believe he wants you to wait for me," a new voice said. It belonged to an old man who walked into our camp out of the mist, wearing black robes and leaning on a staff as black as Excalibur. His face was scarred with a hundred different burns, and where he should have had hair he had tattoos of strange symbols I'd never seen before.

"Merlin!" the others spat and drew back from him. I sighed and relaxed a little. I hadn't been able to come up with a backup plan in case this hadn't worked, so I was glad to see him.

Merlin shuffled over to Arthur and stared down at him, then grunted. "So, he is finally dead," he said.

"He will not be the only one to die this night," Galahad said, coming over to Percival's side with his weapon drawn.

"And who has done the terrible deed?" Merlin asked, looking at me. And I knew I had him when he kept on looking.

I put my sword to his throat. I ignored Gawain's sword, which was still at my throat. It was that kind of scene.

"Where is the dragon?" I asked him.

"Now, what would *you* want with the dragon?" he asked. The way he said it made it sound like he was talking only to me and not the others.

"The dragon has the Grail," I said. "We would have the Grail."

He smiled a little. "The Grail holds no answers for you," he said.

"The dragon," I said, prodding him with the sword.

He studied me a few seconds longer, then shrugged a little. "The dragon hides in the impossible places. If you want to meet it, then you must find a way to draw it into the world of the real."

"And how do we do that, magicker?" Percival demanded.

Merlin cast a glance at him. "You must offer it something equally impossible. Something it will covet."

"Like me," I said. Merlin looked back at me but didn't say anything. His expression was all the answer I needed, though.

So I ran him through too.

None of the others tried to stop me, not that they could have, anyway. They just stared in confusion.

No blood came from Merlin's wound, only dust. And when he cried out in pain, more dust spilled from his mouth. "I am not the dragon, fool!" he said.

"No," I said. "You are Judas."

He just stared at me for a moment, more dust trickling out of the corner of his mouth. Then he chuckled. "How did you know?" he asked in that voice made of a thousand voices.

I tried not to let my relief show. I hadn't actually been certain. This could have been awkward.

"It was what the others told me," I said, twisting the blade hard enough to make him cry out again. He dropped to his knees as the knights stared. I have no problem admitting I thoroughly enjoyed his pain. "Giving Arthur a gift that would ensure Camelot never comes to be. A weapon from the age of the older gods. This is just like Rome, isn't it? You want Camelot to fall before it's even been built. You don't want humanity to have something that perfect."

He grinned through the pain at me. "And Camelot has fallen, hasn't it?" he said. "It has died with Arthur. It could have been but it never will be."

"I don't know what you're talking about," I said, straight-faced. "Arthur isn't dead."

"I felt you slay him . . ." Judas said, looking over at Arthur slumped against Excalibur still. And all the knights looked at their dead king as well.

I waved my hand and resurrected Arthur. It was a showy move, and it took most of my remaining grace, but it was only fair because, as Judas pointed out, I had killed Arthur. But he was dead no more.

Arthur gasped for breath as he looked around himself. And then he saw Merlin and rose to his feet. "Magicker!" he hissed.

And now the others stepped back and stared at me. I couldn't really blame them. But this wasn't the time or place to explain things.

"Arthur still lives," I said to Judas. "And so does the dream of Camelot."

Judas looked back at me. "Very well," he said. "If you want the dragon, you shall have it. *Hic verum gradale*," he whispered, and mist came out of his mouth when he spoke.

"What are you saying?" I asked.

"I am calling the dragon," Judas said and laughed, and coils of fog rolled out of his mouth and wrapped around me.

Now that I finally had him, I fully intended to force him to tell me the truth about my past, and why he had done what he had done to me. But I knew that was going to take time. In fact, I wanted it to take time. I wanted to draw it out. So I had to take care of the immediate problem first and then enjoy myself with Judas later.

"What is the dragon?" I asked. I looked around the mist as the other knights formed a circle, backs against each other. Strange sounds came out of the mist – moaning and shrieking noises. And a low rumble as if something large was stirring.

"It is your nightmares and despair made real," Judas said. "Among other things."

And then the city I'd seen in my dreams formed out of the fog around me. It was as if I were suddenly in a city of Heaven. Beautiful, crystalline towers disappearing into the mist overhead. Statues of smiling men and women in the squares, and ornately carved fountains. Perfectly formed cobblestones under our feet. Trees with branches bent heavy with fruit. A smell of baking bread in the air.

"Camelot!" Arthur cried.

"It is where the dragon has hidden itself," Judas said, laughing even though he was still on his knees, still on my sword. "In the impossible."

And then Gareth screamed, and we turned to see a pack of bears dragging him off. They were made of the mist itself. We started forward to help him, but then more things came out of the mist. A skeleton with an axe attacked Percival. A huge dog with three heads lunged at Tristan. A woman with worms at her breasts reached for Gawain. They were all mist.

"Now we are truly in the belly of the beast," Judas said, and I knew from his words that somehow all of these things were the dragon.

A young man in black armour stepped out of the mist and raised a black sword at Arthur. The sword looked like the twin of Excalibur.

"Prepare yourself to die," he said. "Father."

Arthur stared at him. "What madness is this? I have no son."

"In Camelot you do," the youth said. "But I would have no father." He lashed out at Arthur, who parried with Excalibur, and the blades shrieked as they touched. Then the mist grew so thick we couldn't see each other. I could only hear the sounds of battle, and the screams.

Once again, it was just Judas and me.

"All right, the dragon is my nightmares and despair," I said. "How do I kill it?"

Judas shook his head at me. "When you fight the dragon, you are fighting yourself," he said. "There can be no victory in that. That's why it is the dragon and not some other beast."

I twisted the blade in him again, just to hear him scream. I did wish it didn't sound so much like a joyous scream.

"Why?" I said.

"Why destroy Camelot? Because it would have ushered in a new age of light to keep the darkness at bay. It would have redeemed you." He spat dust at me. "But none of you are worthy of redemption. You belong to the darkness, not the light. I'm simply keeping you in your place, as I have done so many times before."

"I've been thinking a lot about what you told me in Rome," I said, "and I think you're full of shit."

Now he looked a little less joyous.

"I don't think you're trying to keep us where we belong," I said. "I think you're trying to keep us from where we belong. We're not beasts who dream of blood and anarchy. We dream of Camelot. And before that we dreamed of Rome, and before that the Garden. And before that maybe we dreamed of other places that lifted us out of the mud and shadows. Because if we ever manage to build a place like that, then your time is done. I've seen Camelot, and I know there's no room for something like you in it. You'll fade into dust just like the rest of your kind, whatever they were. The blood and mud is where you belong, not us."

I shoved the blade down into the ground, pinning him. Like he'd once pinned me. It didn't feel as good as I'd hoped it would, but we were just getting started.

"This time the blood and mud is where you're going to stay," I said.

"Who says I'm even here?" Judas said, impossibly smiling again. "How do you know I'm not just another dream of the dragon?"

I paused. He made the sort of point only a trickster could make. I looked around but there was no one else to help me figure out what was real and what wasn't here. I was lost in nothingness.

I thought about killing Judas quickly. I certainly wanted him dead, before he had a chance to escape again. But I couldn't kill him yet. Not until he told me what I wanted to know about myself. Before I could get to work on him for that information, though, a massive serpent's head formed out of the mist in front of me, and I no longer had a choice.

I ripped the sword from Judas and his scream was lost in the cry of the dragon as it lunged at me. I slashed part of its face off, but it only melted away. And those jaws snapped shut on me.

What to say of being swallowed by the dragon? It burned and it choked and it seared and it smothered and everything else you can think of. I tried to swing my sword again but the mist pressed in on me like a solid thing, preventing me from moving. I really was in the belly of the beast now, or I would be shortly. I screamed – not in pain or fear, but in rage at being so close to Judas and then having this happen.

But the screaming kept up after I'd run out of breath. The very air around me came apart in a scream and I fell to the ground. At Arthur's feet. I realized the sound was coming from Excalibur in his hand. The blade was clean but Arthur was drenched in blood. Some of it leaking out of the holes in his armour where he had been run through.

"I don't know what you are," he said, "but save yourself."

I cast about for Judas instead, but he wasn't there. He was gone.

And the dragon came at Arthur and he threw himself into its maw, slashing madly with Excalibur, and I was lost in the mist again.

I'd like to say I stayed to help him, that I fought at his side until the dragon was slain. But, instead, I ran blindly through the fog, swinging my sword in hope of striking Judas by chance.

And I stumbled out of the mist and fell against one of the stones of Stonehenge. The mist still wreathed the area, but it was fading now, even as the sounds of battle from within it grew louder. And then Gawain fell out of the mist, collapsing to the ground with dozens of wounds on his body. And Percival stumbled out after him, waving his broken sword at something that didn't follow. And one after another the knights emerged from the mist, all of us bloody and broken.

All of us except Arthur.

When the mist finally faded completely, leaving us alone in Stone-henge, Camelot was gone and Arthur was nowhere to be seen.

"The dragon has taken him," Percival said, gasping for breath.

I wondered if Arthur had found the Grail. If it even existed.

"And it has taken Merlin," Gareth said, clutching the stump of his right hand and rocking back and forth.

I scanned the area for Judas, but his body was nowhere to be found. I felt too tired to even swear. I felt like Arthur must have when he saw the Camelot he could never have.

"Merlin betrayed us," Gawain said.

"He is slain," Tristan said.

"He betrayed us," I said, "but I don't think he's slain."

"No," Percival said, and he spat on the ground where Camelot and the dragon had been. Where Arthur had vanished, and his kingdom along with him. "It was that bitch of a faerie queen. She tricked us into going after the dragon." He looked at me. "And you were the one who brought her to us."

I thought about arguing with them, but maybe they had a point. Besides, Judas was as gone as Arthur and Camelot and the dragon. And the Grail, if it had ever existed at all. There was nothing here for me anymore.

Also, there were more knights than me, and they were still angry that I'd killed Arthur in the first place, let alone everything that had happened since then. So I found a horse and got the hell out of there before they could regain enough strength to raise their weapons again and come at me.

And so ended my days as one of Arthur's noble knights.

AN UNEXPECTED SALVATION

I don't know how long I was lost in the faerie pub before something broke Morgana's spell and woke me.

An irritation in my head, like a mosquito's whine. I tried to block it out but couldn't. It took me a few minutes, or maybe days, to realize what it was.

Words.

"Cross. Awaken, Cross. Cross. Awaken, Cross."

Cassiel.

I opened my eyes. I was face down on a table in the pub. The air was still and silent around me. Musty. No lights, but enough of a glow came in through the windows that I could see.

"Cross. Awaken, Cross."

"All right," I said. "All right."

I pushed myself up and looked around. And thought maybe I was still dreaming.

I was surrounded by bodies. All the people I'd been dancing and drinking with the previous night. They sat slumped in chairs or collapsed on the floor. Mummified, their flesh shrivelled, bones sticking through skin in some of their faces. Their clothes rotted. Those black rings still on their fingers though.

Wait. Not everyone was there. I didn't see Morgana or any of her entourage.

And another detail: the glasses on the table looked fresh, with beer and

Scotch and wine still in them. I struggled to make sense of it.

I'd been on many a battlefield in my life, and one thing is always the same when there are dead bodies other than me involved – flies. But there were none of them here, none of that usual drone of them going about their business. There was just the stillness. And the voice coming down through the fireplace.

"Cross. Awaken, Cross."

"I'm up," I said, and I was. I staggered over to the fireplace and peered inside it. There was no one there, of course.

"Do you live?" Cassiel asked. A whisper from somewhere far above.

What a stupid question, I thought. Then I looked down at myself to check.

"I think so," I said.

"You are ensnared by the faerie," Cassiel said. "Your quest is now one of liberation."

My mind was still a bit muddled, but I think he meant I had to escape.

"I can't," I said.

"Are you bound physically as well as spiritually?" Cassiel asked.

"No," I said. "I just haven't found what I need yet."

I turned away from the fireplace –

– and collided with a dancing woman as the music started up again. She laughed and took my hands and swung me around, passing me off to another woman in the crowd. And it was all laughter and drinks again, and the women kept spinning me around, one to the next, until I found myself in Morgana's arms.

"I know what you're doing," I told her. Which wasn't exactly true, but I've found it's often better to pretend you know what's going on. People are less likely to try to stab or shoot you then. Or suck the life out of you and leave you abandoned in some empty faerie pub in a field somewhere for the rest of time.

"And what might that be?" Morgana asked.

"You're trying to turn me into one of the others," I said. "One of the fey."

She smiled and put her finger to my lips, and suddenly I couldn't talk. She drew me closer in her arms, and her eyes flashed the same red as her hair.

"You are not like the others, though, are you?" she said. "I have to admit, I've thought about hiding you away from the world for the rest of time, so that you stay mine. There are underground chambers no mortal has stumbled across yet. There are others who've wronged me who have yet to be discovered again, centuries later, and who will never be found again. Even I've forgotten where they are." She spun me around and around, faster and faster, until the crowd was a blur. "But you're not the type to stay forgotten, are you? Any more than you're the type to stay dead."

I didn't try to answer that. I couldn't speak anyway.

"And who knows what would happen when you bloom again?" Morgana said. She shook her head. "No, it's better to just play with you for a time."

And with that she led me to a room upstairs, a room with detailed tapestries of forest hunts on the wall and a bed fit for a queen with green blankets, and we did the sorts of things you did in a bed like that while under a spell like I was.

After, she touched her finger to my lips and I found I could speak once more.

"Is there anything you want to say to me?" she murmured.

"Actually, there is," I said. "When you said my kind took Mona Lisa, which kind did you mean exactly? Mortals or the other kind?"

She sighed and rolled off me, taking the blankets with her. "You are all mortals," she said.

And then I woke to find myself alone on the bed, which smelled musty. Morgana was gone, the blankets crumpled around where she'd been. The tapestries on the walls had fallen to the floor, and rich patterns of mould were in their places.

"Cross. Awaken, Cross."

I looked at the window. Daylight through the dusty pane. The voice coming through it, distant and distorted.

"Cross. Awaken, Cross."

"I'm here," I said.

"Cross. You must seek your escape, Cross."

"Not yet," I said. "I think I'm making progress."

"You are serving no purpose now. You must escape in order to find Mona Lisa."

"Yeah, well, maybe things would be moving along quicker if you'd been honest with me from the start," I told the window.

"I have told you no lies," it said.

"Maybe not," I said. "But you sure left a lot of things out."

"You did not ask the questions to the answers you have learned."

I shook my head. I couldn't believe I was having this discussion. Especially with a window.

"I don't think I can leave, anyway," I said. "Not until Morgana is done with me."

"Unbar the door then," Cassiel said. "Unbar the door and your salvation will be free to enter."

All right. Sounded simple enough. It took me three or four days, though. I got up and walked out of the bedroom and into a full-scale dance involving everyone in the pub. I woke up on the dance floor underneath a pile of bodies. I pulled myself out and caught on to the bar to steady myself. And the bartender offered me a glass of the new Scotch that had just arrived, a mixture of smoke and fire that had been aged for a hundred years, he told me. I woke up at the end of the bar in a pile of broken glasses, blood smeared everywhere around me. I got up and staggered to the door and then found myself arm in arm with a group of men singing a song I didn't even recognize, in a language that had been dead for centuries and never had a name. I woke up lying on a tabletop without my shirt. I threw myself at the door and knocked off the bar that locked it from the inside. I stumbled through, but fell into bed with the queen again.

"Why would you want to leave this?" she asked, laughing as she rode me.

So it went.

I'd been there weeks or months when my salvation finally arrived. As usual, it was from an unexpected source.

I was jamming onstage with the band, channelling some crazy mix of Celtic rock and funk, when the door opened and he came in. Everyone did their usual routine, turning to toast the newcomer and offer him a drink and welcome him inside for as long as he wanted to stay, which, of course, was forever. But their welcomes died in their throats at the sight of him, and even those of us onstage stopped playing.

The newcomer was wearing a long coat with the collar turned up, and gloves and a hat. A scarf wound tight around his face. To most people he'd pass for an eccentric or maybe a burn victim. But not me. I knew him. It was the mummy.

"Son of a bitch," I said as it came into the faerie pub, and Morgana turned from her table to look at me.

"Cross, what have you done this time?" she asked.

Before I could say anything, the mummy went to work.

It saw me on the stage and pushed through the crowd, knocking down a man and a woman. Other people tried to stop it, ripping its hat and scarf away, revealing its wrapped head underneath. Those empty eye sockets didn't move away from me, not even when the bartender hopped over his bar and clubbed the mummy across the back with a cricket bat, knocking it to its knees for a second.

"For Christ's sake," I yelled at the mummy. "I don't even have it anymore."

My appeal to reason worked as well as it usually does. The mummy swung a fist back into the bartender's face and sent him sprawling to the ground. Another man rushed the creature and it caught him by the throat and squeezed, until the skin of his neck tore and dust poured out. The man went limp and the mummy tossed him aside too.

I took off the guitar and went to put it on its stand, then decided against that. I might need a weapon. The rest of the band looked back and forth between the mummy and Morgana, uncertain whether they were supposed to keep playing or not.

Morgana's eyes were fiery slits as she got up and came over to me, climbing on the stage and ignoring the mummy wreaking havoc in her court. Everyone was trying to stop it by piling on now, like they'd piled on me when they put me in the irons, but it just shrugged them off or smashed them off or kicked them off. It was about halfway across the room to us. There was nowhere for me to go. I tried to come up with a plan, but the only thing I could think of was how badly I wanted a drink.

"An explanation," Morgana said to me. "*Now.*"

"I'm not really sure how, but it followed me from England," I said. I decided to leave out the bit about Cassiel telling me to open the door so it could enter. "I think I've got a curse."

"You never thought to tell me that before?" she said.

I shrugged. "You didn't ask."

She put a hand to her head and closed her eyes. I looked at Puck and the other faerie. They were still at the table, laughing and placing wagers on the mummy's odds against the room. Well, at least someone was having a good time.

Morgana seized me by the collar and pulled me to her as the mummy grabbed a chair and started clearing the crowd with it.

"How do we stop it?" she said.

"It's after me," I said. "Let me go and it'll follow."

She gritted her teeth, then shoved me away from her. "Very well, you're free to leave," she said. "I have what I wanted from you anyway."

I didn't know what she meant, but now was not the time for that kind of conversation.

"I'm not going until you tell me who took Mona Lisa," I said.

The mummy was nearly at the stage now, leaving a trail of bodies behind. I'll give the revellers credit – they were doing their best to stop the mummy despite the growing body count. They were laughing hysterically and toasting each other with drinks before throwing themselves at the creature and stabbing it with forks and knives from their tables. But the mummy kept coming, even though it had been dealt a dozen wounds that would have been fatal to anyone else.

I lifted the guitar like an axe as the mummy reached the edge of the stage, shaking off the men and women clinging to it. And then the room fell silent just like that, and everyone was dead and mummified on the floor again. Everyone but Morgana. She stood beside me as alive as ever, her arms folded across her chest as she glared at me.

I looked around for the mummy but it was nowhere to be seen. I spun in a circle with the guitar raised to check behind me. There was no sign of it except for the open door through which it had come. I could see the parking lot outside, full of old cars, the windshields dark with dust.

"Where is it?" I asked.

"It's still in the glamour," Morgana said. I took that to be the faerie name for wherever it was that everyone in the pub was alive and drinking and fighting mummies and such instead of lying dead on the floor.

"Why isn't it here like the rest of us?" I asked, looking around the room. The mummy wasn't anywhere to be seen among all the other bodies.

Morgana shrugged. "I guess it's not like the rest of us. We've never had anything already dead come into our midst." She shook her head. "What's the mortal saying? Live and learn?"

I put the guitar down in its stand, which was covered in cobwebs. I saw the amplifier was on, so I reached over and turned it off.

"Given what I've seen of it so far, I'm pretty sure it'll find its way out," I said.

"Yes," she said. "So you'll have to go."

"Yes," I said and waited.

She sighed. "If you want to know who took Mona Lisa, ask your angel friend. After all, it was an angel that took her."

"What do you mean?" I asked.

"An angel stole her from the mortal queen," Morgana said. "But I don't know which one or what it's done with her since, so don't bother asking."

Well.

I bowed to her. "I thank you, my queen," I said. "Both for the information and the hospitality." It took some effort to force the words out, but I was trying to turn the other cheek and all that. Plus, I had to admit I had been less than gentlemanly to her over the centuries. We'd got off on the wrong foot with that whole Arthur thing. So call it even. "And now, for the safety of your realm, I'll be on my way."

She slapped me across the face and smiled. "Do come back and visit sometime," she said. "Without your friend."

I smiled back at her. "No offence, but I think I'll pass." Not that I held out much hope for avoiding her. It was a small world, and our paths would likely cross again.

Before I could leave, she bit down on one of her fingers. When she drew the finger out of her mouth it was bloody. She spat a black ring into her palm and pressed it into my hand. It was like the rings the fey wore. Now that I held it, I saw it was bone.

"When you need to return to me, just put this on," she said. "And trust me, you will need to return to me." She smiled that smile of hers again.

"Is it some sort of binding trick?" I asked.

"It helps keep the fey in the glamour," she said. "And it will help you find your way back to the glamour. To me."

"Why would I want to return to you?" I asked.

"You'll want to see your child, I imagine," she said.

And then she was gone, just the scent of her left in the air. I closed my eyes and sighed.

Well. This was an interesting turn of events. I suppose that's what Morgana had meant when she'd said she had what she wanted from me.

Faerie. They were as bad as angels sometimes.

I opened my eyes again. Time to get on with it. I put the ring in my pocket and went out to the parking lot. I doubled over the instant I stepped outside. The hunger was back as soon as I left the pub, along with something else. A longing worse than any I'd ever felt before. It tried to drag me back inside. Maybe Morgana owned my soul now after all.

Things just kept getting better and better.

I straightened up and forced the feeling down deep inside, like usual. The therapists probably wouldn't approve.

I looked around for Cassiel but of course he wasn't there.

"You want to tell me about this other angel?" I yelled into the wind. But there was no answer.

Goddamned angels.

I brushed the dust off my rented car and hit the road again.

AN ANGEL'S TRAP

I'm sorry.

I was telling you about Penelope.

You'll understand if sometimes I need to take a break from that.

And if you don't, well, you didn't know her like I did.

I stayed with Penelope for a few days after resurrecting, recovering my strength and stretching out the kinks of death. I tried to think about my next move, but I didn't have one I could see now that Gabriel had likely disappeared again. So I just followed Penelope around the woods as she looked for things to photograph.

The more I was around her, the more that feeling of familiarity grew. Normally I was agitated after resurrecting, and hungry. But there was something about Penelope's presence that calmed me. Maybe it was a gift she had. Or, to be more accurate, another gift. Because I discovered she really could see things that other people couldn't. She wasn't a fraud, like I'd suspected at first.

We climbed a hill so she could take a photograph of some moss-covered rocks in a jumble at the top. Each of the rocks was larger than me.

I couldn't see anything special about them and said as much.

"That's because you think they're rocks," she said.

I looked at them again. "Aren't they?" I asked.

She studied them and then set up her camera. "I don't think so," she said. "I think they're bones."

Now I saw what she saw. But I hadn't until she'd pointed it out.

"Can you step clear of the shot?" she said.

I stood to the side and let her work. "What do you think they're bones from?" I asked.

She shook her head and moved the camera to the side for a different angle on the bones. "I don't know," she said. "But maybe someone in one of the spiritualist associations will."

I doubted that, but it was probably better if they didn't know. Some things are better left forgotten and hidden away under moss.

Another day, we set out on a hike with no destination. When I asked Penelope where we were going, she just shrugged. "Let's see where the day leads us," she said.

The day led us to a waterfall. She set up the camera and took photographs of the black rocks behind the water while I gazed into the depths of the pool. The water was as dark as the rocks, but even without using any grace to sharpen my vision I could make out the claw marks all along the bottom of the pool. Massive gouges in the stones. I didn't point them out to her. She shook her head at the falls.

"Maybe there was something here once," she said. "But I don't think it's here anymore."

Maybe she was right. And maybe whatever had been here was on its way back. I didn't want to stick around to find out so I breathed a sigh of relief when she packed up her camera and pushed her way back through the underbrush rather than set up a picnic lunch.

At night she told me about all the things she'd seen in her travels. The footprints of dwarves in an abandoned mine in Oregon, where torches lit on their own at night.

A white horse that came out of a foggy field in Michigan and spoke in a foreign tongue to her before galloping off. She thought the language may have been Gaelic but she wasn't sure.

A mermaid's body washed up on rocks on an inaccessible part of the New York coast. When she came back with her camera, the tide had carried it away again.

There was no way she had stumbled across all of these things accidentally. One strange encounter in a lifetime, maybe. Two, unlikely. Three, impossible. Which meant that if she was telling the truth she had a sense for the supernatural like I had a sense for the angels. And with each day that passed I was less inclined to doubt her.

Given that, it probably wasn't happenstance that she had stumbled upon me in the graveyard just as I was resurrecting. This suspicion was confirmed when she added a new photograph to the wall one night. Me erupting from the ground with a mouthful of dirt, knocking over the simple wooden cross that someone had stuck in my grave.

"I thought you were photographing a sasquatch when we met," I said, but she only shrugged.

"This is what the camera saw," she said.

I could have used that moment to tell her about myself, but I didn't. I liked her, and, as I mentioned earlier, people don't tend to stick around when they learn about my true nature. I didn't want to drive her away.

She continued to share the last of her supplies with me at night – the cans of beans and some hard chocolate bars. One night she even brought out a bottle of wine. We took turns drinking straight from the bottle, because there weren't any glasses in the shack.

When the bottle was nearly done, I asked her if she'd ever photographed any angels. She shook her head. "I'm not even sure any are still alive," she said, looking out the window.

"How do you know they existed at all?" I asked her.

"I'm here, aren't I?" she said.

Okay. *Interesting.*

"What exactly do you mean by that?" I asked, but she smiled and waved a finger at me.

"I should be the one asking you the questions," she said. "Not the other way around."

Fair enough, but that was a route I didn't want to go down, so I opted to change the subject instead.

"What are you going to do when your supplies run out?" I asked.

"Go get more supplies," she said. "And find a new place to explore. Who knows what I'll find there?"

It felt like one of those moments where I could have leaned in for a kiss, but I didn't. Maybe I should have. Maybe things would have turned out differently. Maybe they would have turned out the same. But they turned out the way they turned out.

A couple of days later it was time to hike back to civilization, and I decided to show Gabriel's cave to Penelope. I don't know why. Maybe because I felt so comfortable with her. Maybe because I felt I owed her something for caring for me after my resurrection. Maybe I just wanted to show off to her. Maybe maybe maybe.

We woke up and I told her to get dressed in whatever she had that was closest to climbing gear.

"Where are we going?" she asked.

"If I told you, it wouldn't be a surprise," I said.

"I don't want to find myself in a grave like you did," she said. "Not yet, anyway."

"Nothing's going to hurt you when I'm around," I said, which was less a promise and more a simple statement of fact.

"I've heard that before," she said, but went behind the curtain to change anyway.

I took her to the mountain where I'd fought Gabriel. It would have been an impossible climb for her in the winter, but it was summer now, and most of the snow was melted, so it was just almost impossible. I pointed out the area where the cave was hidden to her before we started, high up the slope. She looked at the mountain for a long time.

"What's up there?" she finally asked.

"These days, I don't know," I admitted. "But I imagine it'll be something you want to photograph."

She studied me for a moment. "This is where whatever happened to you happened to you, isn't it?" she said.

"We should get moving before the day gets too hot," I told her.

And so we went up the steep slope. She let me carry the camera for the first time. Fair enough. We only talked once on the way, when we paused on a ledge to drink from her canteen.

"What will you do if you ever find an angel?" I asked.

"I'm not looking for any angel," she said and squinted upward. "I'm looking for a very specific angel."

"Which angel?" I asked.

"We should get moving before the day gets too hot," she said. She was an intriguing woman, Penelope.

And so onwards and upwards we went, until we reached the entrance of the cave. We hung to the side of the mountain a few feet under the opening, catching our breath. When I looked down at the thousand or so feet to the ground, I had a feeling of déjà vu. Penelope's face was white, as were her hands holding onto the roots of some scrub tree that had once grown up here, but she was still with me.

I didn't sense Gabriel inside the cave, so I wasn't worried. Someday I'd learn to not be so overconfident. Someday.

I heaved myself up into the cave and then reached down for Penelope and pulled her in before some stray wind carried her off the side of the mountain. Only when she was safely inside did we examine our surroundings.

It was more or less like I remembered it. The drawings in blood were still on the walls, and the cross made of bones was still in the back corner of the cave. The ice sculpture of the true face of Christ had melted, but my climbing axe lay on the floor of the cave where the sculpture had been.

Penelope stood in the cave entrance, staring. She didn't even move for her camera, which I leaned against one of the walls.

"What is this place?" she asked.

I considered telling her the truth, that it was an angel's lair. Or had once been an angel's lair anyway. But then she'd want to know how I knew, and what I knew, and that would just lead to too many other awkward questions. So I just skipped that whole subject.

"I came across it climbing," I said.

"Is this where you fell?" she asked.

"Close enough," I said.

"It's a long way from here to the graveyard where we met," she said.

I reached down to pick up my climbing axe and buy some time while I considered how to answer that. As it turned out, there was no time to answer.

As soon as I picked up the axe, the bones of the cross all fell to the cave floor. For a second I thought maybe I had brushed against them and knocked them to the ground. Then they moved around on the floor, reassembling themselves into another shape. A giant man. Or, to be more accurate, a giant skeleton.

"Cross," Penelope said from behind me, in a remarkably calm voice, all things considered. "What exactly is happening here?"

A trap, I wanted to tell her. I didn't know if it was triggered by me specifically picking up the axe, or if it would have happened had anyone picked up the axe. But it didn't matter now. The trap had been set, and I had sprung it. Like so many other traps I'd walked into in the past. Now the only thing to think about was how to survive it.

The skeleton stood up, and it towered over us. It wasn't a human skeleton, but it was humanoid. It had a large skull and fangs, and long, bony talons. I had no idea what sort of creature it had once been.

"Is it a yeti?" Penelope asked.

Well, yes, that made sense. It could have been a yeti. Originally. Hell, maybe it had even been a sasquatch. But all that mattered was what it was now. Which, I was pretty sure, was a golem. Animated no doubt by Gabriel to slow my pursuit.

It slashed out at me with those long talons, and I parried with the climbing axe like I was parrying a sword blow.

"I think we need to climb back down," I told Penelope. *"Now."*

Instead, she went for her camera as the golem snapped at my head with its fangs. I batted it away with the axe, which didn't seem to do much more than inconvenience it.

"This is not the time for photographs!" I yelled at Penelope.

"I can't think of a better time for photographs!" she yelled back.

The golem didn't say anything, just tried a one-two gouge-and-disembowel trick with its claws that kept me busy defending myself with the axe. I guess it was a small measure of mercy that Gabriel had left the axe so I at least had something to defend myself with. He always was a little too committed to honour and other forgotten ideals.

The problem with golems is there's no real way to kill them. They're pretty much indestructible until their power source runs out. But that could work to my advantage, because in this case I had a hunch what the golem's power source was. It had been crafted by an angel, after all.

So I threw myself at it and buried the axe in its skull as hard as I could and released the grace trapped inside it. And as it spilled out I took it in.

And sprung the second trap.

The cave walls shook and then started to come apart. Rocks flew everywhere, bombarding me. I knew instantly what Gabriel had done. He hadn't only breathed grace into the golem. He'd also breathed it into the walls of the cave itself. When I drew the grace from the golem, I also drew the grace out of the walls. And the cave collapsed upon us.

There was no time to shout at Penelope to run. There was no time for her to run anyway. There was no time for anything.

Except.

I used Gabriel's grace from the golem to give myself the speed and power of an angel. I lunged over to Penelope's side as the walls and ceiling of the cave came down and I pulled her into my arms. Then I threw us out the entrance as the mountain reclaimed the cave, burying the golem, and we fell into the sky.

Penelope screamed, but only for a few seconds. Because then I used the last of the grace I'd taken from the golem to sprout wings like an angel's. I hated to do it, but Gabriel was in my mind, so it came naturally. We glided down toward the forest below.

Penelope wrapped her arms around me and stared at me. "You're an angel," she said.

"Not even close," I said.

"What are you then?" she asked.

I shook my head. "I don't know," I said.

And then the last of Gabriel's grace burned away too soon, and my wings melted away, and we were falling once more. I turned us in midair so I would take the brunt of the impact, and then we were crashing through the trees, and I figured that was it for that life.

There was darkness for a time. And then there was light.

And I came to in the cabin in the woods. After I was done the usual thrashing about and such, I looked around and saw Penelope sitting on a stool beside the bed. She had a bandage wrapped around her forehead and there was another bandage on her arm. I could feel more bandages on all my limbs. She leaned forward and put her canteen to my lips.

"I imagine you need this more than I do," she said.

I scratched at the beard on my face and estimated there was about a week's growth there. I took the water and drank, then handed it back to her. She didn't say anything else. Right. I was going to have to provide an explanation.

"I guess it was our turn to be favoured by fortune," I said.

"It took more than fortune to save us from that fall," she said. She looked at my shoulders, where my wings had been. "You were on the verge of death. Your injuries should have been too grave to . . ." She peeled back some of the bandages wrapped around my chest. The skin underneath was pink with fresh scars.

"It's a long story," I sighed.

She got up, and I thought maybe she was going to leave now that I was alive and well again. Just like all the others that had left me over the years. Instead, she went to the cupboard and opened it. There was a last can of beans and a single bottle of wine left. She opened both and brought them to me.

"I ran out of everything yesterday," she said. "I was going to have to leave you here when I went back for supplies. I was wondering whether I should bury you again or not."

I gobbled down the beans and drank half the bottle of wine in one gulp. I thought about the fact she would have come back for me. Then I sat up and stretched. I was still in the same clothes I'd been wearing when I died and I could feel the air on my back from the rips where the wings had burst through my shirt.

"Sorry about your camera," I said. "I'll get you a new one."

"Why don't you tell me who you are and we'll call it even," she said.

I got up and wandered around the cabin, working out the kinks. I looked outside. It was a sunny afternoon. The birds were talking to each other and the spiders were eating things in their webs and the clouds continued to move overhead, uncaring.

"I'm not really sure," I said. "It's complicated."

Penelope didn't say anything else, just waited.

So I told her. I told her who I was, or maybe more accurately, what I was. I gave her the brief notes rather than the whole history, but I did tell her about Gabriel and what had happened in that cave. And then, when I was done, I waited for her to run away or call me mad or do any of the usual things any other mortal had done when I'd revealed the truth about myself.

She didn't do any of the usual things. Instead, she took the wine from my hand and drank some herself. She studied me some more. And then she nodded.

"All right, that explains a lot," she said.

I didn't really know what to say to that, but I had a feeling an apology of some sort was in order. "Sorry about almost getting you killed," I managed. "I really did want to show you that angel's lair."

"We should join forces," she said.

I shook my head. "I'm sure your spiritualist friends are all very interesting, curious people," I said, "but I don't want to get involved with them."

"I meant you and me," she said.

"What would we do together?" I asked.

"The same thing we do on our own," she said. "Hunt angels."

Really, how could I not fall for her?

WHEN ALL ELSE FAILS, GO TO AMERICA

I drove back to Dublin, thinking things over as I went.

This particular trip hadn't exactly cleared things up for me. It may have even cost me my soul. I wasn't sure on how such matters worked. And let's not even talk about the child business for now.

The faerie had traded Leonardo da Vinci dreams for Mona Lisa, dreams I was willing to bet made their way into his sketchbooks and inventions. But there was no way of finding out why he'd had a gorgon in the first place. He'd disappeared a long time ago and no one was really sure if he was dead or not. I'd believe it when I saw the body. But maybe not even then.

I could have searched the dead for him, if I had more grace. But I didn't, so I couldn't. Besides, there was no guarantee he'd be able to help me any more than Morgana had, which wasn't much.

So, who could help me now?

Cassiel was obviously no use. If he knew where Mona Lisa was, he wouldn't need me. And he was apparently playing his own game in this matter anyway. He had as many secrets as I did.

I was pretty certain Victory had told me all she knew. I couldn't see any reason for her to hold anything back if I was trying to save her sister.

Morgana seemed to think herself done with Mona Lisa once she'd given her to the queen.

Which left the one outstanding mystery of this whole situation so far:

the art dealer on the train. Or, more likely, Judas masquerading as the art dealer. What was it he'd said?

I'd take the Mona Lisa *to America.*

Sure, it was probably a trap. But it wasn't like I had any other ideas.

I checked into a hotel in New York with a fresh batch of stolen ID and credit cards. Sometimes I think I single-handedly keep the anti-fraud departments at most banks in business. I showered and shaved and then slept for twelve hours. It was evening when I got up. I went out into the streets and browsed the night markets and the twenty-four-hour stores. I went back to my room with new clothes and remade myself once more. Then I settled in at the hotel bar until closing, tipping the bartender well with my stolen credit card to keep the drinks coming. Well, here I was in America. Now what?

Private collectors, the art dealer on the train had said, back when I still thought he was an art dealer. If he were trying to sell the original *Mona Lisa*, he would try to sell it in a secret auction for private collectors. Maybe it was a clue, maybe it was a trick, but it seemed as good a place to start as any.

So, all I needed to do was track down some rich people who collected ancient mythological creatures who weren't so mythological after all. How hard could it be?

"You have any idea where I can find people who collect gorgons and magic skulls and that sort of thing?" I asked the bartender.

He shook his head without acknowledging there was anything odd about the question. A veteran bartender. Well, you never know unless you ask.

I ordered another drink to fortify myself. Tomorrow was going to be a very long day.

After a time, the bartender told me he had to close the place and wished me luck in my search. I went to the lobby and used one of the hotel's computers to research art dealers in the city. I made up a list and printed it off as the sky outside turned grey. I ate breakfast at the hotel café and was glad to see Americans still did bacon and eggs better than anyone else. I had a couple of coffees to offset the hangover that was starting to set in, and then I went out onto the streets of New York. I bought a phone and loaded it up with a prepaid card, then found a print shop and had some business cards made with my new phone's number on it. Then I started making my rounds.

Fortunately, art galleries, like car dealerships and restaurants, tend to be found in clusters. I was able to hit two or three on the same block and then take a cab to the next group. Repeat. My approach in each was more or less the same. Walk in and wander around, trying to figure out what the hell the paintings or sculptures were, until someone came over to see if I had money or not. The conversations tended to go something like this:

Me, looking at a pile of empty candy wrappers on the floor: "What exactly is that supposed to be?"

Dealer in a suit worth more than most people in the world make in a year: "It's a statement about the exhaustion of consumer culture."

Me, shaking my head and sighing: "What's the point of this after Duchamp?"

Dealer, looking me up and down – evaluating me: "What exactly are you in the market for?"

Me, handing him my card: "Something like the *Mona Lisa*. Only more real."

I figured there was no sense talking in code. The dealers who didn't know what I meant would just think I was old-fashioned or an eccentric, or both. The dealers who did know what I meant – well, those were the ones I was trying to find.

Me in another gallery, watching a machine that consumed rotting vegetables on a conveyer belt at one end and extruded their waste at the other: "Is this actually art?"

Dealer in some sort of leather suit: "It's a statement about art. And humanity. And spirituality."

Me, handing him my card and thinking I really needed to get into the business of taking rich people's money from them: "I'm in the market for some real art. Specifically, the *Mona Lisa*."

Dealer, studying me much like the last dealer did: "The *Mona Lisa* is in Paris."

Me: "Is it?"

Even if these dealers weren't the ones I was looking for, maybe they'd spread the word about the odd customer they'd had, and the right one would find me.

I hadn't paid for voicemail on the phone, and I kept it turned off all day so no one could reach me. I wanted to build a sense of mystery. It was kind of like dating.

I didn't turn the phone on until the end of the second day, after I'd hit the last of the galleries on my list. That one featured a human corpse in a refrigerated display case, opened up to reveal its emptied-out insides. All the organs had been removed.

"Let me guess," I told the dealer. "A comment on the hollowness of our consumer culture."

"Ah, you're a collector," he said.

I just shook my head and handed him my card. "Call me if you get anything like the *Mona Lisa*," I said.

I left the gallery and turned the phone on and it rang almost immediately. I wondered how long the caller had been trying. I walked down the street until I found a doorway leading up to some lofts. I stepped into its shelter and answered the phone without saying anything.

"I think I may be able to help you find what you're looking for," a man's voice said.

"You're a little late," I said. "I've already found her."

There was a pause, and then the man said, "I don't think that's possible. Not if you're looking for what I think you're looking for."

"You're right," I said. "Sorry, that was a bit of a test. I wanted to make sure you were genuine."

"I wouldn't exactly call myself that," the man said, "but fair enough. Now then, the question is if I help you, what will you do for me?"

"It doesn't sound like we're talking about money," I said.

"I don't need money," the man said. "What I need is a service performed."

"What kind of service?" I asked.

"An exorcism," he said.

OF EXORCISMS AND OTHER BUSINESS VENTURES

As it turned out, I had some experience with exorcisms. Back in the sixteenth or seventeenth century – I can't really remember which now – I worked for a while as a travelling exorcist. I rode around Germany on a dark stallion, wearing all black, and got rid of people's supernatural woes for them. It didn't pay all that well – my clients were usually peasants and what passed for middle class back then – but well enough to keep me supplied in sustenance and spirits, although not necessarily in that order.

There was an epidemic of demonic possessions in Germany back then. There was also a plague of the dead rising from their graves, so I doubled as a zombie killer. Coincidentally, both problems tended to start when I entered an area.

It usually went something like this:

I'd ride into the village on my horse, which for the first visit wasn't a black stallion but a dull brown mare. I wore simple clothes and a simple look. I'd have lunch or dinner in the village tavern. During my meal I'd study my fellow diners and try to figure out from the way the others treated them which ones had money. I'd listen to the conversations until I'd learned the names of everyone in the inn. Then I'd pay my bill and go on my way, just another weary traveller passing through. On my way out the door I'd wet my fingers in a little flask of holy water I'd obtained – real holy water, not the knockoff stuff you get in churches – and flick a few drops onto my future customers' hair or feet or wherever it was they were least likely to notice.

That night, I'd circle back and ride through the village again, when everyone was asleep. I'd look for the light of the holy water, because I can see the grace glowing in it. I'd stop at whatever shack or house where I found it and slip inside. I'd pick my target: the wife sleeping in bed with the man I'd marked earlier, a son or daughter in another room, sometimes elderly people who'd fallen asleep with bibles in their laps. Then I'd summon a random dead soul into their bodies and slip back out before the screaming started.

A possession is a simple thing: it's two souls fighting for control of one body. Sometimes it's genuinely demonic, but it doesn't have to be. Throw an extra human soul into the body and the same thing will happen. Especially if the new soul is someone who's been dead for a while and doesn't know what's just happened. The trick works even better if you use a soul who doesn't speak the local language. Then, in those moments when they do manage to gain control of the body, everything they say is going to sound like gibberish. Or a demonic tongue.

Once my summoning work was done, I'd ride out of the village again and spend the next couple days lounging about some lakeside or forest camp. Then I'd change into my black clothes, use a sleight to make my brown mare look like a black stallion and ride back into the village. Usually by this time the local priest would have failed in his attempts to exorcise the demon/confused soul – you need real grace to perform such an act, after all – and the villagers would be getting ready to burn the entire family. That's when I'd make my mysterious appearance, along with a stock line about being drawn there by the stench of evil. I'd offer to banish the offending demon and save the village from an imminent invasion of hell-spawn – for a price, of course.

And if I couldn't find a wealthy enough mark in my first visit, I'd just come back at night and raise the entire graveyard, so the village was overrun with the walking dead. Then everyone would pay me what they could after I knocked the souls back out of the zombies with a palm to the forehead and an amen, and I'd ride out of there with a heavy purse.

I know what you're thinking, but it beats working for a living.

Besides, every now and then I would stumble across a real demon and get rid of it. So there's probably some karma balance there somewhere, right?

No, I don't think so either.

WHAT WE TALK ABOUT WHEN WE TALK ABOUT DEMONS

I followed the caller's directions to a small gallery on a quiet street I won't name to protect the innocent, if there are any. The rest of the street was low-rise apartments, a coffee shop and a dry cleaning place. There weren't any other galleries in sight, and I hadn't visited this place in my rounds. So much for me being the mysterious one.

The gallery had no name and no hours or any other information listed on the door. In fact, the door was locked when I arrived and I had to knock. While I waited for someone to answer, I studied the gallery through the glass windows. Paintings hung on the walls instead of conceptual art. Landscapes and portraits of people who weren't celebrities. Very old-fashioned.

So was the man who suddenly appeared at the door to unlock it. I hadn't even seen him walk up. He wore a suit and tie and looked like he wouldn't have been out of place in a bank. He opened the door and studied me for a moment.

"So you're the one," he said, before finally stepping aside to let me in.

He took me to the rear of the gallery, where the landscapes gave way to colour abstracts of the classic kind: some Rothko knockoffs, a piece that could have been a genuine Borduas if I didn't know better, a couple of homages to Pollock.

There was also an espresso maker, which I mistook for a sculpture until the man made me an espresso with it. I liked this place more with each moment that passed. He handed me the cup and sat down behind a nearby desk with a dead plant on it. It was only then that he spoke again.

"My name is White," he said. "Before we continue, I have a question."

"I have one of my own," I said. "How did you find me? I never visited this gallery."

"A good dealer is always checking in with his contacts," he said without changing expression. "You hear about the latest artists. You hear about what people are looking for."

"And are other people looking for the same thing as me?" I asked.

"No," White said, smiling a little. "That's what caught my attention. A group of people looking for the same thing usually means people just following a trend. One person means someone with a true interest. A genuine collector."

"I'm not a collector," I said.

White shrugged. "And I don't have what you're looking for," he said. "But I can help you find the person who does."

"You said you had a question," I said.

White nodded. "I'm not your average dealer," he said. "And I have contacts most people don't have. I've heard things. A man looking for the Mona Lisa no one knows about. A man who isn't what he seems to be, or even what he once was. A man who should be dead. And let's not even talk about the angels for now."

We studied each other for a moment. I wasn't entirely convinced he was human. Then again, I wasn't entirely convinced he wasn't human either. My daily dilemma. I decided to get straight to it.

"What do you want?" I asked.

"I want to find out if you're who I think you are," White said. He pushed the dead plant on his desk toward me, then leaned back in his chair.

I looked at the plant, then back at him. He didn't say anything.

I shrugged. I didn't normally like to show off what I could do in public, but it seemed a moot point in this case. I reached out and brushed my fingers against the plant's dead leaves, just long enough to let some grace flow into them. The plant's leaves unfurled and it turned green again. Then it was my turn to wait.

White pulled the plant to him and stared at it for a moment. Then he touched it, feeling the leaves with his fingers. He finally looked back at me.

"So, who needs the exorcism?" I asked.

"I do," White said.

I finished the espresso and pushed the cup back to him. "I'll have another," I said. "This time with whisky. Actually, make it light on the espresso." I had a feeling I was going to have to fortify myself for this one.

I wasn't surprised to see White had a small bar hidden away in a cupboard over the espresso machine. Anyone who works in the arts has a hidden bar somewhere.

I waited until he finished pouring the drink, and then I swallowed it in a couple of gulps and relished the burn.

"So, when you say you're the one who needs an exorcism . . ." I said.

"I'm not really me," he said. "I'm a ghost or something." He waved his hand through my chest – and I mean *through* it – and I felt a chill inside me.

"Stop that," I said, and he withdrew his hand. I was surprised to discover he was a ghost, but I wasn't surprised he was able to take on physical form and make espresso and such. It's just a matter of expending some energy, much like the way I use grace. Use too much and you'll become incorporeal and drift away until you've recharged enough to take on physical form. Most ghosts are actually a little like me.

"A demon took over my body," he went on. "It forced me out. And then it bound me here and left."

I wasn't surprised to hear that either. Most ghosts are souls who for one reason or another have lost the connection to their body. Demonic possession is one of the main causes, but there are others – most of them worse.

I got up and grabbed the bottle of whisky to refill my glass. "Tell me about the demon," I said.

"It was in a painting I acquired a few years ago," he said. He took me through a door at the back of the gallery, into a small room the size of a storage closet. It may have actually been a storage closet at one point. But now it held a painting on an easel in the centre of the room. A pentagram was drawn in chalk on the floor around the painting, and there were faded outlines of other ritual shapes, as well as some books in a pile in one corner. I didn't need to look at them to know they were books on demonology and summoning and that sort of thing. Nonsense for the most part. You couldn't write that stuff down – too much of the process involves things going on in the moment. Demons are very moody creatures, so you have to tease them into coming to you. It's a little like fishing actually – more art than science.

But I didn't bother telling White that because I was studying the painting. It was unremarkable – a Rembrandt knockoff of Christ driving a demon from a man lying in a bed in a dark room. I didn't recognize the demon – it was black and scaly and all claws and fangs, and they seldom look like that. Usually, they're a little more Lovecraftian in appearance.

The Christ didn't look anything like me either, but they seldom do. Artistic licence, I suppose.

The key thing to note about the painting was where the demon was going as it left the body. It was headed for a painting on the wall within the painting, its canvas hidden by a curtain. Cute.

"Who's the artist?" I asked.

"I don't know," White said. "I was unable to find a signature anywhere on the painting, although there was a burned area where one might have been." He pointed to a scorched area at the base of the bed that I had initially taken to be a shadow.

"I tried to restore it," White said. "The demon was bound within the painting and something I did released it."

This wasn't the first time I'd heard of a demon in a painting. Many artworks have souls, and some have demons. Some even have both.

"It went down my throat," White said, not looking away from the painting. "It forced me out. And then it told me I couldn't leave here until I was dead. But I'm already dead. Look at me." He waved his hand through the painting.

"It meant your body," I told him. "It bound you here to keep you from interfering with it while it uses your physical form." I didn't add that it had probably done him a favour by binding him to the gallery. Ghosts running around loose usually bring problems down on themselves. And attract things far worse than ghosts.

"I couldn't do anything but watch it walk out the door," White said. "Watch *me* walk out the door."

"Where did you get the painting?" I asked.

"A regular of mine found it in an abandoned villa on some land he bought in Tuscany," White said. "He shipped it to his home here, but he couldn't sleep once he hung it. He said it made noises."

"What kind of noises?" I asked.

"Muttering, groaning, sighing. Like there was someone in the place with him."

"What's his name?" I asked.

White looked at me and smiled a little. "I may be a ghost," he said, "but I'm still professional enough that I respect the privacy of my clients."

I nodded. Fair enough. "I don't imagine you know where this demon went with your body?" I asked.

White shrugged. "I had an apartment. It may have gone there. But it's been a couple of years now."

I sighed. "Just so we're clear," I said. "You want me to track it down, exorcise it and put you back in your body."

White nodded. "That's my price for the information you want."

I took a long drink of the whisky. If he were human, I would have just beat the information out of him. But ghosts were trickier to work with. It might actually be easier to find the demon.

"All right, give me your address," I finally said. I waved my glass at the pentagram and books. "And stop trying to call the demon back on your own. You may end up summoning something worse."

And then I went out in search of White's life.

The address White gave me for his old place was a brownstone a dozen blocks away. I bought a couple of things at a store on the corner and then made my way over there. It was an apartment building. I picked the lock to the front door in under thirty seconds using a pen and a trick a man in an English prison had taught me a few years back. It's really true what they say about jails being training grounds for criminals.

Inside, I went up to the top floor and then did the same thing to the lock on the door at the end of the hallway – White's apartment. Only it wasn't White's apartment anymore. It was a woman's apartment now, judging by the photos of her with friends on all the walls. I checked all the rooms but there was no one home. Definitely no demon wandering about in White's body.

145

But he'd been there in the past. I did a reading, much like psychics do – the real ones, at least. I saw traces of him flicker in and out of existence around the apartment, spectral, like the ghosts that used to be in the old black-and-white shows on television. Only these were memories instead of ghosts. Everything has memories, even apartments. You just have to know how and where to look for them. One night when I was in Madrid, everyone had the same dream of walking down an alley and finding a secret door that led to . . . well, you really had to be there in the dream. Let's just say it wasn't our dream, it was the city's.

But White, or rather the demon, hadn't stayed in this apartment long. I watched him move around the place in the past, looking at the furniture that had been here then, which was all art deco stuff. He studied the paintings on the walls, which were more knockoffs that didn't match the furniture at all – Renoir and Degas, that kind of style. Not to my tastes and I didn't imagine they were to the demon's either. Maybe he was looking for someone he knew in them.

He faded away and then it was just the present furniture again. The woman's apartment, not White's. I switched rooms and found the demon once more, in the bedroom. He was putting on a shirt and tie. A metal name tag that said Carver. Interesting. It looked like the demon – Carver now – had a job. When demons possessed someone they usually abandoned their hosts' jobs and went on sex and murder sprees. They didn't go looking for employment. I wondered what it was up to.

I lost the demon again and found him by the door. The rooms were all empty of furniture now. Carver took one last look around and then left the apartment. I went to the window and looked out into the street. I saw a moving van outside. It pulled away and Carver got into a car – a sensible, practical sedan.

Mystery upon mysteries.

I took a last look around the apartment like Carver had, but there was nothing left of him. There was just the woman's photos, and likely her memories if I cared to look at them, which I didn't.

I went out the door and back down to the street. I did a fresh reading and watched Carver drive away in his sedan, fading away at the intersection.

I needed a vehicle.

I touched the door of a nearby minivan and used a little grace to pop the lock, then got behind the wheel and used a little more to start the engine. I'd learned how to hot-wire cars in jail too, but the corner store didn't sell those tools. And I never was very quick at it.

I drove to the intersection and stopped, looking for signs of Carver. A flash of the sedan speeding away, disappearing into the traffic of the here and now. I followed, but I couldn't find another sign of him, so I kept driving – turning down streets at random, crossing bridges, cruising parking lots for hours – until the minivan ran low on gas. I pulled into a station and filled up and paid for it honestly. A gift to the vehicle's owner.

I caught another glimpse of Carver on a street of fast-food restaurants, driving the sedan in the opposite direction. I pulled a U-turn in the street, waving at the other drivers who hit their horns, and followed, directly behind him. He flickered in and out ahead of me, his hair growing longer and then shorter, his shirt changing colours. I was watching his life change over what looked like years. At one point he wore glasses but then they disappeared. Eye surgery, I guess. The sedan became a BMW sedan. It looked like he'd picked a good job.

The more we drove, the more frequent and solid the sightings became. Which meant this was a regular route for Carver. It occurred to me I might see him for real, so I did what stretches I could while sitting behind a steering wheel and tried to get in the right frame of mind for an exorcism. Whatever that might be.

The sightings stopped at a bank tower in a business district of other towers and cafés. Everything was closed because the office day was over and the sky was fading to amber. I didn't realize what Carver's destination was until I no longer saw him ahead of me. Then I doubled back and went up and down the street until I saw the parking lot by the bank tower, the memory of Carver's BMW in the lot. I pulled over and parked on the side of the street and looked around until I saw the spectral Carver walk through the front doors of the bank building with a shoulder bag and disappear in the lobby inside.

So, this was where Carver worked.

I checked the clock in the minivan's dash: 7:10 p.m. Carver – the real Carver, not the memory one – was probably home now, wherever he lived.

I just had to use the same tricks to retrace his route to find that home. To find the demon.

I pulled back onto the street and kept driving.

I found Carver – the real, present-day Carver – in a commuter neighbourhood outside the city, a subdivision of houses and trees that looked just like the advertisements you see in magazines. Carver lived in a house that looked the same as the other houses on the street, the only real differences being the colours they were painted. There was a tricycle in the driveway, behind the BMW, and a white cat in the window that watched me park on the street. I got out and stretched some more, and then the front door opened and Carver walked out with a bottle of beer in his hand. He was wearing shorts and a T-shirt and sandals. And a wedding band. He looked at me for a second like you'd look at anyone you didn't know walking up your driveway. Then I saw the end of the world pass across his face.

He reached back and closed the door behind him, then took a drink of his beer.

"I figured you'd come for me one day," he said. "I just didn't think it would be in a minivan." I don't know how he recognized me. Maybe we'd met before and I'd forgotten him. Maybe demons had their own secrets. It didn't matter. What mattered was why I was there.

"I move in mysterious ways and all that," I said, walking across the lawn to him. I stopped a few feet away. I didn't want to push things just yet. Not here.

"Yeah, like the tax people." He looked up at the sky, then up and down the street, and frowned. "Not exactly the way I pictured the end," he said.

"It's never the way you imagine it," I said.

We watched a dog run down the street, trailing a leash behind it. There was no one else in sight.

Carver drank some more of his beer and studied me.

"I'm living a quiet life," he said. "I'm not hurting anyone. I have a wife and a daughter – a three-year-old. A good job. People depend on me. I do my part for them. For society."

I shook my head. "This isn't your life," I said.

"It is mine." He spread his arms wide to take in the yard and house. "I made it. It wouldn't exist without me."

"Sure it would," I said. "It'd just be someone else in that body, that's all."

He glanced over his shoulder at the closed door, then took me by the arm and walked me back to my car.

"Is that what this is about?" he said in a low voice. "The body?"

"I'm afraid so," I said.

"I own it fairly," Carver said. "He broke the bonds and freed me." He let go of my arm at the side of the minivan and shrugged. "I'm a demon. What else was I supposed to do?"

"I understand," I said, and I did. "But it doesn't matter. The man you took the body from has something I need. And you have something he needs. I'm sorry, but you know how this has to end."

He looked at me for a moment longer, then looked back at his house. I gave him the time. I'm sometimes stupidly generous that way. I say stupidly because a few seconds later the front door opened and a woman came out with a young girl. I swear I could smell cookies baking somewhere behind them. It was the stuff dreams are made of. It took me a few seconds to notice the phone the woman held in her hand.

"Ray, is everything all right?" she asked.

Carver turned and smiled at her. "Just a friend from work," he said. "I have to go in to the office for a few hours."

She looked at me, then back at him. "You promised," she said.

"I'm sorry," Carver said. "It's a bit of an emergency." He looked back at me. "Isn't it?"

I could see it in his eyes. He knew what was going to happen, and he didn't want it to happen here, in front of his family. Fair enough. I didn't want that either.

"That's right," I said. "It's a real emergency."

The girl took a step forward. "My story, Daddy," she said.

"Don't worry," Carver said. "I'll be back in time to tuck you in."

Now it was my turn to look up and down the street. Anywhere but at them. I tried to tell myself I was doing this for the better good, but I wasn't even sure about that.

We got in the minivan, Carver still holding his beer, and I took us away from there as fast as I could. Neither one of us looked back. I'm not sure if it was easier for me or for him.

"Ray Carver?" I said. "Seriously?"

He shrugged. "I like his stories. They looked like the sort of world I'd be comfortable in."

I shook my head. "Why couldn't you just be a serial killer or a pope or something?" I said. "That would make things a lot easier."

"I've done all that," Carver said. "I wanted to see what the mundane life was like. I wanted the things your kind always want: The job. The big house. The family."

"Those things are never what you think they are," I said. I didn't tell him he could have run and hid if he hadn't tied himself to those things. If he'd stayed on the move, I probably would have lost his trail eventually.

"It was worth it," he said, so softly I may have imagined it. What could I say to that? I knew how he felt.

I turned randomly at intersections, taking us down one tree-lined street after another, deeper into the heart of suburbia. I was lost in no time, but it didn't matter. I was just trying to find someplace quiet and private to finish our business.

"Is there any chance we can work out a deal so I can go home and read my daughter a bedtime story?" Carver asked. "Maybe I've got something worth more to you than whatever he has."

I shook my head. "Only if you know where Judas is," I said.

Carver sighed. "So that's what this is about."

"That's what this is about," I agreed.

"Would you believe me if I told you I knew where Judas was?" he asked.

"Maybe when I thought you were a demon who'd possessed an innocent man's body," I said. "But not now that I know you're a banker with a family and a mortgage. You and Judas don't move in the same circles anymore."

He chuckled. "Fair enough." He finished the rest of the beer in one swallow and put the empty bottle in the minivan's cupholder. Then he threw himself at me with all the fury of a hell-spawn.

I should have been on guard for it – he was a demon, after all – but the whole family and suburbs business had lulled me into relaxing. I barely had time to throw up my arm to protect my face when he came at me, punching and snarling. He let his true form show now, his fingernails hardening into claws that raked skin from my arm while his eyes blazed fire – real fire.

There are wards and binding spells and glyphs and such that you can use to keep demons at bay in a pinch. The problem is they're very personal in nature, and you have to know a lot about the demon in question for them to work. I didn't even know Carver's real name, let alone his genealogy, so I had nothing on him. Someone really needs to do a set of demon trading cards someday.

On the plus side, while the exorcism ritual would take some time to put together, he didn't need to be conscious for it.

I let go of the steering wheel and used my left hand to shield my face while I threw a couple of quick jabs at him with my right. It was an awkward angle, but I had a hard jab thanks to some time I spent in a boxing gym with no name in an old warehouse in Louisiana. Carver's head went back so hard he cracked the passenger side window behind him.

But he lunged at me again just as quick and latched onto my hand with his fangs, and I screamed and started hammering him with my left hand to get him off. If his wife and daughter could see him now.

I finally knocked him off my hand, but he took my pinkie with him, choking it down like a gull eating a french fry.

"God*damn* you," I yelled.

"I am going to devour you piece by piece." He laughed. "And then I'm going to let the pieces simmer in my stomach for the next thousand years."

Yes, the demon in him was definitely coming out now.

Then he screamed and clutched at his stomach, and I couldn't help but laugh at him. "Holy blood stings a little more than holy water, doesn't it?" I said, and gave him a few more jabs with my mangled hand to get as much blood as I could on him. It probably hurt me more than him, but it felt good doing it. I don't think anybody had actually eaten one of my fingers before.

He snarled at me and grabbed onto both of my arms. "I *feed* on pain," he said.

Ah, he was that kind of demon.

We both opened our mouths to exchange more witty banter, but then the minivan went off the road and hit something on account of no one driving it. We went through the windshield still holding each other.

We didn't hang on to each for long, though, as he collided with the tree the van had wrapped itself around and I continued on my way, coming to a stop on somebody's front lawn.

I lay there for a moment or two, considering the crows circling overhead in the clear blue sky, and then I felt myself to see if there was anything broken. There was, but nothing I couldn't heal with a bit of grace, and so I went about that and then got to my feet and looked for Carver before he could get away.

As it turned out, there was little chance of that. He was lying on the crumpled hood of the van, his arms and legs bent in ways that I'd seen enough times to realize there was no hope for him. Or maybe I was the only hope. But I'd never know, because just then Carver left White's body and tried to take over mine.

I had time for a glimpse of White's body shuddering as it gave out a death rattle, and then a glimpse of movement in the corner of my eye. I didn't bother trying to look at it. You can never really catch sight of a demon when they're out of a body, unless they've found a way to manifest in their real forms. The less said about that the better.

If they can't manifest, though, they head straight for the nearest living thing. Which in this case was me.

I had a sudden feeling of déjà vu – a sure sign a demon possession was under way. I lashed out with my hand, still mangled and bleeding because I hadn't gotten around to fixing it yet, and caught Carver by the throat. As much as you can catch a wisp of smoke by the throat anyway.

"I don't think so," I told him.

He writhed in my grip and I burned some grace to keep him there while I looked around for someplace to put him.

There. One of the crows had landed in a branch of the tree and was studying White's body like it was a buffet. I threw Carver at the crow – *into* the crow – and it let out a squawk and launched itself into the air. I muttered a few quick words it's wise not to share and sealed the outside of the crow in a layer of grace to keep Carver in it. The crow fell from the air and bounced off the roof of the minivan to the ground. It scrambled to its feet and looked around, then glared at me.

"Better learn to fly," I advised him. "Before the cats in this neighbourhood find you." And I flicked some more blood on him from my ruined finger for good measure.

Carver cawed in what I assumed was an indignant tone, then hopped away, opening his wings and battering them against the ground.

You'd be surprised how many crows are actually demons.

Granted, he'd be a problem again when the crow hit the end of its natural lifespan and freed him with its death, if he didn't get himself killed first. But I can't fix everything that's wrong with the world.

I went over to White's body to see what I could do, but it was too late. The body was dead, which meant White was really a ghost now.

If I had more grace, I could have tried a resurrection, but I didn't have enough of that left after raising the princess and binding Carver into his new home. I had failed.

A crow laughed at me from atop a streetlight. I didn't see Carver anywhere on the ground now, so it could be him up there. But it could be any other crow too. That's just the way crows are.

People were starting to come out of their homes to look at the accident scene, some with phones in their hands. It was time to move on before the difficult questions began. I laid my hand on White's forehead and said a few words that didn't have any power to them, then got the hell out of there.

THERE ARE ALWAYS
ANGELS IN PARIS

Maybe if I'd stayed with Penelope in that cabin in the woods and never left things would have been different. Maybe we'd still be living there now. Maybe, but I doubt it. I don't believe in happily ever after anymore. I've lived too many lives for that.

Penelope and I hiked out of the woods and to a farm where she'd left her car. It took us three days. We camped in clearings where we could look up at the sky as we fell asleep. It looked like there were more stars than people on earth. Maybe there were.

The farmer was a woman who lived alone with three daughters dressed in boys' clothing. There was a grave marked with a simple cross in the yard. Chickens ran back and forth across it.

Penelope paid the farmer for keeping the car, a rusting Ford Model A. We had to clean animal droppings out of the inside before we loaded it up with Penelope's gear. If the woman thought it odd Penelope came out of the woods with a man she hadn't gone in with, she didn't let it show. She didn't let anything show on her face. It was that kind of age.

We drove down to San Francisco, passing shantytowns beside the road here and there, and people walking in the middle of nowhere, dragging suitcases behind them. No doubt all their worldly belongings. From dust we came and to dust we shall return.

We stayed at a hotel in San Francisco. We rented two rooms, because that was the proper thing to do. We ate in restaurants and I bought new clothes for myself with some money I lifted from pockets here and there. I read the newspapers and that's how I discovered the world was at war again, although it looked like things were winding down in Europe. I wasn't surprised. I'd known Hitler was going to be trouble from the moment he got in power – I'd seen his type before. But I was surprised by the fact I'd missed most of the war. I'd been hiking around the forests and mountains looking for Gabriel for longer than I'd realized. I reacquainted myself with the luxuries of a bath and a bed. It wasn't a bad life. I'd led better at times in the past, and I'd led worse. This was enough for me now.

The third night we were there, Penelope took me to a meeting of one of the spiritualist groups. She put all her photos in a couple of envelopes and changed into a black dress. She told me to call her Miss Cassandra as we drove there.

"Is that your last name?" I asked her.

"It's the name I use with the people you're going to meet tonight," she said.

"What's wrong with Penelope?"

"It's not exactly a name with mystery," she said. "And you need a little mystery to get in the inner circles of these groups."

I didn't say anything for a while. And then I said, "So is Penelope a real name?"

"Here we are," she said, smiling and pulling into a long driveway.

The meeting was at a mansion overlooking the city. A man in a suit ushered us in to a dining room, where men and women sat waiting for us. They'd already been at the wine and brandy in the glasses in front of them, judging by the flushes to their cheeks. They wore formal wear like they'd been born in it, instead of being forced to endure it only every now and then. Poor souls.

The man at the end of the table, who actually wore a monocle, stood and came around to kiss Penelope on both cheeks.

"My dear, it is so lovely to have you back from your expedition," he said. "I trust it was fruitful?" He gave me a look that I couldn't read but that said something.

"It was," she said. "I even found myself an assistant." And she introduced me to everyone around the table. She used the name I'd given her, for whatever that was worth. I won't tell you their names. Not out of respect for their privacy, but because I don't remember them. Hey, I've met a lot of people.

The monocle man seated us beside him at the table. He had to pull in a chair from the wall for me. I guess he wasn't expecting Penelope to be accompanied by any friends. I noted he kept his hand on Penelope's arm a moment longer than was proper. I was surprised to notice it bothered me as much as it did, so I quietly did a number on the brandy in his glass, turning it into a cheap vintage.

"Miss Cassandra, do tell us of your latest adventures," he said once he'd settled back into his own seat.

Everyone quieted and looked at Penelope, and she cleared her throat and took a sip of wine from the glass in front of her and then told them how we'd met.

Only it was all made up.

She told them how she'd seen a ghost moving through the woods outside her shack one night. She'd chased it through the forest, and it had led her to a midnight gathering of faerie in a clearing, where she'd found me, tied to a large stone. They'd been about to sacrifice me to some pagan god or another, but she'd driven them off by reading aloud some parts of the bible. She'd been too busy trying to save me to get photographs, but she had come back the next day to capture the scene. And then she pulled out the photos she'd taken that day on the hilltop of the stones or bones or whatever they had been.

The women at the table put their hands to their mouths, while the men leaned forward and stared at the photos before emptying their glasses of brandy. I was gratified to see the monocle man gag on his drink.

"You are so lucky to be alive," one of the women said to me. "Miss Cassandra saved your soul," another said.

"I was lost and now I'm found," I said, mainly because I didn't know what else to say.

The same man who'd answered the door brought everyone plates with small roasted birds on them. Smuggled in from Europe, the monocle man said. It seemed like an awful lot of trouble for a bird, when there were ones in the tree outside he could have caught and cooked, but I refrained from saying so. Instead, I settled for repeating the brandy trick on his new glass.

Penelope kept on telling stories the whole time we were there. She said after she'd saved me, she'd discovered I had no memory of who I was or how I'd wound up in that clearing.

"The faerie cast a spell on him," another woman exclaimed. Maybe she was a prophet.

"I think it's far worse than that," Penelope said. "I think he's a change-ling. Taken from his human parents years ago in order to sacrifice him to their dark gods that night."

They all looked at me and I refilled my brandy from one of the bottles on the table. It *was* an excellent vintage.

"I've brought him back to civilization in the hopes of finding his human family," Penelope went on. "And of saving his soul."

They all stared at me, so I raised my glass. "Let's drink to that," I said.

They were a good audience, so Penelope milked them for what they were worth. She pulled out the photo of the goblin skull in the stream and told them how it would call out in the voice of a lost child, trying to draw people to the water, where they would drown. She pulled out the photo of the grave where she'd found me and said it was home to a family of ghouls. She said she hadn't been able to capture any of them on film but she had photographed their footprints. And then she pulled out photos of footprints in mud that could have come from any beast.

"Did you encounter any vampires?" asked the woman who was convinced the faerie had cast a spell on me.

"If she had, she would not be here to tell us her tales," the monocle man said.

"Oh, but I've heard that they are just dreadfully misunderstood," the woman said.

I'd had enough to drink now that I wasn't as quiet and cautious as I should have been. "Oh, they're misunderstood all right," I said. "Most people think that they just sip a little blood from you on some enchanted evening and then go about their merry way. If any of them got in here, it wouldn't be little birds they'd be eating, I promise you that."

Everyone looked at me now. Penelope gently ground her heel into my foot.

"Or so I've heard," I added.

Penelope went back to making up stories about her encounters with strange and mythical beasts, and I went back to drinking brandy and keeping my mouth shut. I won't bore you with the details. Rest assured, there were more photos and more exotic dishes and more excitement and lingering of hands where there shouldn't have been lingering of hands.

We only stayed a few hours, and then Penelope said we had to be going, that she had a lead to track down regarding my identity. She put all the photos back in the envelopes before handing them to the monocle man. He gave her an envelope in return when he saw us to the door.

"My dear, it is always a delight to see you," he told her. "Hopefully there won't be such a long delay next time."

"I'll do my best to return soon," she said. "But you know I can't predict where the mysteries of the world will lead."

"Indeed." He turned to me. "And I wish you well finding your people," he said, in a way that indicated he hoped I'd never mingle with his people again.

I thought about tearing out his throat but settled for shaking his hand. I made it as painful a grip as I could without breaking anything, and I was happy to see him wince and quickly pull his hand away. Then I turned his monocle into plain glass. We left him at his front door, blinking in confusion, and drove back to the hotel.

Once we had returned to our room, I looked in the envelope he'd given her. It was full of money.

"Why didn't you just tell them the truth?" I asked.

"They wouldn't understand," she said. "They're not like us. They wouldn't believe the truth. I give them the fantasies that I know they want."

"Us?" I said.

"So where are we going to look for the angels?" she said, changing the subject in her usual subtle way.

"There aren't any here," I said. "I can't feel them." Which was probably true enough, although I hadn't been looking that hard on account of enjoying the baths and the clean sheets and all that.

"Where do we go then?" she asked.

I didn't have to think that over too long.

"Paris," I said.

"Why Paris?" she asked.

"There are always angels in Paris," I said.

"I wouldn't have thought angels the romantic type," she said.

"They're not," I said. "They like all the catacombs and cemeteries there. I think it makes them feel at home."

"It's just been liberated from the Nazis," she pointed out. "There's probably still fighting going on."

"Even better," I said. "The angels like blood."

She sold the car to the front-desk clerk at the hotel at a bargain price and we took the train across the country to New York. We threw decorum to the wind and rented a sleeper cabin. We'd shared the same shack in the woods, after all. For once in my many lives I managed to be a gentleman and didn't touch her. I could barely sleep, though. I was too busy wondering why I'd been so overcome with jealousy back at that mansion. Also, I kept thinking about her naked body underneath her pajamas as she lay in the bunk beneath mine, covered by the sheets. I was a man, after all, and not Christ.

We passed through long forests as dark as night and wound our way along the bottoms of mountains where men must have died by the dozens to lay the tracks for the train. We crossed empty, dead farmers' fields, where the houses and broken farm equipment lay half-buried after countless dust storms. Penelope took photos of them with her portable camera. We passed other fields where men and women bent with age were tending rows of wheat shoots just barely out of the ground. Penelope took photos of them, too.

"I thought you only took photos of supernatural things," I said.

"There's a lot you don't know about me," she said.

"Like what you meant when you said Miss Cassandra's friends back in San Francisco weren't like us," I said. "What do you mean, *us*?"

She smiled and took a photo of me with the camera. She didn't say anything, so I didn't speak again either. I wanted some answers before we actually got close to any angels. I needed to know what I was dealing with when it came to Penelope.

Two or three nights into the trip the train slowed as we passed a camp of homeless people living by the tracks. They huddled by their fires and watched us. People from the train leaned out the windows and tossed them chocolate bars, packages of cigarettes and matches, even a few cans of food.

The homeless people left their fires and tents to gather up the things on the ground and lifted their hands in thanks. A few of them bowed their heads in silent prayer, and I turned away from them.

We sped up again and continued on, through more days and nights and empty fields and then villages and towns. After a time, the evening sky began to glow in the distance. New York. When we disembarked from the train and walked out into the city, the moon was red.

We found a hotel and rented two rooms again. I lay in my bed and thought about Penelope on the other side of the wall between us. I wondered if she was lying awake thinking about me.

The next day we flew to Paris. I paid for the flights with money I'd lifted here and there from people on the train. Penelope had never been to the city before – she'd never even been to Europe – so I spent the morning showing her around the sights. Some of them were marked with bullet holes now, and others had been blown up, either by the Nazis or the resistance, but most of the ones that counted were still there. And there was something in the air, something special even for Paris. A sense of freedom and exhilaration. The sort of feeling you always find in cities after a siege has been lifted. We stopped in patisseries and ate croissants and sweets. The last time I'd been in Paris, I'd been drunk on absinthe and on the run from . . . well, I couldn't remember who I'd been running from that time. I preferred this way of travelling.

In the afternoon, we wandered the River Seine. We stopped on a bridge and watched boats drift underneath, all of them bearing multiple French flags. I remember my breath was visible in the air. I remember my skin was cold but I was warm inside. A few lines of Baudelaire came to me.

"'Soon we will plunge ourselves into cold shadows,'" I said, "'and all of summer's stunning afternoons will be gone.'"

"'It was summer yesterday,'" Penelope said, looking up at the grey sky overhead. "'Now it's autumn.'"

I looked at her. "A poetry lover. Why am I not surprised?"

"My mother used to read to me," she said.

I could tell from the way she said it that her mother was past tense. "What happened to her?" I asked.

"She fell from a bridge," Penelope said.

I considered the water once more. "Interesting choice of verb," I said.

Penelope wrapped her arms around herself and huddled in her coat to stay warm. "I don't know if she jumped or was pushed. Or was thrown."

I took off my coat and put it around her. "Who would have thrown her from a bridge?" I asked.

"The angel." She looked at the sky.

"The same one you're looking for," I said, which was more of a conclusion than a question. She nodded her agreement as she shuffled closer to me and turned away from the wind.

"Why would an angel want to kill your mother?" I asked.

"You'll have to take my word for it when I say I don't know," Penelope said.

"Which angel do you think it was?" I asked.

Now she looked at me. "I don't know that either." She was so close I could feel her breath on my lips.

"Then why do you think an angel was involved?" I asked.

"Because it was involved with her entire life," she said. "So I'd be surprised to learn it wasn't involved in her death."

"You're going to have to explain that," I said, but Penelope just smiled at me.

"I don't *have* to do anything," she said, and kissed me.

LIFE AFTER DEATH

All right, I need another break.

I don't want to talk about that right now.

Let's talk about what I did after I managed to kill White's body instead of exorcising the demon inside it and bringing the body back to White.

I went back to the gallery. The door was open, so I let myself in. White was sitting at his desk in the back, with the bottle of whisky. Two glasses – one for him and one for me. I sat down across from him and didn't say anything. The plant seemed to be doing well. That was something, at least.

Judging by how much whisky was left in the bottle, White had been drinking for a while. I figured I didn't have to break the bad news to him – he must have felt it somehow.

"Sorry," I said. There's not really a standard expression of condolence for moments like this.

White shook his head. "Don't be," he said. "You've freed me."

"I killed you," I pointed out.

White shrugged. "I've been dead for a while. At least now I can get on with it."

"What are you going to do?" I asked. It was a worthy question.

Ghosts aren't like normal souls, which leave the physical realm when their bodies die. They've got a few more options available to them. Call it a trade-off for being severed from their bodies prematurely, although most don't see it that way.

White finished off his glass and smiled at me. "I've always wanted to travel," he said.

I poured myself a generous shot of whisky – three fingers, if you must know – and glanced around the gallery. "What about this place?" I asked.

"Make me an offer," White said, and I toasted him with my glass.

"I'm not really the type to settle down," I told him.

He nodded and looked at the gallery himself, like he was seeing the place for the first time.

"I think I'll just leave the door open for someone else," he said.

"Whoever it is may just come in and steal all the paintings," I pointed out.

"Maybe," he said. "Or maybe the person who needs this place will find it. Either way, I'm sure everything in here will find a good home."

I downed half my glass in a single swallow. "While you're feeling charitable . . ."

White smiled. "Ah yes, our bargain. I was wondering if you would remember."

I smiled back at him and waited to see if he'd been bluffing me all along.

"There's an art auction once a year for special collectors," he told me. "It has no name, and it's held in a different location each time. You can only find it if you're supposed to be there."

"Please tell me they're not special collectors like you," I said. "I don't think I can survive any more deals."

"This year's meeting is in Detroit tomorrow night at eight," he said and told me an address. I won't tell you what it is because I don't want anyone finding it. Not yet. You'll understand my reasons for that shortly.

"The collector who currently has Mona Lisa in his possession will be sending a representative to the auction," White said.

"How do you know for certain?" I asked.

"Because he always has and always will," White said. "He's one of the founding members."

"Who is he?" I asked, but White just smiled.

"I've given you enough," he said. "I'm not going to risk what little life I have left by telling you his name."

"So how am I supposed to know who to talk to about Mona Lisa?" I asked.

"Don't worry about it," White said. "His agent will want to talk to you."

"What do you mean by that?" I asked.

"You're exactly the sort of thing he likes to collect," White said.

And with that he got up and went out the door of his gallery and vanished into the night.

I sat at the desk a while longer, considering what he'd told me. An ache in my hand reminded me about my lost finger, so I grew it back and then finished the rest of the bottle on the cab ride to the airport.

A MESSAGE AMONG THE DEAD

Okay. I just needed a drink before I could carry on.

Penelope and I got a single hotel room in Paris instead of two separate ones. We locked ourselves inside it and made love for days. At the beginning she asked me about protection, but I explained to her the body I inherited seemed to be sterile. Some sort of cosmic joke, no doubt. She just smiled and said we may as well enjoy the joke. Then she pulled me to her.

We only opened the door for room service. We kept the doors to the balcony ajar and listened to the sounds of Paris outside, the car horns and the music and the laughter of people passing below. We breathed deep of the smell of baking bread and coffee, of cigarettes and cooking meat. Of the stuff of life.

The whole thing was a surprise to both of us, but it also had a sense of inevitability about it. And something else for me. I'd slept with, well, hundreds of people in my time. Maybe more. I'd lost count, if I'd ever been counting at all. I couldn't even remember most of them. Maybe I just wanted to forget them, the way they wanted to forget me when they caught a glimpse of my true nature. But Penelope was different. Penelope was the first lover who came to me *after* she found out what I was.

But, of course, it was much more complicated than that.

We finally went out for lunch one sunny afternoon. Who knew what day it was? We sat on the patio of a café for hours. Penelope read a newspaper article about Amelia Earhart, who'd disappeared years earlier and who was still missing. I sipped my coffee and watched the world go by without us. Life was as perfect as I could imagine. I knew it wouldn't last. The perfect moments never last. That's what makes them perfect.

"I met her once," Penelope said.

"Who?" I asked.

"Amelia Earhart," she said. "She came to the meeting of an association I belonged to once in Boston."

"You belonged to it?" I asked. "Or Miss Cassandra belonged to it?"

She smiled. "Lady Hippolyta belonged to it. But Amelia didn't. She just came because she wanted to know what sorts of spirits might live in the sky." She glanced up at the clouds drifting overhead. "I told her there were a lot of people who would like to know the answer to that question."

I looked over at the newspaper and scanned the other headlines. A story about American troops storming some island or another in the Pacific. A column urging a world court to try the Nazis once Berlin finally fell. Another column warning us all to keep an eye on the Russians after this was over, for fear we'd all become Russians. I could see the way things were going. The way history always went.

"She'll turn up eventually," I said. "They always do."

"Do they?" she said.

I finished the last of the coffee and tried to decide whether I should order another or move on to wine. Sometimes the simplest decisions are the hardest ones.

"You still haven't told me the name of the angel," I said.

"That's because I don't know its name," she said.

"Your mother never told you?" I said.

Penelope looked at me. "Why would she know its name?"

I considered how to answer that. Sometimes angels and humans got together for romance, or out of desperation, or simply out of some personal strategic necessity. It happened. If this were one of those times, Penelope's mother likely would have been on a first-name basis with the angel. But this didn't sound like that. This sounded more like the angel was stalking Penelope's mother. Which also happened. But angels didn't give people that sort of attention randomly. There had to be a reason it was so interested in Penelope's mother.

I signalled the waiter for a wine. There. Decision made.

"All right," I said. "Let's start with the basics. This mysterious angel harassed your mother her entire life for reasons that aren't clear to you." And which may not have been clear to the angel either. They think in mysterious ways and all that. "Now you're hunting him because he may have killed your mother."

Penelope shook her head. "That's not why I'm trying to find him," she said.

The waiter arrived and I took the glass of wine from his hand before he could set it down on the table. "Un autre, s'il vous plait," I said, and drank half the wine in one swallow. The waiter raised an eyebrow but went away without saying anything.

"Tell me then," I said, "why are you after this angel, and what are you going to do when you find him?"

Penelope didn't look away from the clouds. "I'm hunting him because he's my father," she said.

Ah.

I should have ordered the bottle.

"And when I find him," she went on, "I'm going to figure out how to kill him."

I looked back at the street, at all the people passing by. At everyone who wasn't the messy afterbirth of Christ or the offspring of an angel. Now I finally understood why it felt like I'd known Penelope all along. I finally understood our attraction to each other. If the mysterious angel was her father, it meant she was half angel herself. She had grace in her. Not enough that I could actively sense, but it explained why I felt so calm and content around her. I couldn't help but be drawn to her. I wondered how I made her feel.

I didn't ask her any more about the angel. I didn't need to, it was clear what had happened. The angel had forced itself upon Penelope's mother. Maybe the angel kept coming back because of Penelope, its child, maybe for another reason. Maybe it was part of some plan, maybe the angel had gone crazy. It didn't matter. I'd seen this sort of thing before, although I'd never been so personally involved.

"I'll help you," I said. "We'll find it and kill it together."

She put her hand in mine but didn't say anything else on that subject.

We finished our wine and then left the café. I wanted to find the angel as quickly as possible. I wanted to find any angel as quickly as possible. I needed grace before I got too hungry. I needed grace before I couldn't help myself and turned on Penelope now that I knew she had it.

I took her to Montparnasse Cemetery. It's where many of my friends have wound up. More of them have found less respectable graves, in trenches or stormy seas, but such is the way of history. The cemetery is also a favourite haunt of the angels. I'd found more than one here over the years and chased or followed them to somewhere I could kill them in private.

But the cemetery was empty of anything except for the dead and us. Someone else had been here, though. The stone angels that marked tombs throughout the place all held postcards: in their hands, tucked into their wings, jammed into cracks in the stone.

When I pulled the first one out of an angel's broken eye socket, I thought perhaps it was just someone being romantic or having a lark. It was a crumpled card depicting chrysanthemums. When I pulled the next one out from underneath an angel's broken wing that had fallen to the ground, I began to wonder. It was a photo of a Shinto shrine. When I took the third one from the hands of the angel looking down on Baudelaire's grave, I knew something was up. It was a photo of Mount Fuji.

"I don't suppose you're behind this, are you?" I said to the stone rendering of Baudelaire at my feet, but like most of the dead, he had nothing to say to me.

"What is it?" Penelope asked, looking at the postcards. "What do they mean?"

"Check all the other angels," I said, "and bring me back their postcards."

We separated and moved through the cemetery, collecting the cards that had been tucked into each statue and marker that held an angel. We met back at Baudelaire's tomb, with handfuls of them. I tossed all my cards on the ground and looked at them.

Samurai warriors.

Japanese sailors.

The Rising Sun flag.

Cherry blossom trees.

Penelope added her cards to my pile.

A street scene from Tokyo.

A woman in a kimono.

An ink painting of trees done in the suibokuga style.

"They're a message," I said, finally answering Penelope's question.

"There's something in Japan," she said.

"The angels have all gone to Japan," I said, nodding. Which explained why we hadn't come across any since my most recent encounter with Gabriel.

"What is there for them in Japan?" Penelope asked, and I shook my head.

"I don't know," I said. "The war, maybe. But if that's where they are, then that's where we'll have to go."

She studied me. "Something bothers you about Japan," she said.

"No," I said, looking around the graveyard. "What bothers me is I don't know who left us this message, or why."

As if on cue, a gust of wind picked up the postcards and blew them into the far corners of the cemetery and out of sight.

A MOST UNIQUE AUCTION

I wasn't surprised I'd found White and freed him – in a manner of speaking – just in time for the annual meeting of the secret group he knew about. There was definitely something or someone working to guide me along the path I was taking. So be it. If there's one thing I've learned over the centuries, it's that everything gets revealed in due time. And if it doesn't, well, it wasn't that important then.

I made my flight at the airport with minutes to spare and settled in to sleep as much as I could. I didn't even notice the turbulence the pilot apologized for when we landed in Detroit.

I hit the first coffee stand I came across in the airport and washed down a croissant and a muffin with a double espresso. I was feeling drained again because of all the grace I'd been burning lately. I was going to have to find another angel soon. It's a shame the essence of demons was the farthest thing imaginable from grace. Carver would have filled me up if he'd been an angel.

After my breakfast on the run, I found the car rental desks and obtained a car. A Ford, it being Detroit and all. I gave the rental agent the latest ID and credit cards I'd stolen, from a man in a suit checking his phone for messages at the coffee stand, and then inspected the car with her. Hopefully this one would lead me to better places than the last car I'd rented.

Once I left the airport, I headed straight for the address White had given me. I was hours early, but I wanted to scout out the place first to check for any potential surprises. To be honest, I didn't think I'd be the only one doing that. Maybe I'd even run into the person I needed to find and manage to skip the entire meeting.

The problem was I couldn't find the address. The area was an industrial park, and all the buildings had been abandoned, their windows boarded up and their overgrown parking lots fenced off with chain link topped with razor coil. But the street signs were still there, and I couldn't find my destination anywhere, no matter how much I drove around.

I finally pulled over to the side of one of the streets and got out. There was no one else in sight to ask for directions, not even a bird. The only thing moving was a plastic bag that blew down the street past the car.

Well, when all else fails, sometimes the direct approach is best.

"Hello!" I yelled. "I'm here for the meeting!"

No one answered but the wind. So much for the direct approach.

I got back in my car and checked the time on the clock. A little before noon. I had a lot of time to kill before the secret meeting in the invisible place started. So I did the only thing I could do in the situation. I closed my eyes and tried to nap.

I'd like to tell you I dreamed of better times, of Penelope and me living back in the shack in the woods, or in Paris, but I didn't. Instead, I dreamed I was back in the pub in Ireland. In Morgana's realm. I stood at the bar and drank an ale that tasted of honey and ocean air. The people all around me welcomed me back by lifting their own drinks in salute. They bore the marks of their fight with the mummy: black eyes and bruised faces and arms in slings made from bar towels. I drank my drink and tapped my foot to the music and saw Morgana come down the stairs, making the entrance like the queen she was. The band struck up a number I didn't recognize, somehow coaxing the sounds of lutes and harps from their guitars and microphones, and the crowd cheered.

Morgana paused on the stairs and smiled at me, and I felt that hollowed-out pain again at being so far away from her. I wanted to go to her, to kneel at her feet, to wait for her touch, even though it was just a dream. Then she patted her stomach, and I noticed for the first time she was pregnant. Very pregnant. She looked as if she were ready to give birth right there on the stairs.

A car driving past woke me. I sat up in my seat in time to see the taillights disappear behind a building at the intersection down the street. Somehow it was night. I'd slept for hours, but I could still feel the hollowness inside me. I could still taste the sea on my lips. So perhaps it hadn't been a dream after all. Well, no time for that now. I started the car and followed the other one without turning the lights on, but by the time I hit the intersection it was gone.

I idled there for a moment, wondering whether I was still dreaming or whatever it was I'd been doing, and then another car, a Jaguar, passed me. I took that as a sign I was awake. I followed it before it could disappear too.

The Jaguar turned down a side street I hadn't noticed before and I smiled and cursed myself simultaneously. It had been the street I'd been unable to find. Unless it hadn't existed before now, it had been here all along, hidden by a sleight. I hadn't even thought to check for illusions. I was getting sloppy in my old age.

The Jaguar went through an open gate into another overgrown parking lot, but this one had a dozen other cars in it. My rental was the cheapest in the lot by a factor of about ten, I guessed. I noticed none of the other cars were parked particularly close to each other, so I gave them all a wide berth and parked underneath a streetlight that somehow still worked. I figured you couldn't be too safe in this neighbourhood.

The driver of the Jaguar, a man in a suit and tie, got out and looked at me as I walked up to him.

"I hope there's not a dress code," I said. "The airline lost my luggage."

He stared at me with incomprehension, and I realized he was the type who'd probably never flown on anything but a private jet and thus didn't know what the hell I was talking about. But then he smiled as he came to the conclusion I had to be joking. Although the smile did falter a little when he looked over my shoulder at the rental car.

"I'm trying to keep a low profile," I said, and his smile came back.

"I also," he said in an accent that couldn't be anything but German. I looked at the Jag and wondered what his regular vehicle was.

He turned and headed for the entrance of the building, which looked to be some sort of older auto factory. I followed him and he didn't object. So far everything was going smoothly. I didn't expect it to last.

The doors to the building were open, and there were lights on inside to welcome us – the kind on metal stands, with cables snaking off to some unseen generator. I figured the factory probably wasn't even connected to the power grid anymore. Judging from the dirt on the floor and the peeling paint on the walls, the place hadn't been in operation for decades.

We went down a hall and into the factory proper. There were more lights in a circle in the centre of the chamber, with folding chairs set up facing a temporary stage with a podium on it. I was surprised to see the factory equipment still largely in place, albeit rusting. There were wide conveyer belts on platforms leading off into the darkness, with chains hanging from tracks on the ceiling overhead. Metal arms hung from bases lining the walls. A forklift was parked in the shadows behind the stage. The sound of dripping water echoed through the room. Very homey.

It looked like we were the last to arrive, because the chairs were mostly occupied. There were only two left empty. Jaguar took one, I sat in the other. Everyone turned to look at me, including the man who stepped up to stand at the podium. I wasn't the only one who wasn't wearing a suit, but I had a feeling my entire outfit cost less than the socks on most of this bunch. I looked around at them. A couple women, the rest of them men. I didn't recognize any of them.

The man at the podium cleared his throat. "I don't believe we've had the pleasure," he said to me.

I smiled at him. "We haven't. I'm here on behalf of Mr. White."

A couple of them raised their eyebrows, but most of them didn't react at all. They were a reserved bunch. I began to worry they might be connected to the Royal Family somehow.

The man at the podium smiled back at me, but it was one of those smiles you see on people who don't actually know how to smile.

"We are glad to see Mr. White back in the business," he said. "His chair has been empty too long. I trust he has finally freed himself from his personal commitments?"

"He's so free you're never going to see him again," I said. "He's retired and I've taken over his gallery." It seemed as good a cover story as any, and I doubted they were going to take this moment to check it out.

Now they all studied me, and none of them were smiling.

"Interesting," the man at the podium said, although I had a feeling it wasn't the word he wanted to use. "Well then, an introduction perhaps?"

"Clement Greenberg," I told them. An art joke. A couple of them chuckled but the rest didn't seem to get it. I didn't know whether or not I should be concerned by that.

"Very well, Mr. Greenberg," the man at the podium said, his face as reserved as ever. Can a face be reserved? Well, his was. "I trust you know how our auction works?"

I nodded. Sure, what the hell. "Let's get on with it," I said.

He looked down at his podium and shuffled some index cards there. "Indeed," he said. "Our first item is a unicorn horn."

Two men wearing black stepped out of the shadows and onto the stage. I hadn't noticed them there at all. They were carrying the horn and held it up for the audience to see.

It was an average enough unicorn horn. It shimmered with its own light and left rifts in the air where it tore its way into other realms. The rifts only lasted a few seconds before they faded, but everyone leaned forward to peer at them. Everyone but me and one of the others. I wasn't interested because I'd seen enough of this sort of thing to know there wasn't much on the other side – usually a meadow with that realm's equivalent of grass and trees, maybe the inside of a building like this one. With any luck, that was it. But sometimes your luck ran out and you found something looking back at you. Something just as curious. That's how some of the demons crossed over into our world in the first place. Best not to make eye contact.

The other member of our little group who wasn't looking at the unicorn horn was looking at me like I was a unicorn horn. A short, bald man whose suit was the plainest of the bunch, and whose shoes were actually scuffed. I suppose he thought he looked inconspicuous, but if you're going to mingle with rich people the best way to stand out is by not looking rich. I say just go for it – throw on the tailored suit and the socks you wear only once and the glasses that cost more than the GDP of some Pacific Ocean islands. Enjoy it while you can.

I nodded at the unicorn horn and rolled my eyes at the bald man, as if to say, "*This* is what they're offering? Who doesn't already have a couple of these acting as night lights in their bathrooms?"

He just kept looking at me without changing his expression. I wasn't sure what that meant, but my vast experience with getting beaten and killed told me that kind of look meant something.

I was a little distracted then, because the people around me started bidding for the unicorn horn.

"A yeti fur," a man with unnaturally perfect teeth said.

"One of the lost books of Atlantis," a woman with unnaturally perfect hair said.

"The jawbone of Moses," a man with an unnaturally perfect build said.

I'd been expecting them to bid cash, but I guess if you already have too much money to know what to do with, you need other excitements. Me, I'll take money over magic and the exotic any day. Only one of those can keep you warm and drunk on a rainy evening.

The man at the podium – the auctioneer, I guess – looked at me, but I shook my head and gave him a smile that said "Show me something worth my time."

"Fair exchange," he said. "A lost book of Atlantis for the unicorn horn." Everyone nodded but no one said anything. It seemed he was the arbiter as well as the auctioneer. Well, I guess you'd need someone to make decisions at an event like this.

The men in black disappeared back into the shadows with the horn and its light faded away. Not your normal shadows then. The auctioneer looked back down at his podium.

"Our next item has been off the market for two centuries," he said. "A leprechaun's foot."

One of the men in black reappeared to hold up the mummified specimen. I winced and looked away. The leprechauns had been a harmless bunch who liked shiny things. Sort of like addled cousins of the faerie. Things went bad for them after the Normans got them confused with lucky rabbits.

There were only two bids this time: a strand of Rapunzel's hair that continued to grow and a goblin's heart, still beating, on a stick. Tough choice. The hair won the day. I tried not to shake my head. It was like trading a stomach ache for a headache.

When they brought the third item out, I figured it was time to make my play. I didn't have anything to trade, so I was just wasting time sitting here. That and I was growing bored.

"The real Kennedy assassination tape," the auctioneer said, and the other man in black stepped out of the shadows and held up a roll of film, the kind that needed one of those old projectors.

"A lost tentacle of one of the Deep Ones," Jaguar said, in a way that implied the capitalization. "Still living." We all stared at him. *How* had he managed to get that?

Well, no matter. It was time to do what I'd come here for.

"Mona Lisa," I said, and now everyone looked at me. I smiled at them. "The real one, of course."

I waited as they glanced at each other, trying to figure out if I was bluffing or not. Or maybe just mad. Then they all looked at the bald man. Which told me what I needed to know.

The bald man finally changed expressions. Now he smiled a little. Never a good sign in those you suspect of murderous inclinations.

"Gentlemen, I'm afraid we're going to have to end this meeting rather prematurely," he said. "I have some matters to discuss with my friend here, and I'll need to do that in private. We'll put everything on hold until next year."

I was expecting an outcry – these were rich people, after all, and we hadn't settled the assassination tape bid yet – but they all just nodded and sighed as they stood up. Even the auctioneer picked up his podium and stepped back into the shadows with it. So that settled who was in charge here. Jaguar frowned at me as he headed for the exit, but personally I thought I'd saved him a fleecing, given that Kennedy hadn't really been killed. Not permanently, anyway.

And then it was just me and the bald man. He stood up and took off his suit jacket and hung it on his chair and then turned back to me.

"I don't know who you are –" he began, and I stood up to interrupt him.

"I'm the guy who's going to beat you," I said.

He rolled up his shirt sleeves as he considered me. He was a real traditionalist when it came to matters of intimidation.

"I wouldn't mind if you did," he said. "But I doubt that's going to happen."

That comment gave me a clue as to his nature. He had the utmost confidence in himself despite facing someone who'd managed to find this secret meeting and who was willing to crash it regardless of all the talk of Deep Ones' tentacles and secret assassination films. That meant he was powerful, most likely supernatural. His statement that he wouldn't mind if I beat him suggested he wasn't happy with his lot in life. I guessed it had less to do with depression issues and more to do with sorcerous bindings and such.

"So what are you?" I asked. "Demon? Golem? Ghost?"

"I was going to ask you the same thing," he said as we began to circle each other, kicking chairs aside to make room.

"Me, I'm just a man," I said. "And you'd be the man of the one I'm looking for, if you were a man."

"What do you want with him?" he asked.

"I don't want anything with him," I said. "I want something he has. Maybe we can work out a fair exchange."

He chuckled a little at that. "What do you have?" he asked.

"Nothing," I admitted. "But I imagine I can come up with a pretty decent IOU."

"I think I'll just take you instead," he said, and we got down to business.

I was expecting the attack to come from him, and I guess it did in its own way. But it mainly came from behind me. There was a scream of metal and I turned in time to see a car frame hurtle out of the shadows at me, knocking over the rest of the chairs. It was one of those huge ones they used to make in the 1970s – two tons of steel if not more – but I couldn't tell the model because it wasn't finished. It was unpainted and didn't have any windows or tires – it screeched along on rims.

I leapt to the right to get out of the way, and even then it grazed me a little. If I'd moved at normal speed it would have driven over me and I would have been just another motor vehicle statistic. I rolled and came up on my feet in time to see my adversary hop over the car, timing it perfectly, and then the car crashed into the wall behind him. I also had time to note there was no driver. I spun in a quick circle, scanning the room just in case, but I didn't see anyone else. And I wasn't driving the car, which left only one other candidate.

"All right, that rules out golem and ghost," I said and threw a chair at him. I didn't expect it to hurt him; I just wanted to gauge his reflexes. He let the chair bounce off him, which confirmed my suspicions about him not being human and all. Sometimes I hate it when I'm right.

"And demon," he said, chuckling. "But we still don't know what you are."

He waved his hand and suddenly tentacles lashed down at me from the ceiling, striking me in the head and wrapping around my limbs and pulling me in all directions. Only they weren't tentacles, they were the chains hanging from the belt on the ceiling. The auction had my imagination working overtime.

I figured my opponent was responsible for the chains grabbing me, so I cast about for a connection between him and them that I could sever. There are a couple of different ways of looking for such things – kind of like looking through a night-vision scope, or maybe seeing in infrared. But there was nothing. He wasn't manipulating the chains. The chains were alive.

Or rather, they were possessed by things once alive. I could see them inside the metal, writhing there to make the chains move and pull at me. And they were screaming as loudly as I was now, in their own way.

Souls.

The chains were possessed by the souls of those who had once been alive. I hadn't seen this sort of thing since the Chinese ghost tank division in the Korean War.

I hit the chains with a minor exorcism spell, the sort of thing every self-respecting priest and tomb robber knows. It did the trick, cracking open the metaphysical chains, so to speak, and releasing the souls to finally die. The physical chains hung limp and I dropped to the ground. But not before I saw who the souls were. They faded into scenes from their lives, moments that summed them up.

A man in grey work clothes watching a woman hang laundry on a line in a yard.

A man lying on a beach, watching a gull circle in the blue sky overhead.

A teenage boy kneeling at the grave of his father, promising he'd look after the family.

And then they dissipated entirely. But they all whispered the same name: Sut.

I stood back up and saw more souls trapped in the car. I freed them the same way. They all said the same name.

I looked at the bald man, who raised his eyebrows at the sight of me unbound and the pieces of metal no longer doing his bidding.

"Let me guess," I said. "Sut."

He bowed his head a little. "Indeed. And judging from your training, I would guess you're a priest. Vatican special collections squad? Or are you rogue?"

"Oh, you have no idea," I said.

He chuckled. "Well, let's find out then," he said and waved both hands at me.

This time the whole factory shook and shrieked and I turned to see a couple of forklifts rushing my way, their cargo arms lifted to impale me. Behind them came what I can only describe as Frankenstein creatures – humanoid shapes cobbled together out of factory parts. Barrels for bodies, hubcaps and tire rims for heads, pipes for legs, strips of conveyer belt for feet, welding torches and metal pincers for arms. An army of them. The human appearance was just for effect – Sut could have just as easily bound souls to individual pieces of machinery and had them come at me. But he struck me as the type who cared about his work. Yeah, I was getting a read on him.

He laughed again as I sighed. "You could just surrender and deliver yourself into my power," he suggested.

I shook my head. "I'm just warming up," I said and I waded into his servants.

By the time I was done it looked as if I'd exorcised every single piece of equipment in the factory. I was surrounded by piles of debris, and I'd gone through so much grace so quickly that I had to lean against one of the forklifts for a moment. It had been possessed by a man whose favourite memory had been drinking alone in a dark bar where the televisions were broken. I was curious before, but I was angry now. There had been hundreds of souls trapped in the nuts and bolts of the factory, some of them for decades. All of them by Sut, if their whispers were to be believed. He couldn't have bound them all in preparation for the annual meeting his little group held here, which meant he must have done it for personal reasons. Which told me exactly what he was because there was only one being that would bother with such an odd form of torture.

"So you're a djinn," I said.

Sut didn't say anything, just studied me with narrowed eyes. The smile was gone now that I'd wrecked his toy army.

I could have stood there all night, making small talk while waiting for my second wind to arrive. But I didn't have all night so I got on with it. I forced myself away from the forklift and managed a smile.

"And if you're a djinn working for someone else, that means he's bound you to his service," I said. "Which means you're no different than this bunch." I kicked a crushed oil can at him. The head of one of the creatures that had tried to take off my own head with a portable power saw.

That made him mad enough to finally come at me himself. Which saved me the trouble of going to him.

He didn't charge me like I'd expected. Instead, he ripped apart in a whirling cloud of shirt and tie and skin and everything underneath. It looked a little like a dust storm in the desert. Then he covered the distance between us in a blink and just like that I was at the centre of the storm.

This day just kept getting better.

I had a hard time breathing, as he was sucking the air out of my lungs while simultaneously battering me with a thousand tiny pieces of himself. It was a handy trick on his part, and had probably served him well over the centuries. How do you beat a dust storm? But he'd never fought anyone like me before. Or maybe he had, but he hadn't fought *me* before.

I grabbed a piece of something hurtling past my face. It was warm and wet and, yes, squishy. I tightened my fist around it and ripped it free of Sut. A handful of bleeding flesh.

He screamed a little and the storm around me faltered for a second, the wind dropping as he tried to figure out what had just happened. I used the opportunity to grab a few more bits of him – best not to dwell on which parts – and ripped them free as well.

Sut redoubled his efforts then, whipping himself into a real storm, one that tried to scour the flesh from my bones. I caught more pieces of him, until he broke away from me with a cry and reformed himself where the podium had stood before. Now he was breathing heavy and bleeding from various parts of his body. He looked a bit misshapen, like he'd put himself back together without all the parts.

"What the hell are you?" he asked.

"Close," I said, and then it was my turn.

I leapt across the room to him and held him in place by the throat when he tried to dematerialize again – holding him bound in his physical shape with the help of some grace. His eyes widened. I guess no one had pulled that one on him before. Every day is a life lesson and all that.

For a moment we struggled against each other, will against will. But then I grabbed a screwdriver off the floor and went to work on him with all the ferocity of an angel, and eventually he fell to his knees with a cry.

"Master!" he said in surrender.

"I'm not your master," I said. "But you can tell me who he is." I *was* growing curious. Whoever Sut was working for had some formidable tricks up his sleeves to be able to bind a creature such as a djinn. That feat would be a struggle even for an angel.

"Jonathan Edwards," Sut gasped. "His name is Jonathan Edwards."

I shook my head. "Don't know him."

"He is a Collector," Sut said. He pronounced it in a way that called for a capital C.

"I gathered that much," I said. "And I'm also guessing he's collected Mona Lisa. The real one. Am I right?"

Sut shook his head. "I'm forbidden to speak of such things."

I prodded him in the chest with the screwdriver, but he held up a hand. "See for yourself," he said. He opened his mouth and spoke but no words came out. He went on like that for a moment and then shrugged. "I have told you everything I know."

I wondered if it was some sort of spell specific to djinn or if it had broader applications. It would have been handy to have for some of my past neighbours.

"What if you write it down?" I asked, but Sut shook his head.

"It just comes out as random lines," he said.

"Lip reading?" I asked.

"Random words," he said.

I thought things over for a moment. I had to admit it was an interesting approach to keeping secrets. Very Tower of Babelish.

"Mind if I get off my knees?" Sut asked. "It's a little uncomfortable."

I nodded him into a chair and then picked another one out of the debris and sat down across from him.

"All right, you can't talk about Mona Lisa," I said. "Can you answer yes or no questions about her?"

"I'm not really certain," Sut said. "It's not a common topic of conversation."

"Let's give it a try," I said. "Does Jonathan Edwards have the real Mona Lisa in his possession?"

Sut opened his mouth to speak but only more silence came out. He looked at me and shrugged again.

"Why don't you just try nodding or shaking your head?" I suggested.

"I did," he said.

"All right. Can you talk to me about Edwards?"

"I think so."

I leaned back and folded my arms across my chest, in order to look more intimidating. Also to rest my sore back.

"Let's hear what you know then," I said.

"The Risen are the alpha and the omega," Sut said, then stopped. He looked at me. "That's not what I meant to say."

"Go on." I sighed.

"The Risen are the first and last." He shook his head.

"Those don't seem to be random words," I pointed out to him. "Who are the Risen?"

"The Risen are the beginning and the end," he said, then added, "I didn't know about this one. I've never had any problem talking about him before."

"It was probably triggered when you submitted to me," I said. I got to my feet, then paused as I thought of something. "How did Edwards bind you?"

"The Risen are the alpha and the omega," Sut said again.

"When did he bind you?" I asked.

"About four hundred years ago," Sut said. "He freed me in an archae-ological dig in a desert that's no longer there." He stopped and raised his eyebrows at me.

I nodded. "Looks like he didn't cover all the bases," I said. "So he dug you out of the ground –"

"Actually, I was in a burial urn in the well-preserved tomb of a pharaoh whose name I dare not speak for fear it will summon him," Sut said.

"Whatever," I said. "How did he dig you out?"

Sut looked confused. "The usual way – with shovels and picks."

"I mean, how did he free you from the urn?" I asked.

"The Risen are the beginning and the end," he said.

It went on that way for a few minutes, until I was satisfied I wasn't going to be able to find out anything else about Edwards beyond what I already knew. Which was almost nothing. Just a typical day at the office.

Now it was my turn to roll up my sleeves. I added a little flair of my own by picking up a metal pipe.

Sut looked up at me with a resigned expression on his face. "What are you doing?" he asked.

"Time to bury you again," I said.

"But I've co-operated with you," he said. "I've submitted to you."

I nodded. "This isn't for me," I said. "This is for all the people you bound in this place." And then I went to work on him with the pipe.

I could have killed him, but I didn't. I left just enough to keep him conscious. And then I bound him into the oil can I'd kicked aside earlier. I took the oil can and hid it deep inside the factory, in a place I was pretty sure only I'd be able to find again. Then I left that place, hoping the sleight that hid it would last a thousand years.

Hey, I never claimed to be a saint.

PENELOPE REVEALS A MIRACLE

Penelope and I left for Japan the day after we found the postcards in Montparnasse Cemetery. Japan was still at war with half the world, but I'd learned over the centuries that you couldn't let some conflict get in the way of your travels. If you did, you'd never be able to go anywhere.

Of course, trying to get into a country at war was more difficult when you were coming from one of the enemy states. We couldn't just catch a direct flight to Tokyo.

We packed our lives into our suitcases and took a passenger plane to Istanbul, where we spent two days waiting for a replacement for some arcane part in the engine. I didn't want to step foot out of the hotel because of what had happened last time I'd been in Istanbul, back when it was known as Constantinople. There are things with very long memories in that city. So we stayed in our hotel room the whole time, making love some more and reading guides we'd bought about Japan. It had been a while since I had been there. Centuries, probably. I'd travelled there after the Shimabara rebellion, when I'd heard Christianity had been outlawed. It had, but one of the other things history has taught me is that prohibition rarely works. Okay, never works. There wasn't any place for me to hide from my past in Japan either, as I kept running into secret Christians who reminded me who I was.

From Istanbul we flew to Karachi and switched modes of transport, boarding a cargo ship I knew of that sailed under a flag so worn and faded it was blank. The flag had once borne a nation's symbols, but that nation didn't exist anymore. The crew didn't look too closely at us, partially because it was their business not to look too closely at their cargo, and partially because I'd cast a sleight to make us look like an unattractive older couple from some northern clime that did horrible things to one's skin. I took it off when we slept together at night so we could still enjoy the bloom of new love and all that.

We sailed from Karachi to Hong Kong, where we paid some money to a British man who looked like Buddha and switched to a regular passenger vessel flying the Japanese flag. We entered Tokyo with the accompaniment of a warm rain. On the way, I adjusted the sleight to give us more of a South Asian appearance. Still old and ugly, though, so as not to attract attention.

It probably wasn't wise to speak English, or any other European tongues, given the war and all, but the few words of Japanese I remembered were so woefully out of date that the dockworkers just stared at me when I tried to ask them where the nearest accommodations were. But we were able to find a cab driver who understood our mimed gestures of sleeping and took us to a hotel.

We slept off the trip into the afternoon and ate breakfast in bed. Then we dressed and went down into the street and began our hunt. If the people we met were curious about our lack of the local tongue, they were polite enough to not show it.

I was surprised at how much Tokyo reminded me of any other city in those days. The virus of modernity had spread even there. We wandered the busy streets until we found a small cemetery hidden away between some apartment buildings. We went through it, but I didn't see any signs of angels. It wasn't really their kind of place. It was all neat and tidy rows of stone markers and swept gravel paths. There wasn't a statue or a tomb in sight, nothing that reeked of brooding loneliness or dramatic suffering.

Penelope asked me what I was looking for, but all I could do was shrug.

"I'll know it when I see it," I said. Like the time I'd found the angel Haniel in a graveyard in Berlin when he'd melted the name off a tombstone with his tears.

We moved on, back into the streets outside and the land of the living. No one paid any attention to us now because I'd adjusted the sleight again to make us look like an average Japanese couple. We'd brought along

Penelope's camera gear and every now and then Penelope stopped us to take photos of things.

A row of monks kneeling outside a bank on one of the main streets, eyes closed, praying.

A man carving strips of meat off a pig carcass in the window of a butcher shop.

A man hung and left as a warning to others, his offence of distributing copies of *The Communist Manifesto* scrawled across the wooden marker at his feet.

It was just like any other place in the world.

For two weeks we toured the cemeteries of Tokyo, but they were all the same: neat, orderly and empty. Every now and then we'd come across another person in them, paying their respects at some gravestone or another. Sometimes they'd bow to us, sometimes they'd turn to watch us move through the place but wouldn't say anything. I wanted to ask them if they'd seen anything odd or unusual lately, but there was that whole language problem. Someday I would start taking my life more seriously and actually apply myself to learning things rather than simply drifting through history. Someday.

When we were done with the cemeteries we moved on to the temples. I knew from the first one that they weren't the sort of places angels would like any more than the cemeteries. They were open-air affairs, at one with the trees and parks surrounding them. Quiet and harmonious, not dramatic and imposing, like the churches of Europe. Not the angels' style at all.

We spent another few days visiting them all anyway. Penelope took photographs of the buildings and of the people praying inside or walking on the grounds. We ate at roadside stalls or in train stations, where people didn't ask too many questions or try to engage us in conversation. I picked up a few words here and there, enough to ask about restrooms and tea. There was hope for me yet. We tried not to hold hands or otherwise show our affection for each other in public, as it wasn't the Japanese way at the time. But it was difficult. It was very difficult.

We found the odd Christian church in the city. They were smaller affairs than the ones back in Europe, as if they were still trying to maintain a low profile, even though Christianity was legal in Japan again. But we didn't have any more luck with them. The priests were mostly Japanese men, but in one a European man in robes was sweeping the pews. I went over and asked him in English if he had seen anything unusual lately.

"Paintings weeping blood," I said. "Statues moving around. The dead rising from their graves and speaking in tongues. Men with wings fighting in the sky. Burning animals roaming the streets." You know, the usual.

He considered me for a moment before answering, perhaps because of what I'd asked him, perhaps because I appeared to be a Japanese man speaking English. "Only in my dreams," he said, and went back to sweeping the dust from the pews.

By the end of the week we'd visited all the sorts of places that were the angels' usual haunts and found nothing. The city felt empty of grace to me, outside of Penelope. The angels were either hiding with more care than usual or they weren't in Tokyo.

I should have been desperate to find them. It had been too long since I'd had any grace. But I didn't feel hungry or empty or any of the usual things I felt when I was out of grace. Instead, I just felt calm and content. I knew it was because of Penelope. Her grace was different from that of the angels. I didn't need to take it from her. It fed me just from her presence. I didn't even care about Judas anymore, or who I was. When I was with her, it was enough. For the first time, I felt accepted. For the first time, I felt whole.

We travelled by train to Kyoto and I stayed up all night in our cabin thinking. I thought that maybe after we killed Penelope's father I wouldn't need to kill any more angels. I thought that maybe Penelope would be enough for me for the rest of our lives together. The only problem, of course, being that she would eventually die and I wouldn't. Not permanently, anyway.

So I came up with a plan for that.

The first night we were in Kyoto we went to the cherry blossom festival along the banks of the Kamo River. We sat on a blanket under a tree and toasted the people sitting around us with sake. The lights of the paper lanterns in the trees were better than any stars. The smell of the blossoms was as intoxicating as the sake.

I was going to tell Penelope what I was thinking about, that she didn't have to die when she was with me. That I could keep her alive. That we could spend forever together. But she had her own surprise announcement.

"I wasn't exactly planning this," she said, "but I'm pregnant." She smiled and shook her head at the wine, like it was responsible.

I smiled back at her. "I'm sorry," I said, "but it can't be." I knew I was incapable of fathering anyone. It had never happened over the centuries, and there had been plenty of opportunities.

"I'm sorry," she said, "but it is." And she took my hand and guided it to her stomach. And I felt it there. A stirring.

I couldn't say anything else. I couldn't do anything else but stare at her. I didn't know what was happening.

"Don't worry," she said, laughing. "It's yours. There hasn't been anyone else for a long time."

"How . . . ?" I said, but I didn't even know what to ask.

"If I have to explain that, I've really misjudged you," she said.

"That's not what I mean," I said. "The thing is, I can't . . ." Again, I didn't know what to say.

She shrugged. "Let's call it a miracle then."

And I realized it was. Somehow, Penelope was changing me.

"Amelia," Penelope said. "We're going to call her Amelia."

"What if it's not a girl?" I asked.

"It's a girl," she said. "I can feel her."

"You are my grace," I told her, and we kissed there, in a sudden shower of cherry blossom petals, as the people around us cheered and lifted their drinks to the heavens.

LOST IN THE GREAT LIBRARY

When I went out into the parking lot in Detroit, the only car left was mine. None of the others had stuck around to see which one of us exited the factory. No honour among thieves and collectors, I guess.

I got in the car and just sat there for a moment. I felt drained after the battle with Sut. I'd already burned up much of the grace I'd taken from Remiel, and I had little to show for it so far. If this kept up, I was going to have to find another angel soon.

I sighed, started up the car and drove it back to the airport. The same woman was working at the rental counter. She gave me the once-over, and I realized my clothes were dirty and torn from the fight in the factory. There was probably blood on my face too, both mine and Sut's.

"So, it was a pleasure trip rather than business, was it?" she said.

"A little of both," I said and took the paperwork she gave me to fill out.

Back in the airport, I booked a flight to Seattle. Sut hadn't given me much in the way of useful information because he wasn't able to but there weren't any spells cast on his wallet. He had a driver's licence with an address on it: 2 Genesis Way. Cute. Another clue to what I was facing, no doubt, but not enough of one to actually figure out anything useful. I doubted the djinn would have its own place separate from its master, so that meant Sut's address was probably Edwards's address as well. And if not, well, I was getting good at figuring out things as I went.

I boarded the plane along with all the people who probably hadn't fought a djinn tonight and took my seat near the back. Someday I was

189

going to fly first class again. Someday. But for now I slipped back into veteran soldier mode and curled up in my seat as best I could to get some sleep.

I didn't wake again until the plane's tires touched the ground in Seattle. I shuffled off the plane along with everybody who probably still hadn't fought a djinn. I rented a car from another woman at another rental agency. This time, just for fun, I used Sut's credit card. I hoped he could feel that in his oil can.

I sat in the car in the parking lot and searched for 2 Genesis Way on my phone, but it told me there was no such address. So much for that.

I wasn't surprised. If it were easy, Cassiel wouldn't need me to do his dirty work for him.

I started the car and headed out of the parking lot. It was time to hit the library.

I drove to the central branch and parked on the street. I didn't bother putting money in the meter. Let them ticket me. Or rather, let them ticket Sut.

The central branch of the Seattle Public Library system – what to say about the central branch? A gleaming edifice of glass and steel angles, it loomed above the street and the people walking past like a collapsing office building. I'd once thought it was everything a library shouldn't be, but I'd come to terms with it over the years and now I even had a certain affection for it. Life is change and all that.

I went inside and browsed the fiction section. I looked for misshelved books. I opened one, read the first paragraph, then put it back and repeated the process with the next one. I got the usual looks from passing library staff, but luckily whoever was in charge of the universe now was kind to me that day. I'd only been at it for a few hours when I found a copy of Calvino's *Invisible Cities* shelved out of place in the A section. I flipped it open and read a random passage: *I entered the great library, I became lost among shelves collapsing under the vellum bindings, I followed the alphabetical order of vanished alphabets, up and down halls, stairs, bridges.*

As soon as I put the book back on the shelf I heard Alice singing "Ring Around the Rosy" in the next aisle.

"Ashes, ashes," she sang, as I came around to her side. "We all fall down."

She was wearing a bloody hospital gown and sitting on the floor, building a house of cards, only it was made of books she pulled from the shelves. She'd reached waist height with it. I was particularly impressed by the balconies.

"I dreamed about you," she said. She squinted at me as if she thought maybe I was a dream now. Who knew? Maybe I was.

I sat down across from her and studied the house. It wasn't quite a mansion, but it would be close enough for most people.

"What did you dream?" I asked.

"Apocalypse, apocalypse," she sang. "We all fell down."

"Sounds more like a nightmare," I said.

"Nightmares are fun." She giggled. "But this was . . ." She chewed on the end of a strand of hair and frowned at the house. "What's the opposite of fun?"

"Apocalypse?" I suggested.

She pointed at me. "That's exactly what it was. All the things that end the world decided to end the world together."

"There are a lot of things that can end the world," I pointed out.

"The Midgard Serpent," she said. "The fifth horseman of the apocalypse. The drowned god under the sea. You tried to save everyone from them."

"I don't do that sort of thing anymore," I said.

"Yes, you do," she said, frowning. "I saw you."

"It was just a dream," I said.

"But it actually happened," she said. "It just hasn't happened yet."

I shook my head. Having a conversation with Alice was like falling down the rabbit hole.

"I need your help," I told her.

"That's why I dressed up," she said, pointing at her hospital gown.

"I don't suppose you know where Judas is," I said.

"Of course I do," she said. "He's in the apocalypse."

Yeah. Well. That didn't surprise me at all.

Time to get on with things.

"What do you know about Jonathan Edwards?" I asked.

She chewed on her hair some more. "Is this a test?" she asked. "Because

191

they have those metal boxes that answer these questions now."

"You mean computers?" I said. "I don't think they're going to have the Edwards I'm looking for. He's at least four hundred years old and has a fondness for quoting the bible."

She clapped her hands together. "I know who you mean!" she said. She pulled one of the books from her stack and handed it to me, and the house wobbled a bit. I looked at the title: *Sinners in the Hands of an Angry God.* By Jonathan Edwards. I opened the book and flipped through it. It was a sermon. The title pretty much summed up the subject.

"Edwards was a preacher?" I said.

"Uh, don't you know all the preachers?" Alice asked. "I mean, aren't they all talking to you?"

"Maybe, but I haven't been listening," I said. On principle, I tried to avoid priests and churches and that sort of thing unless I was hunting angels. One too many misunderstandings.

"Well, you'll like him then," Alice said. "He's dead. It says so right there in the book."

I flipped to the biographical information. An illustration of a stern-looking man gazed out at me. It was true – according to what I read, he died in 1758.

"I don't think this is my man," I said.

"It's him," Alice said. "Books never lie. Except for when they do."

"Do you have any other books about him?" I asked. "Maybe some secret histories that haven't been published?"

But she just coughed up a hairball and then went back to building her house of books without saying anything. So much for Alice providing all the answers to my mystery.

I looked around and saw a library clerk standing at the end of the aisle. She shook her head at us and walked away, no doubt going off in search of a security guard. We didn't have much time left.

"All right, forget that," I said. "I need help finding an address instead."

Alice clapped her hands together. "Oh, I like hide-and-seek."

"I don't need that kind of help," I said. "I need a map."

She pouted at me. "But you can get a map anywhere," she said. "You don't need my help for that."

"Yes, I do," I said. "This address doesn't show up on any map. Two Genesis Way. Here in the city." Then, for her benefit, I added, "Seattle."

"It does so show up on a map," she said. She shoved the house of books and it fell apart in a jumbled mess. In the centre of the ruins was a vellum scroll. I picked it up and unrolled it. It was a road map of Seattle, but it was hand drawn, and the ink looked like blood. The scroll appeared to be a few hundred years old, but the map was up to date. Well, Alice had shown me stranger things before.

There was no index, so I scanned the map until I found what I was looking for. A rendering of a nail, the end pointing at a blank patch of land by the water. It was also drawn in blood. There were no other distinguishing marks anywhere on the map, so I took this to be a sign. But maybe that's just because I hate nails. I never have been any good at carpentry.

I rolled the scroll up and tucked it into my shirt. "I owe you," I told her.

"And you'll repay me one day," she said. Then she went skipping off down the aisle, singing over and over, "We all fall down."

And that was Alice again.

I got to my feet and went down the aisle in the opposite direction before the security guards showed up. When I went out the exit, I half expected the alarm to ring because of the scroll tucked into my shirt. But nothing happened. Just another ordinary trip to the library.

It was raining outside, but my mood was improved somewhat by seeing a parking ticket under my windshield wiper. This day just kept getting better.

Back in the car, I took out the map and looked at it again. Then I put it in the glove compartment for later. I wasn't going to Edwards's place right away. I had someplace else I wanted to visit first.

THE END OF THE WORLD

All right.

This is how Penelope died.

This is how I couldn't save her.

Penelope and I toured the cities of Japan looking for the angels but we were unable to find a sign of even one of them. We didn't carry the camera gear in public anymore. We didn't want to attract any attention. Now that the Americans had started firebombing cities, people were growing suspicious of each other. That was always the way once your side started to lose. No one wanted to believe the enemy was simply better or more technologically advanced. Or worse, had God on their side. Like he'd ever taken sides.

We would have to leave soon if we didn't find anything. I worried about Penelope's safety here, and the safety of our unborn child. If anything happened to me and I wasn't able to maintain the sleight and people could see what she really looked like . . . I wondered if the postcards in Montparnasse had been another trap, to lead us away from the angels instead of to them. To lead us into harm's way. I wondered if Penelope's father was behind it.

We spent so much time in trains and graveyards that I lost track of what city we were in. We stopped at another European-style Christian church that was just as nondescript and generic as all the others in the country. There were no Notre Dames here, no Westminster Abbeys. There was just the Nagarekawa church – a small, humble structure for a small, humble sect.

We arrived there early in the morning. We were following our first possible hint of angels. A ticket agent at the train station had told me she'd heard the sounds of wings flapping over the city for two days even though the sky was empty. It wasn't much – she may even have been mad – but it was something at least. I hoped the local priest would have more to offer us. I wanted to find Penelope's father and kill him so we could leave Japan and head back to Europe, or maybe America. I just wanted to live with my family.

We went into the church and looked for someone else to question. There was only one other person inside, a priest who stood in the sanctuary, staring up at the stained glass windows. Penelope sat in one of the pews to rest while I went over to talk to him. She was already showing with Amelia, and it was growing harder for her to walk around.

"Pardon me, but I have an odd request," I said as I approached the priest. I gambled on speaking English, because I still couldn't manage enough Japanese to speak the words I wanted to ask him. "Have you heard the sounds of wings over the city lately?"

He didn't turn to face me. He didn't even look away from the windows. "It is the sound of the angels gathering to witness the end," he said.

I knew that voice. It was the same voice that had rung in my ears when I'd been born. When I'd died in the sands of the Colosseum. When the dragon had nearly taken me. I grabbed his arm and spun him around to face me.

He was a man I'd never seen before, just another man, and for a few seconds I thought I'd made a mistake. I thought perhaps I was imagining things. But then he changed before my eyes. His eyes turned black and his skin withered to that leathery corpse look. The priest's robes hung on him like they would have hung on a skeleton.

Judas.

"Hello, monkey," he said, smiling. "It's been a while."

I moved on reflex, my body acting before my mind could. I grabbed him by the throat and slammed him down on the altar, so hard the wood cracked in two. So hard I would have crushed his throat if he were a normal man.

But he wasn't a normal man. He was Judas.

I screamed at him, because it was the only sound I could make. It was a mix of rage and joy. I didn't recognize the noise I made, but I must have asked him why he was here, because he told me.

"I am here to witness history," he said. "To watch your kind wreak the kind of havoc I can only dream about."

I didn't let go of him, even when he started shifting his appearance in my grasp. He went from that simple man who had befriended Christ to the Roman soldier who'd gouged out my eyes. Then he became Commodus again. Then the priest from the Spanish Inquisition who'd burned all those villages and men of learning as I followed his trail across the land, then the merchant sailor I'd chased through Greece after he brought the Black Death into Europe. He kept changing, becoming men and women I didn't recognize, but who I had no doubt he had been at one point or another in human history.

"Your kind doesn't even need me anymore," he added. "You are your own destruction now."

I grabbed a piece of the broken altar and ripped it free. I raised it over my head like a stake, ready to ram it through his heart, and he suddenly changed into Penelope.

I hesitated.

And the world became undone in that moment.

I looked over my shoulder to make sure Penelope was still there. She was, but she was on her feet again, halfway to Judas and me.

"Cross!" she said. I half expected her to ask what was going on, and for a second I considered how to answer that. Then I saw she held her stomach in a way that could only mean there was something wrong.

I looked back down at Judas again. Now he was me.

"Kill me and you'll never have the answers you seek," he said.

I thought about killing him anyway. About killing myself. I'd become a different man since Penelope had found me. Maybe it was time to put the past to rest. Maybe it was time to put all my questions to rest.

But the decision was made for me before I could choose.

All the stained glass windows suddenly shattered, and wind howled into the church. The air filled with the sounds of a mighty beating of wings, and Penelope's cries and my own were lost in it. I threw myself to her, to protect her from whatever was happening. Her and Amelia.

I threw myself away from Judas with a curse of frustration.

I knew something bad was about to happen. If Judas was here, something very bad was about to happen.

"What is it?" I said to Penelope, holding her in my arms.

"I don't know," she said, looking down at her stomach. She was as pale as I'd ever seen her. "Amelia. Oh my God."

But God wasn't there to help us. There was only me.

I turned back to Judas, shielding her with my body.

"What have you done this time?" I screamed.

"I've done nothing," he said. He continued to change as he stood. Now he was a Japanese man, a Japanese woman. They were all naked, their skin melted with burns. "Your kind has done it on their own this time. They have become the gods of death." He laughed, but it wasn't the kind of laugh that had any joy in it.

I pulled Penelope outside. There'd be time to deal with Judas later. Judas would always be there. Right now, I had to get Penelope and Amelia away from whatever was about to happen.

But it was too late.

Outside, it was snowing. No, not snow. Pieces of paper. I caught one of them in my hand. A fragment of a postcard – a tree done in ink in the suibokuga style. One of the postcards we'd found back in the Montparnasse Cemetery.

It was a trap. Japan was a trap. But I still didn't understand what kind of trap.

"What is it?" Penelope cried, looking at the snow. And then she couldn't speak at all when the angels started falling from the sky. They filled the air. Hundreds of them. No, thousands. It looked to be every angel left alive, although some of them were so ragged and skeletal I wasn't sure they actually were alive. They were all in their heavenly incarnations – naked, winged men and women with swords and spears and axes that glowed or burned with fire or dripped the venom of older, dead gods. They landed on the roof of the church, and in the yard, perching on the fence and the water fountains and the trees. The earth and stone and wood under their feet smoked, and their wings formed little whirlwinds of fire in the air.

They stared at us but didn't say anything. If they were here for me, there were too many of them to defeat. But if they were here for me, they would have attacked already. Which meant they were here for something else. And whatever else it was had to be something truly terrible to attract this many angels.

"It's the end of an age," Judas said, following us outside. He was still an ever-changing crowd of burned Japanese people.

"Why did you bring us here?" I asked him. I kept myself between him and Penelope. I was still struggling to understand what he was up to.

"The child," he said, and he became a young girl, then a young boy. Their bodies were melted and covered in burns as well.

I spat on the ground between us. My rage was so powerful the ground caught fire where it hit.

"You will not harm my child or Penelope," I said. "I will not allow it."

"It is true I won't harm them," Judas said, looking up at the sky. "But that is meaningless. The child will fall to the same fate as the rest of us. It is as much an abomination as we are."

"Cross," Penelope said. "Who is he?"

But I had no way of answering that. Not really.

"She is a miracle," I said to Judas instead.

"That's what I just said." He chuckled. He looked at the angels, then back at me. "She redeems you, doesn't she?"

"They both redeem me," I said. "Enough that I'm done with you now. I swear, and this is the only time I'll make this offer, but I swear that I am done with you if you just leave us be."

Judas looked at me, and for a moment there was only the sound of the angels' wings. When he spoke next, his voice was almost a sigh.

"That's why I've brought you here," he said. "I cannot abide a redeemed Christ, or even the shell of Christ, any more than I can abide a redeemed humanity. For, one day, you may give them hope again. You may give them peace once more. I cannot *allow* that."

"We're leaving," I said and pulled Penelope toward the street. There were angels in our way, a pair of ebony giants with spears made of even darker bone. I didn't recognize them at all. "We'll take care of your father later. We have all eternity to find him." I didn't add that I no longer cared if we found him. I just wanted to get her and Amelia away from there.

"We don't," Penelope said, looking around. "I don't think we have any time left at all." There were tears on her cheeks as she laid a hand on my face.

"I won't let you die," I said. "Not when you're with me."

"Don't," she said, shaking her head. "Promise me."

I stopped and looked down at her. I didn't want to speak for fear of what she might say. But she said it anyway.

"Promise me that when I die you won't bring me back to life," she said.

I stared at her. "But we can have forever," I said.

"I don't want to be like him," she said. "I want to be human."

And there was nothing I could say to that. So instead I turned back to the angels. "Get the hell out of our way," I said to the ones holding the spears, and they stepped out of our path and bowed.

Too late. Far too late.

"Cross," Penelope said, staring up at the sky. A lone plane flew high above the angels. The sun glinted on something falling from it. Something metallic. "Oh God," she said.

It was too late to run. So I shielded her with my body as best as I could. And I prayed for the first time in many, many years. I prayed for protection. Not for me but for Penelope and Amelia.

"The gods are all gone," Judas said, and now he was himself again. He looked to the sky, and for a moment he looked bent and weary with age, and very, very alone despite the crowd. "Only we remain."

And then the angels all screamed in unison, a terrible noise that tore the sky open, and then Hell erupted all around us and through us.

And that was Hiroshima.

THE WAR AMONG THE ANGELS

I drove out of Seattle and headed north for a couple of hours. I took a side road off the highway, then turned off that onto a dirt road, then turned off that onto an overgrown trail. The car scraped along rocks and tree roots, and branches clawed at the side of the car. Sut's credit card was going to get a real workout with the rental agency. The trail ended at an abandoned farm. The same farm where Penelope had left her car so long ago. The roof of the house had collapsed and the fields were overgrown. A deer ran away at the sight of me. There were three leaning crosses in the yard now. I gave them a moment of silence, which is as close as I come to prayer these days, and then hiked into the woods.

I moved quicker now that I was on my own and not slowed by Penelope and her camera equipment. I reached the shack I'd shared with her as the sun was setting, turning the sky amber.

I hadn't been back here since we'd left. I was surprised to find the place looked much the same as before, only now it was lost in the shrubs and young trees where there'd once been a clearing. A dead, fallen tree leaned against the roof, buckling it, but it hadn't caved in yet.

Memories and longing welled up inside me and mingled as I approached the shack. I thought maybe the longing was for Penelope, until I opened the door and stepped through.

The inside looked the same as I remembered it, too: the simple bed in the corner, the wooden plank on stones we used for a table still set with chipped cups, the clotheslines on the walls where Penelope had hung her photos. It should have been overrun with insects by now, everything rotted away, but it looked the same as the day we'd left it. That may have had something to do with the angel standing in the centre of the room.

He'd gone with the classic look: naked, feathered wings, radiant skin, flowing hair. I realized as soon as I saw him that the longing I felt was for his grace, not Penelope, and I cursed him even though I didn't recognize him.

He put up his hands in peace, and I saw he was unarmed. For whatever that was worth.

"I am not your enemy," the angel said. "I am Aigra. I am your salvation."

"That's funny," I said. "I thought I was my own salvation." I risked a glance over my shoulder, back outside, but I didn't see anyone else. Which didn't mean much, of course.

I searched my memory but his name meant nothing to me. He must have been a minor angel. Or he was lying. Or who knows?

"So, Aigra," I said, "what are you doing here?"

"I am waiting," he said. "As I have been for countless days and nights. Ever since you journeyed away from this sanctuary." He looked around. "I have preserved it for you."

I considered him. Something I didn't understand was going on here. In other words, business as usual. "What have you been waiting for?" I asked him.

"For you," he said.

If he was here to ambush me, that would have been a good line to attack on. But he didn't do anything, just dropped his hands back to his sides and watched me.

I shifted a little to the right, so I was no longer standing in the open doorway. Just in case anyone was sneaking up on me from behind.

"And what do you want with me?" I asked.

"I want nothing but to serve you, my lord," he said. "I am here to offer myself to you."

"That's very generous," I said, "but I'm not really interested in sidekicks."

"You misunderstand me," he said. "I mean I offer my grace to you."

I'd met many angels in my time, and learned there were as many personality types among them as there were among people: there were the

201

warlike ones and the scholarly ones, the passionate ones and the cold, calculating ones. But I'd never before met a suicidal angel.

"If you were looking to kill yourself, you could have come found me a long time ago," I said. "I haven't exactly been hiding from your kind."

"I am not seeking to simply kill myself," he said. "I am here to provide you with aid. We have a common enemy, after all."

"We?" I said.

"The Fallen," he said. "Those of us who have been left here by God to fulfill the Plan." I could tell from the way he pronounced things that he was capitalizing them. Everyone seemed to be capitalizing things these days.

"I hate to break it to you, but I don't think there is a plan," I said. "I think we're all on our own now."

"Have you become one of them then?" he asked, and he looked surprised. It was the first time his expression changed.

"One of who?" I asked.

"The Risen," he said.

I sighed. "Look, I can't keep track of your guys' little cliques at the best of times. Just break down for me what's going on and who the major actors are."

Aigra blinked a couple of times and his wings spread a little. Then he nodded and folded his wings back in. "There is a new war among the angels," he said. "We are divided into camps."

I waited. Nothing new there. The angels were always looking for reasons to get into fights with one another. Sometimes they made up, sometimes they found their own corner of the world or elsewhere to sulk and torture lost souls for eternity. Sometimes, apparently, they hid in abandoned shacks for decades.

"We started off all Fallen," Aigra went on. "Those of us left behind when God hid himself. We waited patiently for his return, and we watched the events of the world but we did not act upon them. Like God, we remained outside of history. And at first our only debates were whether he would be wrathful or forgiving of his subjects when he came back. But then some grew impatient."

I swear night fell in that instant. But I could still see thanks to Aigra's glowing skin.

"They ventured fantasies that God wouldn't return, that he was gone forever for reasons we'd never know. They read us Nietzsche and Beckett and said these men were the new prophets. They said God had sundered the world with his absence. They said it was our job to repair it. They said it was time to intervene again."

"Let me guess," I said. "They became these Risen characters you mentioned. And I'm betting the name means they're the type who want to get biblical on the world."

Aigra nodded once. "They want to recreate Heaven on earth. They seek to supplant God." His wings flared out again. "They seek to supplant you."

"Well, they can have my job," I told him. "I quit a long time ago."

"They are cleansing the world," he went on.

"Cleansing it?" I asked. Yes, it was definitely darker now.

"Removing all those beings that never had a place in Heaven," Aigra said. "The minotaurs, the sirens, the ones that must not be named. They slay those they cannot remove."

"What do you mean 'remove'?" I asked. "Where are they taking them?"

He shrugged. "We don't know. Those taken by the Risen are never seen again."

I was beginning to get a bad feeling about this.

"They will not rest until the earth is naught but Heaven and human," Aigra said. "The angels and their subjects."

Alice, I thought. The gorgons. The faerie. And all the others.

"It is not our duty to protect them," Aigra said, as if reading my mind. "Nor could we if we chose such a path. The Risen have grown too strong."

"What do you care what the Risen do?" I asked. "I would have thought such a world would suit you just fine."

"It is obviously not God's intention or he would have made it so," Aigra said. "The Risen are perverting the Plan."

"And I suppose you want my help in fighting them," I said. I moved around to the wall that had served as our kitchen. Cups and plates still sat on a wooden shelf. I blew dust off them while looking for the knives.

Aigra didn't turn to follow me. "You are our lord," he said. "We will do as you desire."

"I'm not who you think I am," I said, automatically. There. A knife with a six-inch blade sitting on top of the old wood-burning stove.

"You are the closest we have to God," Aigra said.

I sighed. Sometimes there's just no talking to angels.

"And who have the Risen chosen to fill in for God?" I asked. "I'm guessing it's not me, or I would have got the memo by now." I picked up the knife and looked at it. The blade looked like it had been sharpened recently.

"They see you as a corruption that needs to be purged," Aigra said. "They have elected one of their own to rule, another Lucifer." He spat on the ground. "He has taken on a human name to express his supposed humility and devotion. His servitude. His name is Edwards. Jonathan Edwards."

I leaned against the stove and studied Aigra's back. It was all coming together. And yes, I had a very bad feeling about this. What had Cassiel gotten me into?

Of course, Aigra being an angel, there was a distinct possibility he was lying to me.

"Tell me," I said, "why didn't you seek me out before this?"

"There was no point," Aigra said. "We have had few dealings with you since the Resurrection, and little access to your heart and soul. We didn't know if you would be interested in fighting against the Risen or with them. Or fighting for anything."

That one stung a little, but only because it rang true.

"I volunteered to wait for you here after you left," Aigra went on. "Because I believed you might come back in a time of need, when you would be willing to listen to my words. When my sacrifice would not be in vain."

A thought occurred to me, and the knife grew light in my hand.

"How did you know about this place?" I asked.

"You grew careless when you were with her," Aigra said. "We were able to watch you unnoticed. We discussed approaching you then, but we believed you would not have gone to war against the Risen when you were in love. You would not have willingly let go of that life. So we continued to wait and watch. We lost you for a time after the chaos of Hiroshima. That's when I came here and readied myself for you. We have come across you from time to time since then, of course, but we kept our distance. You were much changed after that day, and your thoughts were writing in the dark to us. I remained here. I knew you would come in a time of need."

I thought about the angels hidden away somewhere during all those moments I had with Penelope, and I grew still inside. "You're going to have to wait a while longer," I said. "I'm not going to kill you. And I'm not going to help you in your fight. I've got business of my own with Edwards, but it's just business. I'm going to settle it on my terms, and it won't have anything to do with you or the Risen or anything else. You and your plan can rot in Hell with that other bunch of Fallen."

Aigra didn't say anything.

I meant what I said. I wanted his grace but I wasn't desperate for it. I could walk away from here and leave him waiting for another hundred years. Only this time I wouldn't come back. I'd make him long for me like I longed for Penelope.

I stuck the knife into the wall and started for the door, but he stopped me halfway across the room.

"We could have saved her," he said.

I couldn't help but look at him again.

"We saw her death," he said. "We were there when it was made. When the mortals dreamed the dreams of seraphim and conceived the bomb. When they sent it on its way to you in that lonely plane. We were there when she died. We knew how much you loved her. We could have shielded her. We could have spirited her away from the fires, as a gift to you. We could have brought her back here for you."

I didn't say anything. What was there to say to that?

"We need you angry," he said. "So we let her die." He dropped to his knees. "We need you wrathful, so we let her die."

I stared at him for a moment. He kept on looking ahead, out the door, at the stars that were beginning to show outside. Then I went back for the knife.

And I was wrathful. I was very wrathful.

AND THE GRAVES WERE OPENED

I awoke with a mouthful of dirt.
   I was buried in a grave somewhere.
   I reached out for Penelope, for Judas, for anyone, but there was no one.
   And I screamed to find myself alive and alone again.

LET THERE BE LIGHT

When I was done with Aigra I hiked back to the car. The rage was still with me, despite everything I had done to him. I found myself on the hill with the bones that Penelope had photographed that day. I tore them from the ground and threw them deep into the forest, one after the other, until I couldn't see them anymore. I smashed trees out of my path as I went, and the ones that were too large to smash I lit on fire with my burning hands. I turned the forest into ash and smoke, and my memories along with it. I burned the forest. I wanted to burn all of God's creation.

The heat of the flames stung my eyes, and I felt tears on my cheeks for the first time in ages. I tried to stop them, but then the feelings inside me welled up and I wept there in the burning woods, while still screaming my rage and frustration.

I wept for what the angels had done to me, and what I had done to them.

I wept for what I'd been and what I'd become. I wept for everything I had lost.

I wept for Penelope.

I wept for Amelia.

I made it back to the car as the sky in front of me began to lighten again. The sky behind me was a red haze. I sat behind the wheel and took a few deep breaths to compose myself once again. Then I started the car and headed off to find Edwards.

THERE WAS SILENCE IN HEAVEN

I died and Penelope died and Amelia died.
  I couldn't save them.

JUDAS MAKES A
SURPRISE APPEARANCE

I followed the map Alice had given me to a neighbourhood of luxury homes overlooking Puget Sound on the outskirts of Seattle. They were the sort of places that had metal gates sealing off their driveways and garages so large they could have housed families. I half expected to be arrested by private security guards at any moment.

I couldn't see a street sign for Genesis Way anywhere, but I didn't really expect it to be marked. I found it anyway by driving around and pulling over every few minutes to check my progress against the map. Whoever had inked it had been dead accurate.

Genesis Way was a long, winding paved road behind another gate. It climbed a hill at the water's edge, disappearing behind some trees and emerging again at the top of the hill and ending at a house. It was one of those houses that was all windows – you could see right through it to the cloudy sky on the other side. I've always been wary of such places. As much as you can look inside them, the residents can watch you. Sometimes you couldn't ask for a better surveillance system than 360-degree windows.

There were no numbers on the gate but there was only one house up there, so I figured that was it. I parked the car and studied the place for a moment but I couldn't see any movement or light in any of the windows. No one was home. Or maybe they were but wanted people to think they weren't. Or maybe they were just out buying groceries. Only one way to find out. I got out of the car and popped the gate open with a little bit of all that grace I had and went up the hill to the house.

I was grateful for the fact there were no guard dogs. There always used to be guard dogs in the days before security cameras. Most people think the cameras are better, but trust me, guard dogs are much more difficult to deal with than cameras. I didn't see any cameras either. Which didn't mean they weren't there, of course. But it didn't matter that much – I'd cast a sleight on myself in the car to make me appear like Sut. The faithful servant returns home.

It took me a moment to find the door, because it was glass, too. The only thing that gave it away was a small metal handle. I stood in front of it and looked inside the house for a moment. It looked like every other rich person's multimillion-dollar house on a multimillion-dollar location: couches and chairs made out of some sort of moulded plastic, abstract metal shapes on tables – sculptures or garbage, I wasn't sure which – a couple of telescopes on stands by the windows on the water side. And still no lights or people.

I tried the door, but it was locked of course. I shrugged and hit the doorbell. Sometimes the only option is the best option.

No lights turned on, and no people came to investigate who had wandered to the end of their lonely road.

I grabbed the door handle and let some grace flow from my hand into it. There was no sound at all. Expensive lock. I opened the door and stepped inside.

Into an entirely different house.

I stood in a living room with cozy wooden walls lined with bookshelves. A fire blazed happily away in the fireplace in one wall. The couches and chairs were plush, with cushions that looked as if you might actually want to sit on them. The tables held bottles of wine and other spirits. There wasn't a window anywhere, although old landscape paintings hung where they might be. There was no sign of anything I'd seen from outside.

I paused and looked back through the door. The road I'd come up was still there. As was Puget Sound and the city and everything else. It was just the inside of the house that had changed.

I stepped back outside and looked through the windows. The same, empty modern house with no bookshelves or paintings or fireplace. But when I looked through the door I could see the other place there, waiting for me. I checked for the things I'd usually check for in such a situation, but I couldn't detect any sign of a sleight. It looked like both places were real. You see something new every day.

My options hadn't changed any so I stepped back inside the house and closed the door behind me. It would have been nice to leave the door open as an escape route, but I figured that's not the sort of thing a loyal employee like Sut would do.

I waited for a moment but no one came to welcome me. There was no sound but the crackle of the fire. I pulled out a few of the books on the shelves – they were handbound tomes. Religious texts, mainly, although there was a copy of Aristotle's *Poetics of Comedy* and a slim untitled book by Thomas More that was the real reason he was beheaded. I didn't know any copies of that one still existed.

I put them back on the shelves and glanced at the paintings. Then looked at them longer, for I recognized them. Rembrandt's *The Night Watch*. Lorrain's *Seaport at Sunset*. Turner's *Shipwreck of the Minotaur*. Constable's *Hadleigh Castle*. If I wasn't mistaken, they were the originals. Curiouser and curiouser.

I moved on to the next room, a dining room with a long wooden table set with places for a dozen people. The china held a pattern of fighting dragons. It looked so old it may have come from China itself. The silverware was tarnished with age. The dust everywhere was so thick I could have written my name in it.

The kitchen looked about as used as the dining room, but at least there were a few touches of modernity here: A restaurant-grade stove. A metal refrigerator the size of a small car. I opened it and looked inside, but it was empty. I began to wonder if anyone lived here at all.

I found an answer to that question on the second floor, which was interesting on its own because I didn't remember seeing a second floor from outside the house. In the first bedroom I looked into I found a man sleeping on a bed. The room was empty of everything but the bed – no dresser, no laundry basket, not even a window. The bed was one of those ornate affairs with large posters and a dozen silk pillows, which suited the man because he was wearing the breeches and shirt of an Elizabethan man.

I grabbed him by the shoulder and tried to shake him awake, but he didn't respond. He didn't even stir. I pulled him up into a sitting position, slapped his cheeks, opened his eyes and looked inside, but he gave no response. I did note, however, that his ring finger was missing, just a stump showing where it had been cut off.

I laid him back down. I was willing to bet money that he was a faerie, and he wasn't responding because he was off in the glamour. But given the absence of his ring finger, I suspected he wasn't in Morgana's court. He'd literally severed his tie to her – or someone had done it for him.

I didn't know what that meant. I explored the other bedrooms, but they were just as empty as the rest of the place. All they held were beds that looked as if they'd never been slept in and closets with nothing in them. No windows, no phones, no computers, nothing to connect this place to the outside world.

I went back to the first room to wait for something to happen. I leaned against a bookshelf and watched the fire for a while. I poured myself a Scotch – an eighty-year-old Macallan Angels' Share, if I wasn't mistaken. Edwards had taste as well as money.

I stepped up to Constable's *Hadleigh Castle* and studied it. I'd seen it a number of times over the years, and it was one of my favourites – something about the way the castle overlooking the Thames had crumbled into ruins, with the storm clouds overhead threatening to finish it off. Maybe I identified with the shepherd and his dog wandering the desolation. Or maybe it was just wishful thinking about the fate of the Royal Family. Either way, I knew the painting well, right down to the individual brushstrokes. If this was a knockoff, it had been created by a master forger.

"It's real, if that's what you're wondering," a familiar voice said from behind me. Or rather, familiar voices.

I turned to find a corpse in a suit standing behind me. No, not a corpse. Judas. He just looked like a corpse because he was letting his true nature show. I was so surprised to see him here that I didn't even move. But I wasn't surprised enough to miss the gun in his hand. As usual when guns are involved, it was pointed in my direction. That was the only thing that stopped me from leaping across the distance between us and tearing out his throat for real this time. But it wouldn't stop me for long.

"They're all real," he went on, nodding at the other paintings. "The ones in the art galleries are the reproductions."

For some reason, he didn't seem interested in catching up on events with me. He didn't even call me "little monkey." I remembered I looked like Sut, but I didn't drop the sleight. I'd been in enough situations like this – all right, not quite like *this* – to know something felt wrong here. I decided to stay in character a bit longer.

"This is private property," I said. "I'm going to have to call the police."

Okay, it wasn't the wittiest comment I'd ever made, but I *was* taken by surprise. And I was puzzled that I didn't feel the usual things I felt when I encountered Judas. Rage, confusion, emptiness, the desire to murder like I have never murdered. Instead, I felt . . . hungry.

Judas chuckled. "Sorry, Cross," he said, "but when Sut didn't check in I contacted him and found out what you did. You may as well stop wasting your grace."

So much for hiding Sut away for a thousand years. Well, it wasn't the first time a plan hadn't worked out. I dropped the sleight and let myself look like myself again. I watched Judas closely to see how he'd react. He just smiled and blinked a couple of times as my appearance changed.

"You look like hell," he said. "Almost as bad as the last time I saw you."

"Remind me when that was again," I said.

"The Crucifixion," he said. "But I wouldn't expect you to remember such a minor event as that."

Yeah, all right. Things were starting to come together.

"Well, that's where I have a problem," I said. "Because you look like Judas, but I've seen him since the Crucifixion."

"Oh, of course – the disguise." He chuckled. And then he changed appearances in front of me, becoming a thin, skeletal man. He looked almost identical to the man in the book Alice had given me in the library, once you factored in artistic licence. Unfortunately, he still held the gun. I guess it wasn't part of his disguise. "I've become so used to wearing him that I forgot," he said.

"Jonathan Edwards, I presume," I said.

"Yes," he said. "And you're Jesus Christ."

"Not really," I said.

"No, not really," he said.

That was why I felt the way I did – he was an angel, not Judas.

And I could sense his grace, which is why I felt hungry instead of angry. So that cleared some things up. Although not why he was pretending to be Judas.

"How about we skip the witty banter and you tell me what you're doing," I suggested.

"Certainly," he said. "I'm killing you." And then he shot me in the heart three times.

I've been shot before. In fact, I've lost count of the number of times I've been shot. Musket balls, shotgun pellets, AK-47 rounds – I've been intimate with all of them. And one thing remains the same: they all hurt like nothing you've ever known. Except for the ones that don't hurt. They're the ones that kill you. They don't hurt because you're already dead, and one of God's few mercies is you don't feel the things that kill you.

Edwards's shots didn't hurt at all. Nothing hurt as I fell back to the floor, hitting my head on the edge of the bookshelf. I tasted blood in my mouth but the blood didn't hurt either. I had enough presence of mind to know I was in trouble, but I couldn't even summon up grace to heal myself.

Shit. Not again.

I couldn't look away from Constable's castle until Edwards stepped into my line of sight again and stood over me. He pointed the gun at my head and smiled some more.

Goddamn, I hated angels.

"I don't understand why people pray to you," he said. "You're such a disappointment." Then he pulled the trigger, and I saw the light at the end of the tunnel once more.

MORGANA GIVES BIRTH TO AN IMPOSSIBLE CHILD

I was back in the faerie pub. I had a drink in my hand but I didn't remember ordering it. I didn't remember how I'd got there. I didn't even remember what year it was. My drink tasted like embalming fluid but I drank it down anyway and waved my hand at the bartender for another.

But for once he didn't serve me because he was busy looking at the stage. Everyone in the pub was looking at the stage. The musicians were gone, even though I could still hear them playing somewhere. A slow, deep number I didn't recognize that sounded like a funeral dirge.

Morgana was on the stage now, lying in the bed from her chambers. She was naked and I saw she was full term with the child. She writhed on the sheets and screamed, and that's when I realized she was giving birth.

And then everyone else around me screamed too, echoing her cry. I looked around but no one moved to help her. So I pushed my way through the crowd and climbed up on the stage.

Despite all the years I'd spent alive, I'd never helped anyone give birth before. But how hard could it be?

"Cross," Morgana hissed at the sight of me, and everyone in the pub hissed my name too. It was more than a little unnerving. I looked down at her and saw her belly moving. No, twisting and shaking. Like something inside was fighting to get out, not coming out naturally.

"Forgive me for drawing you away from whatever it was you were doing," said Morgana, smiling at me, "but I thought you might want to be present for the birth of your child." The words sounded even creepier coming out of the mouths of all the fey.

"Don't you have a doctor in here?" I asked, looking around. "All these people and you never bothered to ensnare a doctor?"

"We have no need of physicians," Morgana said, and screamed again. Now I saw it was a scream of delight, not pain. She arched her back, and the baby inside her *surged* down, heading for the exit.

"What do I do?" I asked. I went to take her hand to offer what support I could, but she pushed me away, laughing.

"Hold your child," she said, and the crowd repeated her command.

And then the baby was there, slipping out of Morgana in a stream of blood and more black rings and scraps of parchment and pieces of quartz and snakes that slithered away.

I reached for the baby, but stopped when I saw it. And then, before Morgana let me slip back into death, I screamed.

IN A LITTLE WHILE WE
SHALL ALL BE DEAD

Dying doesn't hurt, not really.

Resurrecting, that's what hurts.

Imagine the pins and needles you get in your arm when it falls asleep. Imagine that feeling in each one of your limbs. Imagine it in every cell of your body. Now imagine if the pins and needles turned into fire. You're not even close to what it feels like to be resurrected.

I woke up screaming. I lashed out instinctively at the threat I remembered, at what had killed me, but Edwards wasn't there. Neither was the room with the fireplace and bookshelves and paintings. Or Morgana and the faerie, for that matter. In fact, the house wasn't there, and neither was the faerie pub. I was lying outside, on the ground.

I tried to sit up but first I had to take care of the vomiting business that sometimes comes with resurrections. When that was finally done, I looked around.

I definitely wasn't in Seattle anymore. I was sitting on a patch of grass on a hillside, but it wasn't the hill Edwards's home had been perched upon. This one overlooked the Thames River rather than Puget Sound. Only it was the Thames from my memory, not the present day. There were no buildings in sight on its banks, no passenger jets in the sky. Just green grass and trees and storm clouds overhead.

I had a bad feeling about this.

I quickly inspected myself. I was wearing the same clothes I had on

217

when Edwards had killed me, although my shirt was bloody now and had three holes in the heart area. Nice grouping. I checked my pockets and found everything was still there – my wallet, the car keys to the rental, even the ring Morgana had given me. I pulled the shirt up and looked at my chest. There were still faint, puckered scars where the bullets had gone in. Which meant I hadn't been dead that long. Maybe a week or so.

I'd resurrected much quicker than usual. Sometimes it took decades. But then I didn't usually have that much grace in my system.

I thought about what I'd done to Aigra. He really had helped me, in his own way. The resurrection had used up most of the grace he'd given me, but I still had enough to defend myself a little. Maybe not against a crazy angel armed with a handgun, but perhaps against a sleepy security guard or something similar. Without Aigra's sacrifice, I'd still be dead and powerless. It was almost enough to make me feel bad about what I'd done to him. Almost.

But there was time to be sentimental later. Right now I needed to figure out where I was. I already had some suspicions on that front, which were confirmed when I turned around.

The ruined castle from the Constable painting. Either Edwards had transported me back in time to the scene of the painting after killing me, or he'd somehow managed to move me into the painting itself. I didn't know how he'd manage either one, so I put the odds at about even.

"Well, this is a new one," I said to no one in particular, because there was no one else there. Not even the shepherd boy and his dog from the painting. It was just the empty landscape and me. I probably would have found it profound, if I were the profound type. But I'm more the practical type, so I started searching for a way out of there.

I went over to the ruins and looked around. There was an overgrown road that disappeared into some trees in the direction where the viewer of the painting would stand. In the distance beyond the forest, a thin column of smoke smudged the sky. So there was someone else alive around here, even if I couldn't see any other buildings. I started down the road, hoping I was imagining all this. I didn't really want to relive the past few centuries – especially the ones without indoor plumbing.

I walked for a couple of minutes before I realized I wasn't going anywhere. The forest and smoke in the sky stayed the same distance away. I looked down at the road. I was still at the beginning. I took a few more steps. I was definitely moving, but it was as if the land ahead moved with me. And the land behind me followed along. I wondered what the Renaissance painters would have to say about that and the rules of perspective.

I tried going off the road, first to my left and then to my right, but the same thing happened. I could go a few feet away from the ruins and then I couldn't travel any farther. I reversed direction and went back down the hill. Everything went fine until I hit some bushes at the bottom of the slope. I reached out to part some branches and they moved away from me. I kept walking toward them and they kept receding. I stopped and pictured the painting again. The bushes were at the edge of the frame. I looked up at the clouds. They moved without moving, if that makes any sense. That is, they swirled and drifted, but they didn't actually go anywhere.

So, trapped in the painting it was. I had to admit, it was a pretty good prison. At least, I hoped it was a prison and not just the place Edwards had chosen to dump my body and never visit again.

I went back up to the ruins and sat on a fallen stone on the ground. I tried to figure out if there was some trick to my imprisonment I'd missed, some escape route that was right there in front of me. I tried to figure out why Edwards was pretending to be Judas, which puzzled me more than the things the angels usually did. I tried to figure out what all this had to do with Mona Lisa and Cassiel, because it sure as hell had something to do with them.

I thought all these things over and came up with nothing. As usual. I looked up at the sky and sighed. I was getting tired of this sort of thing happening to me.

I waited a few minutes, or maybe a few days, before something happened. It's hard to say how long when the world doesn't change around you. But eventually someone chuckled behind me while I was tossing rocks out over the bushes, in the direction of the river. Sure, it looked like I was killing time, but I was also searching for any flaw in my prison that I could exploit, any magical hole I could climb through to make my escape. Plus, I was killing time.

I turned to see Edwards standing at the edge of the road, around the same spot I'd been forced to stop when everything moved away from me. He looked the same as when he'd killed me, only now he'd exchanged the gun for a friend – a large man in a black suit who shone with power. Gabriel. Edwards's angel muscle, no doubt.

"I was hoping I'd run into you again," I said to Gabriel, "but I hadn't quite imagined it being under these circumstances."

He didn't say anything, just smiled. He was the strong, silent, smiling, strong kind, Gabriel was.

I considered my options. I knew that in my weakened condition I couldn't take them both in a fair fight. Then again, I've never really fought fair.

"I expect you have some questions," Edwards said to me.

I nodded. "Why were you pretending to be Judas earlier?" I asked. "And why are you pretending to be that dead preacher now?"

"We must all be Judas from time to time," Edwards said. "Do not concern yourself with him."

"All right," I said. "No problem." Do not concern myself with Judas. Really?

"As for the dead preacher," Edwards went on, "I am not pretending to be him. I am him. Or rather, I was. Once upon a time I moved among the mortals as him and tried to bring them back to God. But people are no longer willing to listen to the divine word. So I let him die, or at least I let the humans think him dead. Obviously, I remain."

"But who were you originally?" I asked. "You know, your angel name."

"The name that God gave me no longer matters," he said. "His age is over. Now it is our age. Which is why you're here."

"When you say 'here,' where exactly is that?" I asked.

But Edwards shook his head and smiled. "My turn," he said. "What do you want with Mona Lisa?"

"What makes you think I want anything with Mona Lisa?" I said, more to stall than to be witty and clever.

"Sut said you mentioned her to get everyone's attention," Edwards said. "You would only do that if you knew of her. And you should not know of her."

"How is Sut anyway?" I asked. "No hard feelings, I hope."

"He is where you hid him," Edwards said. "I left him there to teach him a lesson about failure."

I considered everything I knew, which wasn't much. Edwards was clearly one of those religious angels. I mean the zealot type. Never a good thing in a being with power like that. He hung out with other powerful angels, like Gabriel. He seemed to be protecting Mona Lisa. He knew I was looking for her, but he didn't know why. Which meant that his Judas masquerade had nothing to do with me. Oh yes, he also had a faerie sleeping in a bed in his home. Which wasn't the home it looked like from the outside. And he somehow had the power to move in and out of paintings.

I shook my head. This really wasn't helping.

"You haven't answered my question," Edwards pointed out.

"I'm not sure if we're currently in America or England," I said, "but either way I'm entitled to a lawyer."

Edwards shrugged. He turned and stepped onto the road, and Gabriel followed him. He turned into Judas again.

And they vanished.

No fading away, no puff of smoke, no taking flight on their majestic wings. One second they were there, the next they weren't.

I ran after them in case the portal or spell or whatever the hell they used remained open. I came close to the edge of the road, and the road moved away from me. The smoke reached for the sky in the distance. The clouds swirled overhead.

I sighed and sat down on the fallen stone again. Sometimes, when there's nothing to do but wait, the best thing to do is wait. So I waited. And waited. Night never came, the clouds never went anywhere, the smoke on the horizon never faded. And still I waited.

To occupy the time, I picked up a rock and scratched passages from books and poems on the walls of the ruined castle. I wrote some lines from my favourite Keats poem on one wall:

This living hand, now warm and capable
Of earnest grasping, would, if it were cold
And in the icy silence of the tomb,
So haunt thy days and chill thy dreaming nights
That thou wouldst wish thine own heart dry of blood

So in my veins red life might stream again,
And thou be conscience-calm'd – see here it is –
I hold it towards you.

And, just to lighten the day, I inscribed a bit of Cummings on a tree beyond the ruins:

somewhere I have never traveled, gladly beyond
any experience, your eyes have their silence

Some time later, Edwards returned with Gabriel. He showed up looking like Judas again, and then dropped the disguise when he saw me. Gabriel wore his suit once more. It was tight enough to show off all his muscles. He always was like that.

"How do you get in and out of here like that?" I asked them. Edwards smiled. It looked like it had been made by a knife drawn across his face.

"A trick van Gogh taught me," he said.

I shook my head. "He never taught me anything but to keep an eye on my money while he was in the same room."

Edwards shrugged. "It did require some persuasion," he said. He tugged at his ear in case I didn't get the hint.

"Oh, so you're that kind of angel," I said.

He dropped the smile, which didn't take much. "Are you ready to talk now?" he asked.

"I still don't see my lawyer," I said, because it's important to keep your sense of humour in moments like this.

Edwards nodded at Gabriel, who came at me without saying a word. He didn't even take off his suit jacket. Not a good sign.

Maybe I could have fought him. I certainly wanted to. But I didn't bother. Why waste the grace? I had no weapons, and even if I managed to defend myself, or even beat him, I was still trapped in a painting with no way out. So I let him practise his right hooks and stomach shots for a while. When Edwards finally called him off, he wasn't even breathing hard, although I was.

"I'm sure I don't have to point out that we'll repeat this until you're ready to talk," Edwards said.

I'd been in enough police stations and gulags to know how this was going to go. Eventually they'd wear me down, or I'd grow bored. But no one would come along to save me. No one ever came to save me. So there was no need to drag things out.

I spat blood and nodded. "I think I'm ready now," I said, and Gabriel dropped me and stepped away. I swear he looked disappointed.

"On one condition," I added, and Gabriel stepped forward again, but Edwards held up his hand and he stopped. "I'll tell you what I want with Mona Lisa if you tell me what you want with her."

Edwards thought that over for a moment. Gabriel remained ready to grab my throat and choke the life out of me. The clouds churned overhead without going anywhere.

Then Edwards shrugged. "A fair exchange if it speeds things along," he said.

I got up off my knees and gave Gabriel my best "that's all you got?" look. He gave me his best "you're kind of soft for a punching bag" look. Fair exchange.

"You first," Edwards invited.

I brushed the dirt from my clothes and told him the truth. I told him I was working for Cassiel, who wanted me to track down Mona Lisa for him. I figured I didn't owe Cassiel anything at this point. I told him Cassiel would deliver me Judas if I found and freed Mona Lisa. I even told him about killing Remiel in the church; I didn't want him to think I'd gone soft just because I let Gabriel beat on me.

Edwards shook his head. "I don't understand," he said.

"That makes two of us. Probably three," I said, nodding at Gabriel.

Edwards looked at his sidekick. "Cassiel had not yet taken sides the last I had heard of him," he said. "What interest would he have in Mona Lisa?"

Gabriel pondered the question in thoughtful silence. Or maybe just silence.

"Aigra told me all about your little war," I said. "I'm beginning to understand why God left all of you behind. You must have driven him crazy."

Edwards walked past me and gazed out at the Thames, which was busily flowing nowhere. "Aigra?" he said. "He disappeared so long ago I assumed him dead."

"He is," I said, and left it at that.

Edwards nodded. "Well, I suppose we should thank you for reducing their side somewhat. But the truth is we need to weaken them much more. Too many of the angels still refuse to see the light."

"What light?" I asked.

Now Edwards turned to look at me again. "The new light," he said. "The Risen."

I nodded. "Of course," I said. "That light."

"The war could go on for eternity," Edwards said. "We are too evenly matched. There are others who haven't joined sides. Who don't care about the war. Who don't care about anything."

"Cassiel," I said.

"Among others," Edwards said.

"You want them on your side," I said.

"We care about them as much as they care about us," he said. "They are too few in number. What we need is a secret weapon. Mona Lisa is that weapon. But apparently not so secret if even our enemies know about it."

I added that to all the information I already had. I re-evaluated things and came to the conclusion I still didn't know what the hell was going on.

"I see," I lied.

"I doubt you do," Edwards said without changing expression. He walked over to stand in front of me. He gazed into my eyes for a moment. "Of course, our side would be bolstered even more if Christ himself were to join the cause of the righteous. Imagine. The Second Coming at long last."

"I'm not Christ," I said. "Remember?"

"That is an unfortunate fact," he said. "But you do wield his power."

"And doesn't the Second Coming involve God?" I asked.

"He has abandoned us, so the Risen have forsaken him." He said it with about as much passion as when he'd told Gabriel to use my face for a speed bag.

"But we can have Heaven again, only this time on earth," Edwards went on. "All we need is you."

"I'm done with your kind and your battles," I said. "Live and let die, that's my motto. Or maybe just live and die."

"How poetic," Edwards said. "But perhaps we could sway you from your position."

"I've heard all the arguments," I said, "but I'm afraid I'm just not a believer."

"I know," Edwards said. "That's why I was thinking more of a straight-forward reward."

Now it was my turn to study him. It was kind of like studying a wax figure. "What kind of reward?" I asked.

"Join us and *I* will deliver you Judas," Edwards said. "Once the battle is finished, of course."

"You know where Judas is?" I asked.

"Of course," Edwards said. "It is my business to know such things."

Damn it – did everybody but me know where Judas was?

"The real Judas?" I asked. "Or you know – you?"

"Join us and you will have Judas," Edwards said. "Refuse and you'll spend the rest of your lives in this painting."

"Well, when you put it like that," I said.

"You have always been more human than the rest of us," Edwards said. I had no idea if that was a compliment or an insult. No matter.

"I have only one condition," I said. "You let me talk to Mona Lisa first. So I know this is indeed a worthy cause." I smiled. "Fair exchange."

Edwards thought that over for a moment. Then he nodded. "I will bring her to you," he said. He walked past me and Gabriel followed him with a sad look, as if he'd hoped I wouldn't be quite so co-operative. They disappeared on the road again but this time I didn't bother following them. I just went back to decorating the place with some more literary quotes.

In a little while we shall all be dead. Therefore let us behave as though we were dead already, I wrote on a section of wall. Raymond Chandler.

AMELIA

I don't want to tell you about the baby Morgana had, but I suppose I must.

It was a girl.

Stillborn.

But that's not why I screamed.

She was older than a baby when she came out. She was more a toddler. Probably old enough to walk, maybe even to say a few words.

But that's not why I screamed either.

She looked like Penelope.

And I knew, somehow, that Morgana had reached out and found Penelope's child. Our daughter. And somehow, Morgana had taken her from Penelope's long-dead womb.

But that's not why I screamed either.

Amelia, my daughter, who wasn't breathing, and who was as grey as ash, opened her eyes and looked at me.

And that's why I screamed.

A PICNIC IN THE RUINS

Edwards and Gabriel came back a few hours later. Or maybe it was a few days. Or a few weeks. Who knows? I'd covered most of the ruins in passages from books and poems now – I was just finishing up a bit from Mary Shelley's *Frankenstein* when they arrived. My carving was definitely improving – if I ever got out of here, I had a bright future as a stonemason waiting for me.

This time they brought company. A couple more angels and the faerie I'd seen dozing in the bedroom of Edwards's place. And, of course, Mona Lisa.

They were wearing period costume – the faerie was in the same breeches and shirt I'd seen him sleeping in and the other men were wearing similar outfits. Mona Lisa wore a crimson Renaissance gown with a gold, diamond-patterned brocade. Her hair was up in some sort of elaborate structure, but her face looked the same as it did in da Vinci's painting. When she looked at me I felt my skin heat up. Not out of passion or desire or anything like that – her gaze actually raised the temperature a little. And I noticed the air around her shimmering, like she was giving off heat. Gorgons – they were all special in their own way.

Edwards was Judas once more, of course. "I like what you've done with the place," he said, inspecting my handiwork with the ruins. Only now they weren't ruins. The walls were intact again, the castle restored to what was presumably its former glory, although my writing was still everywhere. I looked around some more and saw the clouds overhead fade away to a blue sky. I looked down at myself and saw my clothes replaced with the same period garb as them. It was like we were a little court. This was more than some minor sleight.

I looked back at them and saw a look of concentration on the faerie's face. Now I understood his role in our little drama. We were in some sort of glamour he was maintaining. I guessed it was different from the one Morgana and her merry crew inhabited because of the obvious effort he was putting into it. Interesting. I had always thought faeries just lived in the glamour – I didn't realize they created it too. File it away under Things to Consider Later.

Edwards escorted Mona Lisa forward with his arm. "My lady," he said to her, "may I present to you Our Lord and Saviour, Jesus Christ."

I couldn't stop from rolling my eyes, so I bowed to hide it.

"We have heard many a great thing about you," she said. Her voice had a crackle to it, like a fire. "We are honoured."

"I am the honoured one," I said, straightening up. "I have also heard many a great thing about you."

"Who would speak of us?" she asked with a smile. She spoke in the plural, just like Victory, even though I knew she was cut off from the others. I guess old habits die hard even for gorgons.

"Your sisters have told me much of you, and they send their greetings," I said, and her smile faded away. She looked, well, confused.

Edwards stepped forward, between us. "We have brought a picnic," he said and clapped his hands together. One of the other angels stepped forward with a picnic basket I hadn't noticed before. I glanced at the faerie again and saw him practically sweating with concentration. When I looked back at Mona Lisa, I saw her face take on the same dazed look as the people back in Morgana's pub. Then she smiled once again. "We do like a picnic," she said.

You didn't need my centuries of experience to see the faerie was keeping her mind clouded. Why, I didn't know. Except that it appeared Mona Lisa was about as much a guest of Edwards as I was.

Edwards guided us to the highest spot on the hill and we took in the view while Gabriel and the other angels – I decided to call them Grumpy and Dopey – set up the picnic.

"Such a lovely place," Mona Lisa said, looking down at the Thames. "Judas, my love, why have we never come here before?" She took his hand in hers.

I tried not to react at the words "Judas" and "love" in the same sentence. I looked up at the sky, at the castle, at the river in the distance, anywhere but at the happy lovers. I stared at Gabriel, who stared blankly back at me. Maybe I wasn't giving him enough credit. I'd probably have lost my wits in this scenario too.

"It is a long and complicated journey," Edwards answered, and from the tone of his voice I suspected he was telling the truth.

The three of us sat on a blanket while the others stood off to the side. I noticed the faerie stayed in Edwards's line of sight. No doubt to pick up on his cues for setting the scene and controlling Mona Lisa. We ate grapes and tore chunks off a bread loaf and drank wine, while a warm breeze caressed us.

"So, how long have you known Edwards?" I asked Mona Lisa. I used his name deliberately.

"Who?" she asked, looking around.

"He means me, my love," Edwards said, putting his hand over hers on the blanket. "Christ likes to grace us with the names of particularly strong believers, as a gesture of respect."

I looked at those hands entwined, then looked away again. The fact they were lovers changed everything. Now I just needed to figure out how it changed everything.

Edwards simply smiled at me, but Gabriel had shifted a little closer since I'd used Edwards's real name. Like he thought I was going to spoil the party or something. I winked at him, but he didn't wink back. Angels – they never know how to have fun.

"Oh, of course," Mona Lisa said. She smiled at Edwards, then at me. "We've been with Judas for decades. He has been most faithful to us. He did not abandon us when da Vinci captured us and turned us over to the rebel angels, who would have locked us away forever. Instead, he worked cleverly to free us."

She talked in the plural like Victory, but she didn't sound anything like her sister. Victory spoke like a gorgon, like the world had once been hers, which it had been. Mona Lisa spoke like a smitten schoolgirl. I doubted it was her natural state. That faerie worked powerful magic.

I nodded at her and forced another smile. "Rebel angels?" I said.

"The ones who kept us hidden away in the pub," she said. "The ones who wanted to dance and sing the world away."

Now I nodded at the faerie. "Well done," I said.

"Those who would destroy the world and its myriad miracles," Edwards quickly added, with a straight face. "Those who took her sisters away."

I considered his words. Either he was lying about what the Risen did with creatures like the gorgon or Aigra was. Oh, which one to believe?

"We thought ourselves forever lost," Mona Lisa said. "But then Judas tricked the angels into sending us to the human queen's prison, where he helped us escape."

I poured myself some more wine. "I've known Judas a long time and I know just what a gentleman he is," I said.

"He has been trying to enlist us to join his crusade against the angels still loyal to their god," Mona Lisa went on. "But we have been hesitant to involve ourselves in their affairs until now." She gazed at Edwards, and I successfully managed not to crush the wineglass into a thousand shards. She was clearly in love with Edwards, who she thought was Judas. But how could anyone – or anything, for that matter – love Judas?

"What changed?" I asked instead of becoming homicidal. Well, outwardly homicidal.

They both looked at me. "You did, of course, my lord," Edwards said, and Mona Lisa nodded.

"He has sung to us the legends of your power," she said. "And shown us glimpses of the Promised Land you will deliver."

"Ah, the Promised Land," I said. I finished my glass and hit the wine bottle again. I hoped it was one of those never-ending bottles.

"The rivers of fire," she said. "The ash winds. The steam pits. Just like the times of old."

I opened my mouth for a witty comment, but I couldn't actually come up with one. First time for everything.

"And our sisters, of course," Mona Lisa added. "Reunited in the time after time."

"About your sisters," I said, but Edwards held up his hand.

"We shouldn't talk about such matters on a fine day like this," he said, and Gabriel took a couple steps closer.

I nodded. "All right," I said. "I apologize, my lady."

"We have no need for apologies," she said. "Only vengeance."

"It's just that they've been hunting for you," I said as quickly as I could. "And if I ever get out of here, I'm going to tell them exactly where to find you."

The wind suddenly turned hot, and she sat up straighter and opened her mouth to say something.

And then she was gone. It was just Edwards and Gabriel and me. The others had vanished. The clouds were back overhead, the castle was reduced to ruins again. Even my dirty, bloodstained clothes were back. Worst of all, the picnic had vanished. I'd been enjoying that wine. Edwards still looked like Judas, though.

"She's in love with the real Judas, isn't she?" I said. "That's why you're pretending to be him." To recruit a secret weapon to win a meaningless war. A gorgon who was in love with Judas, of all the godforsaken creatures.

He sighed and stood up. "It will take some effort to undo the damage you have caused," he said, ignoring my question. "Such setbacks, while not surprising, are unnecessary."

I shrugged. "If I have to choose between being loyal to you or being loyal to the gorgons, I'll take the gorgons," I said.

"You have no choice," he said, and he wore no expression at all on his face now. Or maybe that was just the usual expression on his face. "We have all eternity. Eventually we will break even you. Given time, eventually we would break even God."

I raised an eyebrow at that. "I wouldn't have thought you the blasphemous type," I said.

"The only blasphemous type here is you," he said, and then he turned in the direction of the road and vanished.

"I guess it's just you and me again," I said to Gabriel. "Unless you were planning on following him?"

This time he took off his suit jacket and placed it on a nearby rock. Not a good sign at all.

"You know, I'm going to enjoy killing you when all this is done," I said. He just nodded and then got down to beating the hell out of me.

ASHES TO ASHES

When I came back to life after Penelope died, I screamed to find myself alone in a grave. Only I wasn't truly alone. I was entangled in rotting bodies. I'd resurrected in a mass grave. I spat the dirt out of my mouth and screamed and screamed and screamed but there was no one under the earth who could hear me.

I dug my way up out of the dead and found myself in the desolate wasteland that was now Hiroshima. The city was gone, replaced by the skeletons of buildings and trees. The sky was the colour of ash. It was as if I had climbed out of the grave and into Hell. I didn't have to look for Penelope to know what had happened to her. I couldn't scream any more.

I searched for her in that nightmare and learned what had happened from the people I met as I picked my way through the wreckage. Homeless people who had lost everything and didn't know where else to go. People like me.

Now I understood why Judas had taken on the forms of those burned Japanese people back in the church. He hadn't been transforming himself into people he'd been in the past. He was transforming himself into people who were going to die in the future. Who were dead or dying now. Or maybe they were forms he was planning on taking in order to move undetected through the wreckage and chaos. To create more havoc. No one knew but him.

But I wasn't looking for him now.

233

I found Penelope in another mass grave, a smaller one where they had put women and children. I dug her up and held what was left of her in my arms and wept under the night sky. I wanted to die again to be with her. I wanted to resurrect her. I wanted to burn the entire world.

But I didn't do any of those things.

Instead, I honoured her request. I kissed her and let the grace flow from my lips into her, turning everything she had been and everything she could have been into ash. I collected the ash in a Coke bottle I found lying on the ground, and later I poured it from the bottle into a proper urn. I took the urn with me and travelled the world with it. And wherever I went, I gave Penelope back to the world.

I dropped a handful of ash into the sea as I sailed from Tokyo to Hong Kong.

I let a handful of ash blow into the wind from a mountain peak I climbed in the Himalayas.

I worked a handful of ash into the sand of Saudi Arabia.

I dropped a handful of ash into the water over Victoria Falls in Africa.

I scattered ash along the steps of a forgotten temple in a jungle in South America.

I rubbed ash into a pillar of the Parthenon.

I tossed ash into the wind at Auschwitz.

I sprinkled the last of her ashes into the River Seine, and then threw the urn into the water after them. I stood there a moment longer and watched it sink out of sight. I promised her I would track down her father and kill him in honour of her memory.

And when the last sign of her faded from the water, I went and found a wine bar and drank myself to oblivion and lost myself in the remains of the century.

THE LAST SUPPER

When Gabriel had said his goodbyes and I'd recovered enough that I could sit up without vomiting from the pain, I propped myself against one of the castle walls and reviewed what I had learned.

Sometime in the past Morgana had managed to add Mona Lisa to her collection of fey. Then she'd given her to the Royal Family as tribute, but Edwards had broken Mona Lisa out in order to turn her into a secret weapon to break the stalemate in the war of angels. Although his liberation seemed to be more of an abduction. He was pretending to be Judas in Mona Lisa's presence because Judas and Mona Lisa obviously had had some sort of relationship in the past. A relationship she thought they still had. A relationship I wasn't even going to try to understand. Not right now, anyway. I couldn't bear to think about that. Besides, I wouldn't be at all surprised if Judas had already forgotten her. He didn't strike me as the sentimental type.

And now Edwards was trying to sway her to his side in the battle by using me – well, Christ, anyway – and promises of a heavenly reward she'd never see. That is, she wouldn't see it if Aigra was telling the truth about the Risen wiping out everything that didn't come from the Divine. And it looked like Edwards thought maybe he could turn me into a secret weapon as well.

I still couldn't figure out how Cassiel played into all of this. Maybe he still had feelings for her, even though she was obviously hung up on Judas. Or maybe he and the rest of the faithful had their own plan for a secret weapon. Or maybe there was something I wasn't seeing here at all.

Yeah, it was just another day at the office.

Then there were the other unknowns. I had no idea why the faerie was helping Edwards. I supposed it didn't really matter – the loss of his finger meant Edwards had found some way to bind him, just like Sut – but I'd have to find a way to deal with him to rescue Mona Lisa. Because, yes, I did still plan to rescue her.

And that was the other unknown. Just what was Mona Lisa's power? Victory had called her the most powerful of the gorgons, and all those fire and brimstone feelings around her hinted at something. I didn't even want to know what apocalyptic time she'd come from. I wondered how the hell da Vinci had managed to imprison her in the first place. But he was a cagey soul, especially given that he was mortal. Well, had been mortal. Who knows what he was now. Wherever he was now.

I rested a bit more and then decided I'd better get on with things before Gabriel came back to offer me more encouragement to join their cause.

Edwards was right – I would make a good secret weapon. But he'd overlooked the fact that I had secret weapons of my own.

I pushed myself up to my feet and turned to face the castle wall. I read the Keats passage I'd started with. I read the Margaret Atwood poem. I went down the wall and read a few choice lines of Rosencrantz from the Stoppard play, not the Shakespeare one. I read a passage from Ecclesiastes. I wandered the ruins, reading everything I'd carved into those walls until I turned a corner and found Alice smiling at a little bit of Dr. Seuss I'd added to the other side of the wall.

She was wearing combat fatigues and a monocle, and she was spinning a yo-yo up and down on one hand.

"I like the cat in the hat," she said, "but not as much as I like the stories about the hat going off on adventures without the cat."

I let out a long sigh of relief. I hadn't known if my homemade library would work or not.

Alice kept spinning the yo-yo as she looked around. "I've never seen this library before," she said.

"I made it for you," I said.

"For me?" She did a pirouette of joy.

"I have a favour to ask," I added.

"What kind of favour?" she said. "I think I may have some party favours here somewhere." She began checking her pockets.

"Alice," I said, "I need you to take me with you."

"With me where?" she said.

"To Jonathan Edwards's library," I said.

She looked at me, and for the first time I noticed her eye behind the monocle was green while the other one was blue. Or maybe it had just turned green. You never know with Alice.

"Sometimes I lose people in libraries," she whispered, like it was a secret. "And I can't find them again."

"I'm going to have to take that chance," I said.

She spun her yo-yo a few more times and then smiled. "I know how to keep you," she said and flicked the yo-yo toward me. I caught it and looked down at it.

"Hang on to it and you won't get lost," she said.

"I think I'm already lost," I said, "but all right."

She giggled. "You sound just like the hatter."

She went around the wall, tugging me after her with the yo-yo's string, and I followed her. We went to the other side and then she continued on, circling the wall again. By the third time, the view hadn't changed any.

"Alice," I said, "where are we going?"

"I can't remember where I came in," she said. "But I'm sure it's around here somewhere."

I closed my eyes for a few seconds at that. I hoped I hadn't trapped her here as well. Who knew what Edwards would do with her.

But when I opened my eyes again Alice was leading us through a hole in one of the walls I hadn't noticed before, into a courtyard surrounded by more crumbling walls. I'd never seen this place, but the stone here was covered in more writing. Passages from Edgar Allan Poe and Angela Carter and Emily Dickinson, all written in my hand even though I had no memory of writing them. I looked up at the sky overhead and saw it was the same rolling clouds as before.

Alice pulled me to an open doorway in one of the walls, and now we were in a stone tunnel. There was no writing in here, but after a while wooden doors started to appear. Alice skipped along past them, so I restrained my natural curiosity and didn't open any of them.

Which was just as well, because after a few minutes of this the doors were replaced by open doorways that looked into libraries. But not your normal sort of libraries.

There was one in ruins, the roof blown off and the shelves collapsed. Men in overcoats and hats stood in the ruins and browsed the books. It looked like England during the war years, but I couldn't say for sure.

The next one was a library in flames, the books burning on their shelves. I looked inside but didn't see anyone in there, but I did feel the heat from the flames.

Another one was a flooded library, water pouring in through windows up near the ceiling. The books were handbound leather. Water flowed into the tunnel, carrying books with it, and we splashed through them.

We climbed stairs, past a pile of scrolls in a cave and a van with boxes of books parked in the desert. We went down another tunnel, this one lined with wood-panelled walls, past what looked like the reading room in the New York Public Library, and a library on a cruise ship somewhere. We stepped onto an escalator that took us up through a bookstore, with people browsing the aisles, and then the escalator ended in the stacks of a university library.

Alice led me through the books, and after a couple of turns the metal shelves turned to wood. I looked behind us but I couldn't see the university library at all anymore. Now we were in a used bookstore, and then we were in what looked like a home library, and then we were standing in Edwards's living room again, the fire and Scotch welcoming us.

I looked around. The room looked the same as the last time I'd been here, only minus Edwards and his gun. I didn't see a secret entrance or anything to indicate how we'd gotten here.

"I can see why you like this place," Alice said, running her fingers along a row of books on a shelf. "There are some interesting editions here."

I went over to the *Hadleigh Castle* painting and studied it. It looked the same as before. There was no sign I'd ever been in it.

"You're going to have to teach me how you do that someday," I told Alice.

"Do what?" she asked. She blew a gum bubble at me.

"Travel between libraries," I said.

"Each one has its own story," she said. "You just have to keep turning the pages until you come to the story you need."

I should have known better than to bring it up.

"Do you have any more secret libraries we can visit?" she asked.

"Not right now," I said. "And if I were you, I'd leave that one alone for a while. It's not safe right now."

Alice frowned. "For how long?" she asked.

"I'll contact you when it's okay to go there again," I said. "And if I don't contact you, then it's never safe."

I left her there and went down the hall, to the kitchen. I could have just gone out the front door instead, back to the car and far away from here. To hell with Cassiel and Mona Lisa and the war between angels and whatever else I didn't know about.

But I couldn't. I felt honour bound to try to save Mona Lisa now. Not for her sake or even Cassiel's, but for Victory. I'd grown fond of Victory, and yeah, maybe even thought of her as a friend. I guess this is the sort of thing friends did for each other.

That's what I told myself. But the real truth was I still wanted Judas. I'd deliver Mona Lisa to Cassiel, for whatever reason he wanted her, and then he'd deliver Judas. Or I'd get the information out of Edwards somehow.

Fair exchange.

I went through the kitchen drawers until I found a knife with a suitably strong and long blade. Then I went upstairs. It was still empty, just the sleeping faerie on his bed. I shoved the knife into his heart to see if I could break the glamour he was casting, but he didn't react, didn't even stop breathing. Well, no harm in trying. I was going to have to go in after him and kill him in the glamour.

I went back downstairs to the living room. Alice was gone. I hoped she'd heed my advice and stay away from the library I'd made in the ruins.

I poured myself another glass of the Macallan and studied the paintings again. I figured if Edwards was using *Hadleigh Castle* as a prison, he was most likely hiding out in one of the others. I just wasn't sure which. I couldn't see any signs. I doubted he'd chosen *Shipwreck of the Minotaur* because who would want to hide out in a shipwreck? So maybe *Seaport at Sunset* or *The Night Watch*? I shook my head. Neither one seemed his style. In fact, none of the paintings looked like the sort of place rogue angels would hide out with Mona Lisa and a faerie. I was missing something.

I wandered the library until I found it. Some scrape marks on the floor where the bookshelf had been pulled out. Well, when in Rome . . .

I put down the glass on a table and pulled the bookshelf out a few feet. The wall behind it was covered in a painting. Da Vinci's *The Last Supper*. It was on the wall itself, and stretched away into the shadows behind the other shelves. The paint was faded and cracking, and it looked like the real thing, given what I recalled of it the last time I'd seen it. And given what I knew of Edwards, I was willing to bet it was the real thing, although how he'd got it here and what he'd replaced it with, I had no idea.

No matter. I winked at my portrait in the painting and then got down to it before Edwards and his group could make another appearance.

I reached into my pocket and took out the ring Morgana had given me. I took a deep breath and then, before I could think twice about what I was doing, I put it on my ring finger. For a second nothing happened. Then the bone sank into my skin, merging with it, and I felt the change start inside me. It was like the never-ending hunger I had for grace, only far worse. I had a sudden yearning to see Morgana again. The yearning grew, filling me, until every cell of my body screamed with desire, until I screamed with desire, too – and it was desire, not love, and the difference between the two is the difference between me and the real Christ. I stumbled in what I imagined was her direction, and I wept at being so far from her.

I knew all I had to do was think about her, like she'd said. If I focused on her, the ring would lead me to her. Instead, I forced myself to concentrate on the faerie lying on the bed upstairs, even though thinking of anything other than Morgana made me feel so hollow inside I felt like collapsing in on myself.

It was a hunch, but it was the only thing I had.

I told myself the longing I had for Morgana was no different than the hunger I'd had for grace so many times. I'd learn to endure it. I had no choice. I told myself that, but I didn't believe it.

I couldn't see because of the tears. When I reached up and wiped them away, I was inside *The Last Supper*.

It was different than the painting. The walls in the background and the table at the centre of the painting were the same, but Christ and the disciples were gone. They'd been replaced by Edwards and Mona Lisa and Gabriel and the other angels. The table was covered in a feast of fresh fruit and chunks of raw, bloody meat. Edwards and Mona Lisa sipped wine from goblets. The air was smoky, and the landscape outside the windows blazed with fire. The faerie stood off to the side of the table, staring at the scene and concentrating. He didn't even look away when the others turned to me. I glanced down at myself and saw I was outfitted in stained breeches and a torn shirt. The knife in my hand was a rapier now. I nodded at the faerie. That was a nice touch.

Then Edwards, who still looked like Judas, put down his wine goblet and applauded me.

"I was wondering where you'd run off to," he said. "I didn't think it would be here."

The other angels got to their feet and came around the table for me. Things were about to get ugly.

I tried to take off the ring, but it wouldn't move. Not good. But there was no time to deal with that now.

"Sorry to ruin such a lovely dream," I told Mona Lisa, who was looking back and forth between Edwards and me with obvious confusion. Then I threw myself at the faerie and skewered him through the heart with the rapier.

For a moment, everyone froze, or at least that's the way I remember it. The angels paused to stare at what I'd done. Edwards stopped his hands mid-clap. Mona Lisa looked at the faerie as if noticing him for the first time. And the faerie? Well, he kept concentrating on the scene for another few seconds. Then a violet bubble burst from his lips, and a stain spread around the rapier. I pulled it from his chest in a smooth motion – I'd had lots of practice over the years – and the stain spread even more.

"Thank you," he said to me, and then he fell to the ground, skipping the whole slumping to the knees part and opting instead to melt into the floor, seeping through the cracks in the wooden planks. Then he was gone, like mist in the sun.

Another nice touch. I would have appreciated it more if I didn't feel so damned miserable. Once I settled things with Judas, I was really going to have to do something about Morgana.

With the faerie dead, the glamour he'd been maintaining started to die as well. The fires outside the window flared once and then fell out of sight. The smell of smoke in the air faded away. The banquet turned to mouldy mounds of food swarming with flies. The angels' finery drifted apart into spiderwebs that broke as they moved, leaving them naked. I glanced down at myself and saw I was holding the kitchen knife again, and once more wearing the clothes I'd been killed in. To clarify: the clothes I'd been killed in most recently.

"What's happening?" Mona Lisa asked, looking around her, at the tapestries fading into the walls, at the goblets turning to plastic cups, at her dress turning into rags, at Judas turning into Edwards.

"You've been deceived," I said, but that's all I had time for before Grumpy and Dopey spread their wings wide to block her view of me. And then Gabriel leapt over them and descended upon me.

Sure, there were three of them, but I had once been Jesus Christ, their Lord and Saviour – their *master*.

Yeah, they kicked my ass.

I tried to impale Gabriel with my blade like I'd impaled the faerie – oh, *Morgana*! – but he just held up a hand to catch the blade. By "catch" I mean he let me stab him through the hand. Then he swung his arm back, taking the knife with it, only to punch me in the head with the same hand. He didn't even bother to pull the knife out.

Everyone had impressive tricks today.

While I was still trying to figure out whether the white lights I saw were imaginary or from the faerie's fading glamour, Grumpy and Dopey grabbed my arms and slammed me against the wall. I looked past them and Gabriel to see Edwards make a motion with one of his hands, and just like that he was Judas again.

"Look at me," he told Mona Lisa and she did and paused.

"Judas," she said. "What is this place?"

I wanted to shout at her that it was her prison, but I was taken aback by her appearance. Her skin was marked with what looked like the scars of branding irons. Her eyes were empty sockets, just black holes in her drawn face. Her smile was the worst of all. Loose pieces of wire hung from her mangled lips, and the holes still gaped in them where she'd been stitched shut.

Then it was all gone again as Edwards replaced the faded glamour with a sleight. It wouldn't be as good as the glamour, and he wouldn't be able to keep it up, but it might do the trick long enough to cloud her mind with some other enchantment he had waiting as a backup. Maybe he even had another faerie in reserve in one of the other paintings. I knew I had to do something. But Gabriel complicated my efforts when he pulled the knife from his hand and then stabbed me in the stomach with it. Maybe that was ironic. I've never been quite clear on the definition of "irony."

It hurt like hell, but it didn't hurt any worse than my new longing for Morgana. If it were just Gabriel and me, I probably could have dealt with the pain and made a fight of it. But, unfortunately, it wasn't just Gabriel and me – it was Gabriel and me and the other two angels and Edwards.

If there were ever a time for divine intervention, this was it. I didn't get it, of course. But I got the next best thing.

I saw Edwards narrow his eyes in concentration and Mona Lisa's elaborate dress returned, as did his fancy costume. Gabriel now held a rapier again instead of the knife. The tapestries on the walls were back, and the plastic cups were goblets once more. Then Edwards smiled at me. He wouldn't be able to keep this up for long, but it wouldn't take long for his angels to kill me. He gestured with one hand and Mona Lisa looked outside as the fires out there flared back up again and the mummy climbed in through the window.

The mummy.

It must have found a way to escape Morgana and her court.

Beloved, beautiful Morgana . . .

I shook my head to try to clear my mind. Maybe putting on Morgana's ring hadn't been the best course of action.

The mummy glanced around the room and then saw me. It lumbered forward just as Gabriel drew his arm back for another shot at me with the rapier. The angels holding me spoke for the first time.

"Beware," Grumpy said. Or was that Dopey?

"A corruption," the other one said.

"More like a deus ex machina," I said.

The mummy caught Gabriel's arm just as he started to thrust. He turned, surprised, and it threw him across the room, slamming him into the wall hard enough to crack the stone there. Unless that was just another effect added by Edwards.

"You're in trouble now," I told the other angels. "Even I can't stop him."

One of the nice things about angels – and there aren't many nice things – is that they're reliable. They like to fight. The angels holding me let go and threw themselves at the mummy even as Gabriel climbed back to his feet. The mummy grabbed them by their throats and smashed them together, and feathers flew. But they kicked and punched the mummy even as it tried to choke the life out of them – which doesn't work with the angels or any of their close relations – so all it could do was glare at me with those empty eye sockets while they kept it busy.

I held back for a moment, slumped against the wall and feigning a slow death from the knife wound. Not hard, considering how much it hurt. Gabriel bought it and only glanced at me for a second before leaping across the room and ramming the rapier through the mummy's head. Which had exactly no effect.

I used the angels' distraction to run past them and throw myself over the table even as Edwards turned the food back into a banquet fit for something other than zombies. I tackled him and took him to the floor, and we rolled around there for a bit, giving me time to work a bit of magic of my own.

When he finally threw me off – nearly out the window and into the burning landscape outside, in fact – and we stood up, I'd cast my own sleight. Now I looked like Judas, too.

And if you think I hated becoming Judas to try to survive this situation, well, you've underestimated my feelings a thousandfold.

But I've done worse.

No, no I haven't. But I probably will in the future.

I didn't waste any grace on the wound in my stomach. That would have used up most of my reserves, and the sleight covered it anyway. Besides, I had a feeling there were more wounds on the way. I wasn't going to get out of this one alive. But maybe I could still find a way to free Mona Lisa, and

Cassiel would owe me one. Finding out where Judas was after I resurrected was almost as good as finding out where he was now. As long as I didn't die in his form . . .

Mona Lisa looked back and forth between the two of us and sipped her wine. "An enchantment," she said. "How delightful."

I sighed. Or maybe I could just beat Judas's location out of Edwards.

I risked a glance over at the other fight. Grumpy and Dopey had managed to pin the mummy against the wall like they'd held me, and now Gabriel was stabbing it repeatedly with the rapier. Good luck with that.

Edwards opened his mouth to speak, but I didn't give him time for more threats or boasts or invitations to dinner or whatever it was he wanted. I leapt across the distance between us and grabbed on to him, then shut him up with a head butt to the nose. That always shuts people up. It had the added effect of breaking his concentration, and the sleight masking the room faded again. Stone walls, check. Mouldy food, check. Naked angels, check. Edwards as his true self . . . nope. I was going to have to do more than that.

"Judas!" I heard Mona Lisa cry as we struggled. "Judas!" And the sound sent a shudder through me, because a gorgon's cry is like nothing you have ever heard – or want to hear. Especially when it's calling the name of Judas.

"He's an imposter, my love!" Edwards yelled. "Help me kill him!"

"No, he's the imposter," I shouted. Okay, it wasn't the most imaginative thing to say, but do you think you would have come up with anything better in the same situation?

Edwards wrapped his hands around my throat to try to stop me from saying anything else. I tried to pull them off, but he was stronger than me at the moment. This wasn't going well at all. I needed another plan. Hell, I needed *a* plan. But I didn't think I was going to have the time to come up with one.

So I threw some of my remaining grace into my right hand and punched him in the face as hard as I could.

The blow would have taken off a normal man's head. It would have broken through a brick wall. It would have fractured the ground like an earthquake. You get the idea. Edwards took a couple of steps backward, and his eyes glazed over a little, and that was about it. But that was enough.

I felt the air start to heat up around me. And I couldn't help but notice the walls begin to smoulder around the same time my feet began to burn.

"My love – *don't!*" Edwards managed to gasp as he collected himself again. Then he kneed me in the balls – my Achilles' heel, so to speak – and I was left hanging on to him more than holding him. But it was too late. I'd broken his concentration with my blow, and thus broken his hold over Mona Lisa.

We spun around as he struggled to break free of me, and I caught a glimpse of Mona Lisa in her full glory. I didn't know what her power was, but I was about to find out.

Her clothes were gone, burned up in the flames that covered her body. But she wasn't burning up – the fire flowed out of her. She wore it like a gown. The snakes of her hair were made of more flames, and they spat fire at Edwards and me. Smoke poured out of her eyes and mouth. The wire in her lips glowed white hot.

"What have you done to us?" she screamed, and the words were blue flames. Everyone paused to look at her. Even the mummy. I wondered how my dear, sweet Morgana had ever managed to hold such a creature.

Edwards found the strength to throw me away from him. "My love, the imposter has imprisoned you," he shouted at her. "He has masqueraded as me to keep you hidden away from your sisters and your true cause."

Okay, that was well played.

Mona Lisa looked at me. What can I say about that look? I burst into flames. Or rather, my clothes did. She set my clothes on fire with that glare, and it was all I could do to not drop to the ground and roll about in an effort to extinguish the flames. Because that would have been pointless, as the wooden floor was burning now.

Oh Morgana, I am never going to see you again now.

Shut up, Cross, I told myself with a mental slap.

The obvious response to Edwards would have been something like "No, *he's* the imposter who imprisoned you!" But I could see that particular approach wasn't working. So I said to hell with it and went with the only other option I could think of.

"We're both imposters," I screamed, although it was more of a shriek thanks to the flames and burning skin and unbearable longing and all.

"You've been stolen away from the real Judas. He doesn't even know where you are." I could have added he didn't care, but I didn't think that would go over so well with her.

The flames subsided a little as Mona Lisa looked back and forth between us. I tried to bat them out with my hands, but my hands were on fire now, so you can imagine how well that worked.

I'd only been burned to death twice before, once at the stake in England and once in a car accident on a deserted road in a German forest. This time was shaping up to be the worst of the bunch.

"I have rescued you," Edwards said. "I have broken the spell. Finish him so we can leave this place."

In case you haven't figured out his plan yet, I think it was meant to go something like this: He convinces Mona Lisa to finish barbecuing me, and then he helps his henchmen dispose of the mummy. Which would probably mean dumping it in the *Hadleigh Castle* painting or someplace like that, because I was beginning to think the mummy was unkillable. And then he'd have all the time in the world to work some fresh magic on Mona Lisa and cloud her mind again.

But I wasn't going to let him do that. I was going to free Mona Lisa if it meant killing us all – including me. And that's exactly what it meant.

"The real Judas would know where you kissed for the first time," I said. Okay, it was more like I spat out the words. This was killing me. Figuratively and literally.

Mona Lisa stared at me. And then she smiled, which looked kind of like adding a line of gasoline to a fire.

"Tell us the truth and live," she cried. "Tell us a lie and we will burn you from history itself."

At this point in my life, the latter didn't seem like such a bad option.

"On a bridge over the River Seine," I said. If I was going to go out here, I may as well go out a romantic.

"Pray to your gods," Mona Lisa said to me.

"You really don't know me," I said, but she was already turning to Edwards.

"Tell us the truth," she said.

Edwards looked at her for a moment. The other angels continued to struggle with the mummy. The mummy was burning now, too, and Gabriel's wings had caught fire, although he didn't seem to notice.

Then Edwards turned to me and slowly clapped his hands together again. "Well played," he said. "Very well played." And then he dropped the sleight and he was just Edwards again. There was no sign of Judas at all.

Well, fair's fair. I wasted no time dropping my own Judas masquerade. And then there were none.

Mona Lisa howled when she saw our true natures, and the snakes threw themselves at us, uncoiling and lashing out across the distance to score our faces with their burning fangs. The very air itself began to burn in places, scorching my lungs until I couldn't breathe, and the flames from the floor leapt up all around me. The walls began to melt. The da Vinci painting we were in was turning into a Dalí painting.

The other angels finally let go of the mummy and took flight, screaming. But it was no good. Their wings were melting and there was nowhere for them to go.

Edwards seemed more philosophical about the whole thing. He shook his head at me. "You can stop me, but you can't stop the Risen," he said. "We are legion."

Then the snakes wrapped themselves around him like a hundred fiery constrictors and I couldn't see him at all anymore. When the snakes snapped back to Mona Lisa's head, there simply wasn't anything left of him, not even ash.

I'll give him credit – he didn't scream.

Mona Lisa turned to me then and I held my arms open to welcome my fate. I was getting tired of this century anyway. But before she could do to me what she'd done to Edwards, another angel came hurtling through the window from outside. Cassiel. He was naked like the others, and his wings were smoking but they weren't burning yet.

He landed between Mona Lisa and me, facing her, and kept his wings up out of the flames. "The River Styx," he told her. "The River Styx is where we kissed for the first time."

She stared at him for a moment, and then his wings crumbled into dust and blew away. His skin melted, turning white and then ashen, like a corpse's. And his body took on a gaunt, not-quite-human shape that was all too familiar . . .

Oh, for Christ's sake.

Mona Lisa's snakes reached out to caress his face. He didn't flinch away from them, just held out his hands to her. The flames faded from her skin – but not the rest of the room – and she stepped into his embrace.

"A boat of bones," he whispered. "The songs of the dead. The end of time."

"Judas," I swore. There was no other way to describe how I said his name.

He turned to face me. It was him all right. I'd been played like I'd never been played before. I was too disgusted with myself to even attack him right away. And too near death. I could barely stand.

"I told you I would deliver you Judas," he said. "And I have kept my end of the bargain. Just as you have kept yours."

I thought about maybe picking up one of the fallen weapons and killing him with it. But instead, I just rested my burned hands on my scorched legs for a moment. I took note of the black spots marring my vision, but I wasn't sure if they were ash or just my eyesight starting to fade.

"As you might expect, I have a few questions," I said through gritted teeth and charred lips. "Like why the hell you dragged me into this. Why didn't you just rescue her yourself if you knew where she was?"

Judas smiled as Mona Lisa embraced him. Her snakes caressed his face like Penelope had stroked my hair when we lay together. "How could I have succeeded where even you have failed?" he said.

Fair enough.

"I'm going to die here," I said. "But I'll die trying to take you with me."

And the snakes hissed at me as Mona Lisa straightened and pushed Judas behind her.

"Yeah yeah yeah," I said and grabbed a knife off the burning table. The blade and handle were both white-hot from the fire, but whatever.

"Wait," Judas said and pulled Mona Lisa back before she could annihilate me. Damn him. "I have met the terms of our bargain, but I feel perhaps that is not enough."

"Perhaps not," I agreed, continuing on. I threw a jab at his face, but it was just a feint to cover the knife thrust to his stomach. I sank the blade in deep, to the hilt. And then it kept going. My hand erupted out the other side of him, and ash poured out. Mona Lisa screamed, but Judas waved her off.

"You have earned that, or I have deserved it," he said. When he spoke, cobwebs spilled out of his mouth and drifted through the air around us. Other than that, he showed no signs of being affected by the wound. "And now I will give you what you deserve. The answers you have so long sought. The secrets of your existence."

I paused in pulling the knife back out of him for another shot. It was the only thing that would make me stop.

"I'm listening," I said.

He chuckled. "I thought you might be." He leaned close, so that when he spoke the cobwebs floated out onto my face when he whispered the words I had waited so long to hear: "I don't know who you are. And I don't know why you came to be. I don't even know how."

I swore a handful of forgotten curses at him. "This is not the time for your tricks," I said and ripped the knife free. More ash filled the air. I rammed the knife deep into him again, through his heart, through him, before Mona Lisa could kill me.

He cried out in pain but didn't try to stop me. He just stood there and shook his head. "You can't kill me any more than I can kill you," he said. "That's because you don't know me any more than I know you."

And Mona Lisa shoved him aside and cast her fiery gaze upon me. The air was a howling firestorm, but it wasn't so loud that I couldn't hear his words.

"I am not the one to blame for your existence," he said. "I am not the one who put you in that body. I suspect the body made you all on its own. Maybe it sought to heal itself when Christ's soul departed for the happy never after, and it created a new soul to fill the void. You."

And then he grew wings again, this time made of smoke and bone, and he caught Mona Lisa in his arms and leapt out the window before she could destroy me. All I could do was scream my rage at them as they disappeared into the burning sky outside.

And then there was more screaming behind me and I turned to see the other angels completely aflame now. Gabriel threw himself out the window after Judas and Mona Lisa, to who knows where, but the others just battered themselves against the ceiling like moths.

And there was still the mummy. It stumbled across the room toward me, burning like a torch as it came. I had to give it credit for persistence.

And I decided then that I was going to make one good thing come out of this unholy mess. Everyone else had been making sacrifices. Morgana, when she had freed me, although she had taken much in return. Aigra, who had given everything to me. Hell, Judas had even sacrificed Remiel to me, if you wanted to look at things charitably. And maybe he *had* told me the truth about myself, as unpleasant as it was to hear. Now it was my turn. I wasn't going to use the last of my grace to try to find some way to escape. I was going to use it to free the mummy from its curse. I was going to let it die a man. I was going to use the life my body had given me to give it life. It wouldn't be much of a life, considering the circumstances, but whose really is?

So I resurrected it.

It took the very last of my grace, and I dropped into the flames in exhaustion after I did it. I had nothing left. But the mummy stopped coming at me and gasped for breath. Then it started tearing off its burning bandages. I saw a man's fresh skin underneath, saw his young face with glistening new skin when he ripped the fiery strips from his head.

Then the world flickered around me and started to go dark. I thought I was finally passing out, until I realized it was just the flames dying. I looked at myself. My skin was scorched black, but I wasn't burning anymore. The floor wasn't burning. The walls had frozen mid-melt.

I looked around. The angels lay moaning where they'd fallen from the air, smoke rising from them, but the fires had been extinguished on them, too.

As for the mummy, he was now a naked man with gleaming bronze skin and golden circlets around his arms. A pattern of diamonds I didn't recognize was tattooed around his neck. His eyes were the same gold as the circlets. I could see grace radiating from him, more than I'd ever seen from angels. It was a shame I was too hurt to do anything about it.

He stood above me and smiled. "You may have resurrected a dead man," he said, "but in doing so you have birthed a god."

"If you say so," I said, or something equally as eloquent.

"It was my destiny to join the ranks of the lords upon my death, as it was for all the pharaohs," he said, and I remembered the sign on the sarcophagus case in the British Museum, which had said pretty much the same thing. "But I was cursed with the undeath by a priest. I could not rule the afterlife. I could do nothing but watch my realm crumble into dust, until the ghosts came and made me their slave."

"I'm guessing by ghosts you mean the British," I said. I figured I might as well make small talk while I waited to die.

"Do not speak unless told to speak," he said, although not in an unkind way. Fair enough – he had stopped the flames. Now all I had to contend with were my burns and stab wound and deep, insatiable longing for Morgana. And I had to face all that without any grace. I kind of wished he had let the flames kill me so I could have some peace.

He looked out the window and his eyes turned black. "It was a curse with a hidden blessing, though," he said. "The afterlife is gone. The afterlife itself has died. I would have died with it. And now I am free to live as a god where I will, for as much time as this realm has left to it."

Okay, he could be a problem. But I vowed he wouldn't be mine. I was going to stay clear of gods and angels for a time. And gorgons.

He looked back at me and put his hand on my shoulder. It felt cool and soothing on my tortured skin. "I owe you a favour," he said. "You have freed me from my curse and given me a new realm, a new time to rule. I will give you a blessing in return. I will give you the gift you have given me."

"Don't tell me you're going to resurrect me after I die," I said. "Because I can manage that on my own."

"No," he said, "I'm going to resurrect you before you die." And then I felt more of that coolness flowing through his hand and into me, spreading throughout my body, and it was unlike any grace I'd ever felt. It didn't make me feel any more alive – it soothed the pain and made me feel light and insubstantial. And then I realized it was because I was actually becoming insubstantial. Either the room was fading away around me or I was fading away – I wasn't sure which. Either way, I hoped I was heading back to Morgana's court. I really needed a drink now.

"We will meet again before the end of time," he said before I drifted away completely. "Remember who spared you then." And then everything was the familiar white glow of the light at the end of the tunnel.

AMEN

Only rather than this glow fading into black like it usually did when I died, it faded away into a spotlight overhead. I squinted against its glare. I felt cold metal on my back. On my naked, unburned skin. I felt the chill of air conditioning. I felt no pain at all. Other than the usual existential kind, anyway. I saw Anubis and Osiris and the other dead gods looming over me, welcoming me to wherever the mummy had sent me. I tasted blood in my mouth.

And grace.

I tasted grace in my mouth to go along with the blood.

A fresh drop of blood landed on my lips and I sucked it in, savouring it. I felt a shiver of electricity flicker briefly through the screaming emptiness that was my longing for Morgana.

I saw the angel perched on a pipe hanging from the ceiling overhead. Cassiel. A cut on his wrist. The blood dripping down from it to my mouth.

Where was I?

I sat up and looked around. I was back in the British Museum. I was in the same room the mummy had been displayed in. I was lying in the case he'd been in. I was in a healthy body again, showing no signs of burns or stabs or bullet wounds or any of the other treats of the last few days. Except for the black ring on my finger. I guess the Egyptian god didn't want to do anything about that. Or couldn't do anything about it.

A drop cloth that had been covering the case was pulled partially away. A sign beside the case said *This Exhibit Closed for Maintenance*. Anubis and

Osiris were just statues on pedestals. There was no one else in the room. I didn't need someone to tell me the museum was closed. The bastard had sent me back to where our relationship had started.

I chuckled my appreciation and then looked up at Cassiel. A fresh drop of blood from his wrist hit my lips.

"Is it really you this time?" I asked.

"It would appear to be me," he said.

"You know what I mean," I said.

"I am aware of your meaning," he said. "But what I am or am not is of little relevance to the matter at hand."

"It's of relevance if you're Judas," I said.

"I am not Judas," he said. "I have never been Judas."

"What if I don't believe you?" I said.

He flicked some more blood into my mouth. "Do I taste of Judas?" he asked.

The truth is I didn't know what Judas tasted like. But whatever his flavour was, I doubted it was the grace of the angels. Just like I doubted he would willingly give me strength.

"Why are you giving me grace?" I asked.

"There is a need for your services," he said.

"Oh no," I said, climbing out of the case. "I'm not falling for that again."

I looked around for the exit. I had to get back to the faerie pub and Morgana.

Cassiel watched me but made no move to follow. His blood dripped into the empty case. It was all I could do to not throw myself back in there and lick it up. Anything to distract me from thoughts of Morgana. I tried to pull the ring off my finger again, but it was really stuck on there. This wasn't looking good.

"There is nothing to fall for," he said. "The need is as genuine as it may have been with Mona Lisa. But this time I am indeed Cassiel, not Judas."

I stared at him. "You *knew* about all that?" I asked.

"I am a watcher," he said, studying me without blinking. "I know much that others do not."

"And you didn't try to stop Judas from pretending to be you?" I said.

"Judas has taken on many forms over the millennia," Cassiel said.

"None of them have been of any import to me."

"What about the Mona Lisa?" I asked. "Is she of import to you?"

"The painting or the gorgon?" he asked.

I closed my eyes. "Did everyone know she was a gorgon but me?" I asked.

"I appreciate the artistic merits of the painting," Cassiel said. "And of course the rituals of binding that were involved in its creation. But it is of no matter. The gorgon and I were once lovers, so yes, she is of personal interest. But that has nothing to do with you or the matter at hand."

"But it did," I said.

Cassiel paused. "It did what?" he asked.

"The fact that she was of personal interest to you did have something to do with the matter at hand," I said. "Only it was Judas's matter, not yours."

Cassiel finally blinked. Maybe it was his way of showing surprise. Or confusion. Or maybe impatience. Or maybe he just had to blink every few thousand years to keep his eyes moist. "I am . . . unclear as to your meaning," he said.

"You know everything that happens, right?" I said.

"I observe," he said. "I undertake the sacred duty of documentation."

"To hell with your sacred duty," I said. "Just tell me if I'm correct."

I waited for him to blink again, but he didn't. Ah well. I'd check again in a thousand years.

"Judas pretended to be you for two reasons," I said. "One, so I wouldn't kill him outright. Two, because he knew about your fling with Mona Lisa."

"'Fling' is an inaccurate way of describing our relationship," he said.

"I'll take that as a yes," I said, carrying on. "He chose to be you because he knew I would go to Victory for help once I was in the Louvre to check out the painting. Victory knew about your fling with Mona Lisa because of her sisterhood with the other gorgons. Judas probably figured because you were involved Victory would feed me a few details about Mona Lisa that maybe she wouldn't have told me otherwise – like the fact that Mona Lisa is a gorgon. Only it wasn't you who was involved, it was Judas. But she didn't know that."

"Again, 'fling' is the wrong word," Cassiel said.

"After that, he knew he just had to sit back and keep an eye on me," I said. "Once I learned about Mona Lisa's secret, I was able to start figuring things out for myself. Judas only stepped back into the scene when I got stuck, like when I was in the faerie pub and he pretended to be you again, or when I needed a nudge in the right direction, like when he pretended to be the art dealer and told me to go to America."

Cassiel didn't say anything, just studied me.

"It was all low-risk stuff for him," I said. "Nothing where he'd have to stick around for long and chance me figuring out what was really going on. And I'm betting he knew where Mona Lisa was all along, right? He just didn't know how to get her out. Not until I got all Philip Marlowe on the case."

"That is an acceptable version of events," Cassiel said. "Except for your description of the relationship I had with Mona Lisa."

I still had questions, of course. Like how Judas had been able to follow me so effectively without me noticing him. I'm usually better than that at picking up tails. But that wasn't the real important question. The real important question I asked Cassiel: "Were you there in *The Last Supper* with Judas and me?"

"I was not there," he said. "I will never be there." Whatever that meant.

"Let me rephrase that," I said. "Do you know what he said to me there?"

"What he said is history," Cassiel answered.

"So you do know," I said.

"History is the known," he said. "That is what makes it history."

Right. I tried not to grind my teeth out of my head. "Was he telling the truth?" I asked.

"The truth is an unstable element with Judas," Cassiel said.

"Was he telling the truth when he said he didn't put me in this body?" I asked. "Was he telling the truth when he said this body created me?"

Cassiel stared at me for a long moment. He flexed his wings. He looked away, then back. It was the most flustered I'd seen him get.

"Yes," he said. "Judas told you a truth in that instance."

I closed my eyes and waited for a while. But it didn't work. When I opened them again, the world was still there. Cassiel was still there. I was still stuck in that body.

"So it's true," I said. "I am nobody."

"You are Christ," Cassiel said.

"No, I'm not," I said.

"It is also true that you are not Christ," Cassiel said.

I sighed, because there was nothing else to do. Two thousand years after I was born, I finally had an answer to who I was, and whether or not there was a reason for my existence. And that answer was I was an accident. I wondered if God even knew I existed.

"One more question then," I said. "Where can I find Judas now?" I still wanted to kill him. He had it coming, after all.

"There is no time for that," Cassiel said. "There is only time for feeding on my grace and growing strong again, before we return to La Sagrada Familia."

"Remiel's nest?" I asked. "Why would I want to go back there?"

"Judas did not lure you to Remiel's nest," Cassiel said. "Judas lured you to Remiel's station."

I had a sinking feeling at the sound of that. "Station?" I asked. "Like stations of the cross?"

"La Sagrada Familia was Remiel's guard station," Cassiel said. "When you slew Remiel, you slew the guard of the crypt."

"The crypt," I said. That sinking feeling kept going lower.

"What lies in the chamber underneath La Sagrada Familia," Cassiel said. "What La Sagrada Familia was constructed to contain."

"No no no," I said, backing away until I bumped into a wall. "This is not my fight."

"With no one to guard it, it has awoken," Cassiel said. "It is breaking free of its prison. It must be stopped."

"Call your friends," I said. "Summon the Risen. Appeal to the Faithful. I don't care. This has nothing to do with me. I'm going after Morgana. I mean Judas." I didn't even want to know what lay underneath Gaudí's church.

"It has everything to do with you," Cassiel said. "You slew the guard. You set the awakening in progress. It is your responsibility."

I considered his words in silence for a moment. And then another one. Hell, I may have thought about them for the rest of the night.

"Judas will always be there," Cassiel said. I wasn't sure if he was telling me to be patient or if he was getting metaphysical.

Finally, I nodded at the blood in the case. "Get me a goblet or something," I said. "A coffee cup. Anything."

"A grail awaits you," Cassiel said, nodding at the drop cloth. I lifted the cloth and saw a thermos sitting in the foot of the case, amid the shards of broken glass. I pulled it out and unscrewed the lid. It was full of Cassiel's blood.

"How did you know I'd agree?" I asked.

"I see all the deeds that are and all the deeds that have been," he said. "I see all the paths that can be from those. In no path did you refuse."

"Do you see me kill you in any of these paths?" I asked him.

"I see you kill me in all of them," Cassiel said without changing expressions. "But not until many years from now."

I looked down into the thermos, at all that grace waiting for me. I thought about Judas and everything he had done to me. I thought about what I'd learned about myself, that I was nobody and there was possibly no reason for my existence. I thought about Morgana and how much I missed her. I thought about my vow to kill Penelope's father, who was still out there somewhere, waiting to be found. I thought about how much I loved that Gaudí church, and about how much I loved Barcelona. I thought about all the people sitting in cafés around the city right at this very moment, drinking their good wine and enjoying their good lives while something they couldn't imagine woke from slumber beneath their feet.

"Damn you to hell," I told Cassiel and I drank down his blood.

Damn you all to hell.

AFTERWORD

In the beginning was a vague idea.

Many years ago, I read an article about the Shroud of Turin, the burial shroud that had supposedly been used to wrap Christ's body and bore his likeness in its fabric. That in turn reminded me of a poem I had read in university, "The Dream of the Rood," which told the tale of Christ's crucifixion from the perspective of the cross that bore him and was left behind.

Then I began to wonder what if Christ's body was like that cross, a vessel for the divine spirit in this physical realm but abandoned when that spirit moved on to wherever it went. What if that hallowed body were still out there somewhere, like the fragments of the original cross and all the other relics of the Crucifixion?

And then I thought, what if another soul somehow found its way into the body to replace the spirit that had left it?

And lo, Cross was born.

I knew instantly that I had a complex and intriguing character with lots of potential. I also knew I had to make him the opposite of everything Christ is for dramatic tension. So right from the beginning Cross was a drunken, murderous, immortal antihero.

But what to do with a character like that?

I wrestled with the question in the weeks that followed, and one idea after another slowly emerged.

First, I knew someone born into a body like that would hunger for the heavenly grace that had left it, so chasing that grace had to be a central motivation for Cross, one that would drive the action of the book.

Next, I knew I needed to start the book in a setting as interesting as the character. I immediately thought of La Sagrada Familia, the famous Gaudí church in Barcelona. I had been fascinated by the church ever since I visited it on a tour of Europe, because it's such a weirdly beautiful and delightfully strange place. I love the way it takes the grandeur and spectacle of religion and makes it completely alien yet compelling at the same time. So I knew it was the perfect place to start the Cross book because of how much it reflected him.

Now that the book was starting off weird, I had to maintain that tone. I started thinking about other things I had seen on that Europe trip, many of which also found their way into the book. I'd been struck by the *Mona Lisa* painting when I had seen it – not because of the woman in the painting so much as the landscape she inhabited, which struck me as eerily apocalyptic. And just like that, the title came to me: *The Mona Lisa Sacrifice*. But who was Mona Lisa in this book, and what was that apocalyptic landscape?

The answer came with another famous work in the Louvre: *Winged Victory of Samothrace*, a truly divine Greek sculpture missing its head and arms. It's one of the most captivating works of art I've ever seen for reasons I find hard to define. That's the way art works sometimes. And because art is a living, evolving thing, I decided to make Victory a living creature (in a way). In honour of her Greek heritage, I made her a gorgon. And because there was more than one gorgon, that allowed me to draw a connection to Mona Lisa, who I decided also needed to be a gorgon.

At some point I realized Judas had to make an appearance in the book, because what better nemesis for Cross than the one who had betrayed Christ? I made him a trickster god both to explain his longevity and his original betrayal of Christ, and now I had all the characters necessary to develop the plot, which turned into a twisted mystery that revolved around an even more twisted romance.

And that made me realize I needed a true romance for Cross as well, as a sort of counterpoint. And a motivating force to drive his revenge, because someone like him would need a reason to see this quest through to the end rather than just walk away to get drunk for a century when things went sideways. So that led me to Penelope, who started out in the early drafts as human but then became half-angel in the later versions. Someone like Cross would need a special counterpart, after all, a lover who was just as strange and intriguing as himself.

And then, just because Cross is complicated, I gave him a faerie queen as an additional lover. And not just any faerie queen, but one who is deeply involved behind the scenes of our world, and who is as much a creature of myth as Cross himself.

And Amelia? Well, I wasn't quite sure why Amelia needed to be in this world, but I knew that she did. Such is the way with children.

I wish I could remember where the idea of Alice as a sidekick came from, but I can't. And given her nature in this book, I suppose that's fitting.

There were many things that brought me joy in writing *The Mona Lisa Sacrifice*. Working out the mystery of why Cross needed to track down the missing Mona Lisa – the gorgon, not the painting – and what would happen when he did. Creating a wild and weird magical world within our own – something that infuses our often banal and dreary existence with the grace of myth. And, of course, discovering Cross and the cast of characters that populate his world.

But nothing brings me as much joy as publishing this tale so others can follow Cross's (mis)adventures and lose themselves in his world.

I hope *The Mona Lisa Sacrifice* brings you as much joy and intrigue as it has brought me. Thank you for being part of this story.

Peter Darbyshire is the author of six books and more stories than he can remember. He lives near Vancouver, British Columbia, where he spends his time writing, raising children and playing D&D with other writers. It's a good life.